I0747720

Respect
Yourself

Respect Yourself

a novel

JOYCE ASONG

NKENGASONG
— PRESS —

Copyright © 2023 by Joyce Asong

All rights reserved
Published in the United States of America by Nkengasong Press LLC
www.nkgpress.com

This is a work of fiction. While, as in all fiction, the literary perceptions and insights are based on experience, all names, characters, places, and incidents either are products of the author's imagination or are used fictionally.

Library of Congress Cataloging-in-Publication Data
Names: Joyce Asong
Title: Respect Yourself
Identifiers: LCCN 2020925544
ISBN 978-1-7363084-6-2 (paperback)
ISBN 978-1-7363084-7-9 (hardcover)
ISBN 978-1-7363084-8-6 (ebook)

PRINTED IN THE UNITED STATES OF AMERICA

Design by Asya Blue
Cover artwork by Thee Prince Melo
Author photograph by Ayo Photography

For the marginalized worldwide—be the change you want to see in the world

Respect Yourself

CHAPTER ONE

The unwelcome feeling of sweat beading on my forehead grew worse as I climbed the stairs. I had my mattress pad and comforter piled nearly up to my eyes. I was eager to get all my belongings into my dorm room. The move-in couldn't be over fast enough.

Mama and Papa stood near the elevator, a few floors below, waiting for the car to descend so they could wheel a cart containing my mini-fridge, lamp, microwave, and suitcases into the elevator.

I was out of breath by the time I made it to my room on the fifth floor. I arrived before Mama and Papa. When I opened the door, I frowned. In my haste to get all my belongings into my room, I had told Mama and Papa not to organize anything.

"Just leave them on the floor," I told them.

I dropped the bedding on an empty desk and got to work, creating piles and stacks by category. The boxes containing my toiletries went in the bathroom that connected our room to that of our suite mates. I kept the suitcases containing my clothes in the little hall to our room, where twin wardrobes stood, and I slid the plastic bin containing my books and art supplies under the bed I chose.

"You packed too many things," Papa said when they finally arrived. He wheeled the cart into my room, leaving it by the door.

"No, I didn't. I don't have that much stuff."

"You packed a lot."

"Well, I need to be comfortable."

Ever since we loaded his car that morning, Papa had been complaining about how much I was bringing. His constant complaints were irritating, even though I was certain it was his way of saying he was going to miss me.

Mama and Papa lugged my mini-fridge and large suitcase from the cart, while I did my best to unpack neatly. I did not want them to think they'd left a mess when we went downstairs to say our good-byes.

An hour later, we were about to leave when Mama said, "Wait, let's take pictures for Nana Ola."

"Mama, my room is a mess," I protested. "Let's take them outside."

"Nana Ola won't care about the mess. We should let her see where you will sleep."

"Okay," I muttered.

Mama stood by my side, encircling my waist with her left hand. Thanks to my growth spurt a few summers prior, the top of her head barely reached my chin.

I didn't like taking pictures, especially impromptu ones. Today, I indulged her this once. She had been hurt when I turned down her offer to cook a batch of Cameroon food and store it in the mini-fridge.

It is not that I didn't like my mother's cooking. In fact, I loved it. I also loved my native food, especially *ekwang*. *Eru* was wonderful eaten with *fufu*—I could go on. The problem was, these foods did not have the best smell, and once heated, they had a way of lingering in the room. I didn't want my roommate to see me as the weird girl with the strange, stinky food.

I could still remember the day Mama boiled *miondo* when Michelle came over. Michelle and I had grown close, so I was no longer hypervigilant about what I thought were the embarrassing parts of my African culture.

Michelle pinched her nose in disgust. "Humph, do you smell that?"

"Smell what?"

"That smell, it smells like old food," she scowled.

When I sniffed, I realized that yes, miondo did smell funny.

Nonetheless, I could have had Mama prepare foods that did not have a strong scent like *jollof rice*, *koki corn*, *koki beans*, or pepper soup, but I had another reason for refusing Mama's food. Earlier that day, I had listened to Michelle raving about her writing program in California. Despite my begging, Mama and Papa had refused to let me attend the program—under the tutelage of my favorite author, Esther Collins.

"Say cheese—smile wider, Foma," Mama said as Papa stood beside me, holding me close.

"That's enough," I said, squirming free. "Let's go."

"Okay, okay, we're finished. Nana Ola will love these pictures."

Nana Ola was my eccentric, vivacious, and sophisticated grandmother. I loved her, but her decision to return to Cameroon months earlier than planned still upset me.

On our way down the elevator, Papa cleared his throat and said in his formal way: "So, for eighteen years, you have been with us. We have advised and guided your path so you make the right decisions. Today, we will leave you and hope that what we have taught you will continue to guide you as you enter adulthood."

I stifled the urge to roll my eyes. He was always talking about making the "right decision." Who was he to tell me what the "right decision" for my life was?

"Focusing on your studies is the most important thing. You have seen how hard your mother and I have worked to get where we are today. Just eight years ago we came to this country with almost nothing, but look at us now," he said, slowly separating his hands.

"Yes, Papa, I understand."

"I see I am annoying you. I just want to make sure to put things into perspective before we leave. This country provides you with so many opportunities. To attain all you want, you must put in the work."

"Opportunity comes in a variety of forms," I said. "Like writing."

Papa raised a bushy eyebrow. Minus the few gray hairs on his neatly cut head and mustache, he was the same tall, slender man with dark brown skin who valued education above all else.

He ignored my comment. "You have Paige's information, right? She has done very well for herself at this university. Stay close to her and follow her example."

That summer, Paige had been one of my supervisors at my esteemed internship position at Papa's hospital. I had no choice but to accept the internship, since Mama and Papa refused to let me choose the creative writing program. Still, Paige was the highlight of my hospital internship. She was a biology major entering her senior year of college. Attending medical school was her goal upon graduation.

"Yes, Papa. I have her number," I said curtly.

We hugged and kissed at the corner of my dorm building. As I was going back in, I turned back and saw Mama still standing there, waving. Then she dabbed her eyes with the tissue crumpled in her hand. I felt a pang of loss as well. Although they annoyed me, I was going to miss my parents.

As I placed the last of my clothes inside my wardrobe, I heard a skirmish right outside the door. *That must be my roommate*, I thought.

When the door opened, in stumbled a tall girl with long blonde hair and the bluest eyes. Two others, who I presumed were her mother and father, stood behind her, storage bins in hand.

"Hello," the young girl said as she extended her hand. "I'm Kara. You must be my roommate?"

"Hi, I'm Foma."

We awkwardly shook hands. My grip was too tight, and her hands were sweaty.

"Hello, Foma, we're Kara's parents," her father said, while her mother smiled too tightly. She broke off contact by bending down to place a clear bin on the floor.

"Been here long?" Kara asked me.

"I got here about four hours ago."

I retreated to get out of their way. Feet stretched before me, I sat on my already made bed. I self-consciously studied the campus map in my hand, while watching as they lugged in suitcases, tubs, and lamps.

Since I found out the school would be placing students with roommates at random, I felt uneasy because I had hoped they would allow Michelle and me to room together. I was an only child who had never roomed with anyone, even in Cameroon. Now I didn't just have a roommate, I had a white roommate. I stole a glance at Kara and her parents, observing their pale skin. My eyes reverted down to my brown hands that held the map. I was curious to know what they thought about me.

My classmates at St. Joseph Academy who looked like Kara acted like I did not exist all four years of high school, and I wondered if Kara would do the same this year. I heaved a sigh of relief for having the foresight to not accept Mama's food. I was already different enough.

When Michelle texted me to ask if I had arrived, I jumped to my feet, happy for an opportunity to leave them alone.

I gasped as heat and humidity came rushing at me while I pulled the heavy glass door open. Mama had plaited my hair in individual braids, securing each lock between the long artificial hair she used. That morning she had gathered all hundred or so braids into a firm bun at the top of my head. My braids would prevent the hot, sticky air from reducing my hair to a puffy and frizzy mess.

I took my light sweater off and tied it around my waist. Our room had been cold when we arrived because the air-conditioning had been on full blast. Covertly checking the map in my hand, I began what looked like a long trek to Michelle's residential dorm on the west side of the campus.

Even though I considered myself lucky that we were attending the same university, I still could not believe that she had gone behind my back and applied for that writing program without telling me. She would never have known about it if not for me. I had no idea she had an interest in writing. Mrs. Lawson, my AP English literature teacher at St. Joseph Academy, had told me about the opportunity. She knew that Esther Collins was my favorite writer.

I loved writing. It was my favorite pastime, a way for me to express myself. I had exercise books full of my poems, prose, and short stories. When I was upset, writing poems or just scribbling down my thoughts calmed me. After Michelle came back from California, I tried my hardest not to act like I was wildly jealous.

I knew I was halfway to Michelle's dorm when I approached the Sterling Student Center. The tall glass building housed the bookstore, student activity centers, and a host of different offices. I stopped to read the notices on a bulletin board off to one side:

THE AFRICAN STUDENT ASSOCIATION Welcomes You! We Would Like to See You at Our First General Body Meeting of the Year. Come Join Us to Learn More About Our Organization! FOOD WILL BE SERVED!!!!

The bottom of the flyer gave the time, place, and location of the meeting. I made a note of the information.

Sterling was empty but for a few students seated at a booth, deep in conversation. I sighed a breath of relief when I stepped into the cool building. I was sticky from sweat. I stopped in an inconspicuous corner and sniffed my armpits, relieved to smell the sweet scent of my passion fruit deodorant. As I descended the stairs, I saw an array of fast-food restaurants. They were all closed.

Eight minutes later, I texted Michelle to let her know I was outside.

"Hey, you," Michelle cooed when she opened the front door to let me in. We hugged, and I followed her upstairs—her building did not have an elevator. I panted, out of breath, as we climbed up the third flight of stairs.

"How'd you get your stuff up here?" I asked.

"The old-fashioned way," she said, flexing her right bicep. "Of course, my dad and uncle did most of the heavy lifting."

Inside her room, she introduced me to her roommate, Eva. I noted that she and Michelle could be sisters. Eva was short and thin. Her caramel brown skin was several shades darker than Michelle's extremely light complexion, but an equal amount of shades lighter than mine.

Right away I knew this was not the right time to air out my grievance with Michelle. As she unpacked, I looked around their old, musty room. Rust lined the windowpanes that held Michelle's fan in place. I was thankful for my almost brand-new dorm building. I welcomed the gush of cool air that touched my legs.

"So, I was waiting to tell you," Michelle announced. "Remember how I won that award for my short story at the end of SAWP?"

Michelle told me that throughout the summer, they referred to the program, Sacramento Artistic Writing Program, as SAWP.

Burning slightly, I nodded my head for her to proceed.

"Well, Esther Collins liked my work so much that she entered it in a writing competition with a $10,000 award. She thinks I have an excellent shot of winning."

"Oh, that's nice," I said.

"I find out if I won in a few weeks, I think."

I nodded again. She knew how much I had wanted to go.

She went on and on about SAWP and her new friends. Soon I couldn't take it any longer. I told Michelle I had to go.

"So soon?" she asked.

"Yeah, I'm really tired. I need to lie down."

She frowned. "Okay."

"Don't worry, I know my way," I said when she attempted to follow me out the door.

When I got back to my dorm, it was almost six o'clock. Kara and her parents were still there, but they told me they were heading out to dinner. I got on my bed and plugged in my earphones, book in hand, and a few minutes later, they left.

I was still sitting on my bed, feeling all alone, when shortly after their departure a student opened our door, without knocking, and peeked inside.

"Oh," she said when she saw me. "I'm Shannon. I'm one of your suite mates. I was looking for Kara."

"She left for dinner."

"Okay," she said, and swiftly she popped her head back into the bathroom and shut the door.

I had just placed my head down when the door opened again. "You are a student here, right?" Shannon asked.

My nostrils flared as I looked at Shannon's pale face, cupped by a brown bob hairstyle. *No, I decided to randomly break into a dorm room*, I thought of telling her, but I gave her a tight smile. "Yes, I am a student here, and this is my room," I said finally.

Before Shannon could say anything further, I heard another girl say, "Is that Kara?"

"No, it's our new...suite mate," Shannon responded.

Now standing beside Shannon was a girl the same complexion as Michelle. She was about my height, with long black hair that was ironed bone straight. I exhaled, reassured by her light brown skin.

"Hi, I'm Foma," I said, looking directly at her, ignoring Shannon. I flinched when I saw the frown on her face.

"I'm Jessica," she said coldly as she looked at me skeptically, her mouth upturned.

I fidgeted, made aware of my dark brown skin.

"Nice to meet you," Shannon said before they turned around and closed the door behind them.

The sound of the door closing made me feel more alone.

CHAPTER TWO

Biology and chemistry were my first two classes of the semester. I tried to take diligent notes, but the professors went over everything unreasonably fast. In biology, I looked around the large lecture hall at my counterparts. Those who were paying attention looked just as lost as I did.

I have to do some major studying after this class, I thought as I took copious notes on material that I did not understand, even though I had completed my readings before class.

When I walked into the cozy classroom where my freshman English class was being held, I was grateful that the air felt less stuffy than that of the lecture halls from which I had just come. I sat down and was fishing through my backpack for my notebook when I felt a tap on my shoulder.

"Hey, you had bio and chem this morning, right?" the voice asked.

I looked up to see a short, dark-skinned black girl with puffy, curly hair in a half ponytail.

She must be African, I thought immediately. We had a way of spotting each other.

"Yes, I did. Are you a bio major too?"

"Yes," she said. "Oh, my goodness! Did you understand anything?"

"Nope!"

"Me neither." She sat next to me and introduced herself. "I'm Ife."

After class, my friendly new classmate asked me to go with her to Sterling to grab a bite to eat. I wanted to, but I had promised myself that after English class, I would go to the library and try to make sense of my class notes from that morning. Plus, Sterling was on the other side of campus. I had planned on eating in the dining hall near the library.

"I wish I could go with you, but I have other plans. We can exchange numbers, though, and maybe have dinner together?"

"Sure, which dorm are you in?"

"McKee Hall."

"Oh yay," Ife replied. "East or West?"

"West. Don't tell me you live there too."

"I live in McKee East."

"That's awesome! We can definitely grab dinner then. Just let me know!"

At the deserted library, I found a cubicle overlooking the wide lawn that stretched out front. Tall trees surrounded the turf. It was windy that day, and the tree branches were swaying from side to side. When I opened my planner, a sheet of paper fell out. I immediately noticed Papa's handwriting.

Before starting college, Papa and I sat down and looked at the requirements for the best medical school programs in the country. He wrote the GPA requirements as we researched, and there it was, his handwritten list of the GPAs I needed to have by the end of my four years. *Overall GPA: 3.8, but preferably 3.95 / Science GPA: 3.5, but preferably 3.65.* Papa had added the "preferably" part. Seeing that got me annoyed all over again.

I understood how important education was in the African culture. Even grade schools in Cameroon fostered an environment of competition among their students. Mama and Papa's educational expectations for me were made clear when we moved to the United States eight years prior. Before my first day of class, Mama and Papa had sat me down and told me that mediocrity was not acceptable.

"From now on, I don't expect to see anything other than A on your report card. This is America. You can become whatever you want if you are intelligent and you work hard. Your mother and I are also students now, just like you. We promise to study hard to make sure we can provide a good life for you, and you have to promise us you will also work hard."

Minus a few Bs in my advanced classes at St. Joseph, I had kept up my end of the bargain.

Feeling inspired, I was diligent and spent several hours at the library.

As I made my way back to my dorm, I checked my phone and saw that it was just after 4 p.m. So, around 9 p.m. in Cameroon. I searched through my phone for the pin numbers of several international calling cards that Mama had given me days ago.

I called Nana Ola. I knew she would be up, because my grandmother hardly slept.

"Hello, who is calling?" The nasally voice of Susana, Nana Ola's house girl, roared through the phone. Her English had gotten much better.

"It is me, Foma."

"Fomanju, nah how o?" she asked.

"I am fine, how are you?" I asked.

Before she could respond, I heard Nana Ola in the background. She was speaking sternly to Susana in our tribal language—the Nweh dialect. Even though I could not make out what she was saying, I surmised she was chastising Susana for making small talk with me. She was constantly complaining that Susana wasted our minutes, although the pleasantries with Susana only lasted thirty seconds at most. That was Nana Ola for you, never shy to voice how she was feeling, even over the most minor infraction.

"Hello, my baby, how are you?"

"Good evening, Nana Ola. I am fine, how are you?"

"By God's grace, I am doing well, my university girl. Today was your first day of class, correct?"

"Yes, Nana Ola."

"Tell me all about your day."

I recounted my classes to Nana Ola, and then I could not help but to complain about Michelle's winning the award for best story and Esther Collins entering it into a writing contest with $10,000 as the winning prize.

"Fomanju, have you told your friend about how you feel, like I told you to do months ago?"

"No, I haven't had the opportunity. But she should know that what she did was wrong."

"If you feel someone has wronged you, tell them how you feel…"

When the pause went on long enough, I asked, "Nana Ola?"

I did not get a response. We had lost our connection. Connection issues were common with international calls to Cameroon. I decided I would call her back on a different day. We only had two minutes of credit left, anyway.

Ife and I had dinner after I got back to my side of campus. Michelle had texted me to ask if I wanted to get dinner with her and Eva, but I had declined.

When I met Ife at the courtyard that connected our two buildings, she introduced her friend Neema. In the dining hall, we got our food and sat in a back corner.

"Where are you from?" Ife asked.

"Cameroon," I said. "You?"

"Nigeria."

"Ahh! My neighbor!"

"How long have you been in America?"

"I've been here since I was ten."

"Well, I've been here since I was three," Ife replied smugly.

Nothing annoyed me more than when Africans felt that coming to America at a younger age gave them an advantage. I tried not to roll my eyes.

"Neema is half African American, half Nigerian," Ife volunteered.

"That makes sense," I said. "I couldn't place you."

Ife laughed because she knew what I was talking about. When we'd met that morning, we both deciphered that the other was African. But looking at Neema, it was not immediately obvious.

"Yeah, I know. Many Africans can't tell that I'm also African."

"How do you two know each other?" I asked.

"We're suite mates," Neema answered.

I tried to conceal my annoyance. Everyone around me appeared to be happily paired up while I was stuck with Kara, Shannon, and Jessica.

"Are you going to the ASA meeting on Wednesday?" Ife asked.

"Yes, I saw the flyer. Are y'all?"

"Yeah! We can't wait!"

When I got back to my dorm room, I found Kara, my suite mates, and a few others from our floor in our room.

So much for me winding down and sleeping early, I thought.

I gathered my clothes and towel and went to the bathroom to take a shower, hoping that when I came out, they would've moved to another room. Yet in the week since orientation had started, our room had turned into the favorite meeting spot. Kara always insisted that they come to her.

After I finished showering and got dressed, I walked out to find them still in the room, cackling as they looked through Kara's high school yearbook.

I picked up my biology textbook from my desk, got my ear-phones out of my backpack, and sat on my bed. I hoped the sweet sounds from the Afrobeats songs that plunged into my ears would drown them out. However, I could not do that without piercing my eardrums, so I eavesdropped.

"And yeah, we had this random Asian girl, Amy, in our class. She was super smart, though," Kara continued.

"They're always smart," said Casey from down the hall.

"You can't say that. That's racist," her suite mate Jennifer corrected her.

All conversation stopped. The left side of my face burned as I felt their stares. It annoyed me that Jessica was staring at me as well—wasn't she also a person of color?

The day before, Jessica, Shannon, and Kara had been talking about becoming a part of Greek life when Kara asked Jessica, "What are you?"

"What do you mean?" she responded.

"What's your…ethnicity?"

"I'm not black!" Jessica responded quickly, sounding offended.

Just like tonight, I had felt the group turn to look at me.

Then, without knocking, someone opened our door.

"What's up, ladies!" It was Jared with Mark and Thomas, from across the hall.

The girls giggled.

Black guys like Jared annoyed me. In high school, I had met plenty of guys like Jared. Those guys who only hung out with white boys and only gave white girls the time of day. Of all the times he had been in our room over the past two days, he had barely acknowledged my presence. Tonight was no different.

Kara gave Casey a knowing look when Jared made a beeline right to her side. Casey looked annoyed. I'd heard whispers that Jared had a crush on Casey, but the feeling was not mutual.

"We were just looking at my yearbook," Kara said.

"Oh, okay. Let me take a look-see," Jared said in a mocking tone as he took the yearbook from her hands.

"Where are all the brothas?" he asked as he scanned the pages. The girls giggled.

Of course, he only cares about the brothas being in the pictures; he has no interest in us sistas, I thought.

"We only had, like, one black family in my town," Kara said. She had told me she lived on the outskirts of Boston.

"I'm from central Pennsylvania, and we too only had a few black families in our town," Shannon added.

Maybe people are racist because they grow up in towns where they have little interaction with black people. So they just assume the worst of us.

"Only three black families in both of your towns?" Jared asked. "Well, madams, I am happy to bless you with my presence." He took a bow, and the girls giggled.

This scene was straight out of a high school movie where the white kids had a token black friend who was there seemingly to amuse everyone and bring color—literally and figuratively—to the group.

"Her roommate is black too," Jessica said.

Jared glanced over at where I sat, pretending to be reading. He did not respond to Jessica's statement.

Kara and her crew eventually left the room, off to play beer pong on the foldable ping pong table in Jared and Mark's room. We were just days into the semester, and the ping pong table had already gained notoriety on our floor. I sighed. It was going to be a long year.

CHAPTER THREE

Thanks to my budding friendship with jovial Ife, I met other freshman African students. We soon developed a small network who dined at the Freeman Dining Hall. Our group of eight girls joined tables and sat at the back near a series of tall glass windows.

After dinner on Wednesday, we went to the ASA meeting. All eight of us got on the shuttle and headed to Sterling, where the ASA meeting was being held in one of the empty rooms upstairs. As the bus approached, we saw students walking into the building.

Ife and I sat near each other toward the front of the shuttle, so we got off first.

As we walked toward the building, a student began walking beside us.

"Going to the ASA meeting?" I asked.

"Yes," he responded.

"Okay, we'll follow you. We don't know where the room is."

"No problem. I'm Chad, the vice president of ASA. You all must be freshmen."

"Yeah? Is it that easy to tell?" I asked.

"Yes, it's pretty obvious. Freshmen travel in packs," he said as he pointed to the group of six girls right behind us.

We looked at each other and laughed.

The meeting was refreshing. From the second we walked

into the room, I felt at home. African music was playing and people were chatting and enjoying themselves before the meeting officially began. African accents, both natural and manufactured, were strewn about. I happened upon a heated discussion about which jollof was better: Nigerian jollof or Ghanaian jollof. I didn't mention that our Cameroon jollof rice was too good to even bother comparing.

As they argued, someone said, "I am going to get pizza."

"Pizza!" another student said in disgust as he took a big bite of the pepperoni-covered pie that he was eating. "Where is the fufu and *egusi* soup?"

"Look at your face!" another girl said, "then stop eating that pizza in your hand!"

He grinned as he took another bite. This was the sort of camaraderie I loved.

Gillian, the president of ASA, began the meeting shortly after she arrived. As she spoke, more people streamed in. Soon, the room was almost full. I was happy to see so many Africans on campus.

Gillian started the meeting by explaining the purpose of ASA: to provide African students with a home away from home while on campus. She also said that ASA was an all-inclusive organization, not just reserved to African students—all were welcome. Then she announced openings on the ASA board; they needed a secretary and parliamentarian.

After the meeting, I went to speak with Gillian about becoming the secretary, and she gave me a form to fill out and bring to the next meeting. Also, Chad introduced me to some of his friends. Chad was from Sierra Leone, he said, and he was a sophomore engineering major.

"Who decided that you were going to be an engineer? You or your parents?" I asked.

"They gave me options, and I chose one."

"What were the options?"

"Engineer or doctor," he said. We both laughed. Typical African parents: whether they were from Sierra Leone or Cameroon, they were always pushing us to strive for the most respected degrees.

"What's your major?" Chad asked.

"Biology."

"Is that what you want to do?"

"Yes, since I was little, I have always wanted to become a doctor," I said.

"Good for you. Come with me, I can introduce you to some other biology majors."

I followed him, and he introduced me to a girl with thick-rimmed eyeglasses, then left us to talk.

"My dear, please be careful o because this major is not one to play with. So many people come in as biology majors and say they want to be doctor, but by the end of the semester, a lot of them change majors o," she said in the thickest African accent. She was from Ghana and had come to the United States to attend college and then medical school.

"Why is that?" I asked. I understood why, but I wanted to get her perspective.

"Because it is difficult. People start the major saying they know science. This college science is difficult o. You must be attentive from the very beginning or things will not end well. Here, I need to give you my number in case you have questions. I can even give you my notes from last year."

"Oh, thank you!"

After we exchanged numbers, I looked around for Ife and Neema. I had lost track of them.

It was already 8:45 p.m. when we exited the building. Because of the evening shuttle's unpredictability, a group of us who lived in the same area walked together. I made it back to my dorm by nine.

Jessica, Casey, and several guys from our floor were lounging around in our room. Thomas was sitting on Kara's bed with his back to the wall, and Kara sat between his legs. Mark was seated in my chair.

"Excuse me," I said as I approached my desk.

"My bad," Mark said as he got up. I placed my backpack on the chair.

I had my 9:15 class the next morning so I went into the bathroom, preparing to take a shower.

While I was in the changing area—the curtained-off space right before entering the shower—Shannon opened the first curtain, just as I was about to pull open the second curtain to enter the shower.

"Oh," she said, her face twisted in a look of repulsion.

I shrieked and looked back at her in shock. She closed the curtain and went away without saying a word.

Still rattled, after my shower, I kept my towel around me as I got dressed in the changing area.

When I entered our room, they hadn't budged.

"Can you take it to the other room?" I asked Kara.

"Let's go to our room," Shannon said, without even acknowledging my presence.

"I don't want to go. I want to stay here," Kara said.

"Well, I need to read for class, and I can't do that with you guys in here," I said.

"Maybe you can read in the lobby," Kara replied.

That didn't sound very reasonable, but I asked, "Will you all be done in an hour maybe?" They were just lying there, talking.

"Sure."

After I situated myself on a comfy armchair in the lobby, I saw Kara and her group of five strolling down the hall.

Why hadn't they just left when I had asked them?

Although I had already gotten comfortable, I called it a night and went back to our room. I was too tired to study.

As I tossed and turned on my pillow, trying to get comfortable enough to sleep, I remembered a school incident just after my family had immigrated. My entire sixth-grade class went to the library. As my luck would have it, the librarian wanted to talk about Africa. As soon as she said this, most of the students turned to look at me because I was the only one in my class who was from Africa. I squirmed in my seat uncomfortably. Even Michelle and her friends were eyeing me.

Displayed in the book from which the librarian read were different pictures of barefoot African children who wore dirty, tattered clothing, and their hair was unkempt. The background showed muddy houses and huts where presumably the children lived. Also shown in the book were pictures of women with buckets of water standing on top of their heads with the support of loincloth rolled into a halo shape.

Under the picture of one of the women was text that read, *Every day Achia walks three kilometers to fetch water at the nearest stream. It takes her approximately one hour to make this trip.*

There were also pictures of men dressed in nothing but a skirt-like cloth that covered the lower half of their bodies. They held up long sticks and their faces were painted with a white chalky substance. Also, their feet were bare and they wore anklets made of small, colorful metal beads. Behind them were more mud houses, and in front of those houses, women were crouched over a large fireplace above which hung a large pot propped up by sticks that had been planted in the ground. The orange and red flames from the fireplace were clear and vivid. This was a portrait of Africa that I had not experienced.

I waited for the librarian to turn the page to show us pictures of the other side of Africa, the side I knew—the side where people lived in concrete houses fully equipped with bathrooms and kitchens, where children wore neat clothes, and shoes, and where the buildings were just as tall and nice as the ones in America. I waited to no avail. The librarian continued to show those same images of indigent African people, living in impoverished areas. To say the least, I was embarrassed. The librarian followed up this presentation by telling us to appreciate everything we had, as the children in Africa had so little compared to us. This statement elicited more stares from my classmates.

When we were returning to our classroom, Billy, a white class-mate, came up to me and asked to see the palms of my hands.

"Why do you want to see my palms?" I asked him.

"Would you please just show me?" he asked.

Hesitantly, I turned my hands over, and immediately a look of disappointment covered his face.

"Oh," he said.

"What?" I demanded.

"My dad and I were watching the news last night, and a woman from Africa was talking and we saw her palms. They were very dark and had spots on them. But your palms are very light, lighter than your skin. Why is it like that?"

I didn't know how to respond. As I looked at my palms, because of the look of disgust that filled his face when he spoke about the woman's dark, spotted palms, my initial instinct was to be proud that my palms were light and not dark and spotted like the lady's he had seen. Then I was overcome by an unsettling feeling.

"Get out of here, Billy. Leave Foma alone," Michelle said before I could gather my words.

As we walked to class, I looked down at my palms and asked myself why they were lighter than the rest of my skin. Was that normal? I observed Michelle's palms and saw that they were almost the same color as her skin.

That evening, I posed this question to Mama. "Huh?" she asked in response.

"A boy at school asked me why my palms were lighter than my skin. Even my friend, her palms and her skin are the same color," I explained.

"Foma, I don't understand the question."

"Mama, let me see your hands," I said as I flipped them over. "Your palms are light just like mine, but your skin is also dark like mine."

"Foma, that is just how God made us. It is perfectly normal, dear. Please, don't pay attention to that stupid boy."

I smacked my pillow at the vivid memory, and the sound of it brought me back to my dark dormitory room. Here I was in college, and it looked like I would have to play the palm game all over again.

The following day, Michelle and I met for lunch. The night before, she had texted saying she missed me and asked if I was free for lunch. I frowned when I arrived at Sterling and found that she had brought Eva. I had thought it would be just the two of us. I wanted to finally tell Michelle how I felt about the SAWP situation.

I joined them in the middle of the food court. We ate as we swapped reports of our first week of school. Michelle mentioned that the Black Student Association (BSA) was having an event that evening. The BSA was the first multicultural association on campus, founded in the 1960s by African American students who felt ostracized at the predominantly white institution.

"We should go! Remember that rapper who had that reality television show with his family?" she asked.

I thought about it for a second. "Oh, yeah, I do."

"He just published a book, and he's gonna be speaking at a BSA event this evening. Eva said she wants to go. I can get all three of us tickets."

Eva nodded her head in agreement.

"Okay, what time?"

"It starts at six."

"Cool."

Shortly after, Eva excused herself because she had class. This was my opportunity to tell Michelle how I felt.

"Michelle, I want to talk to you about SAWP—" I began.

"Oh yes, oh my gosh, I was waiting for her to go. I won! I got the ten thousand dollars." She was more excited than I had seen her in a long time. "I didn't want to say anything while Eva was here."

I bit my tongue. I didn't want to spoil the mood by telling her how I felt. So, I put on my best smile and congratulated her.

"I wanted to tell you so bad last night, but I thought it would be best to tell you in person!"

"I'm happy for you," I lied.

Michelle went on and on, drifting into how she was rethinking her psychology major. Her newfound fame as a writer was causing her to rethink her decision to become a psychiatrist. As she spoke, I tried my best to be supportive, the smile still plastered on my face.

When I arrived at Sterling that evening, Michelle and Eva were waiting for me. I had contemplated making an excuse for why I couldn't make it, but I did want to go. Soon, we were forging our way into a crowded hall and found some empty seats.

My mood immediately lifted when the sweet sounds of old school rap proliferated around the room. I swayed from side to side in my chair, excited about seeing my first celebrity in person. Then the DJ reduced the music to an echo, and Larissa, the president of BSA, came on stage and introduced the rapper. He walked on to the blasting of one of his most famous songs. The cheers inside the hall were deafening.

His speech was motivating. It covered concepts from his book. He spoke about controlling your thoughts because they create the lives we live. This hit home, as I considered the negative thoughts I was having toward Michelle.

Then he spoke about meditating to maintain a calm and positive mind—inhaling the positive and exhaling the negative. He also spoke about setting goals and relentlessly pursuing them, and distancing yourself from toxic people.

After his speech, Larissa moderated the questions-and-answers part of the event, bringing the microphone over to those who raised their hands. The last question of the night made me cringe.

"How can us black students in a university that is predominantly white channel positive thoughts in an environment where we deal with microaggressions or outright racist behavior from our white counterparts?" Larissa asked.

Here we go, I thought.

I sank down low in my seat in embarrassment, even though I understood the frustration of feeling like an "outsider" on our own university campus. Just hours prior, I had been taking a nap in my room when Kara came in with one of her friends.

"Who's your roommate?" I heard the girl ask loudly in a valley girl accent.

After a bout of silence, the girl responded, "Oh!"

I had not heard what Kara said, but I knew what had happened. The girl had assumed I was another white girl. Kara must have mouthed, "She is black."

To me, there was nothing per se racist about this. It was a consequence of us attending a predominantly white university. Although I understood other black students' points of view, it made me uncomfortable. Despite the color of our skin, didn't we all have the same opportunities?

As I slouched down in my chair and brought my hand to my face, I looked up to find the rapper looking at me disapprovingly. I changed my stance; I assumed he disapproved of my mortification over Larissa's question.

CHAPTER FOUR

"Hi, Foma."

Seeing Paige on campus, not in the hospital, was surreal. She had replaced the low bun she sported that summer with springy curls that cascaded around her face.

Months earlier, when Paige found out we would attend the same university, she suggested I take part in the mentorship program the school offered for black students. The program paired incoming black freshman students with black upperclassmen, usually in their same major. She said if I liked, she would ask to be my mentor.

Working with Paige that summer had been terrific. As the internship progressed, we met plenty of doctors who congratulated the four of us high school graduates on being the few selected out of many who applied for the opportunity. The compliments felt good.

I remembered how she helped me after I made an embarrassing error on one of our lab assignments.

"Foma, don't beat yourself up over this. You've been doing a superb job. We all make mistakes. Trust me, I've made a fair amount myself. The most important thing is that we learn from them," Paige had consoled me.

When I stood up to greet her, I held out my hand awkwardly.

"Don't shake my hand. Give me a hug!" she said as she reached in. We hugged awkwardly, mostly because I was so stiff.

"I'm gonna get coffee before we talk. Do you want anything?" she asked.

"No, thank you."

I had been waiting in the café near the library. I picked up my schoolbag from the chair I was saving for her and hung it behind my chair.

"So, how're your parents and grandmother?" she asked as she sat down.

"They're all doing fine. My parents helped me move in, and Nana Ola went back to Cameroon a little over a month ago."

That summer at the hospital, Paige had met my parents because Papa sometimes came to our unit to take me out to lunch. I was always embarrassed when he came, but Paige loved speaking with him about medical issues. I introduced her to Mama and Nana Ola when they came to pick me up from work, and from then on, Paige had a good rapport with them.

"I'm sure you miss her a lot. Your grandmother is a hoot."

"Yes, I do."

"So, how was your first week of classes?"

"It went by fast. There's so much to learn, and so little time to learn it!"

"Yeah, yeah, trust me, I know."

Paige was so active. She was one of the school's ambassadors; she gave tours to prospective students. I had even seen her face on the cover of the school's incoming students' booklet. She blushed when I asked her if she was the girl I had seen on the cover. I learned that she was also the president of the Pre-Med Society.

"Take the quizzes seriously! From my experience, your performance on that first quiz will dictate how you do in the classes for the rest of the semester. Do not fall behind because it will be very difficult to catch up."

I nodded. She wasn't telling me anything that I didn't already know. When I told her about the study schedule I had set for myself, she agreed that it was effective.

"You should also look into a study group. It can be helpful to study with other students because we all have different strengths and weaknesses. Yours will become very clear with a study group."

As we were ending our meeting, Paige said, "Since you're done with class for the day, do you wanna study over at my place? I live in an off-campus town house."

"Sure, I would love that."

We walked outside and jumped into Paige's car. It was a shiny silver car—more luxurious than the vehicles that Mama and Papa drove.

After a bunch of turns, she pulled over and parked. "Welcome to my humble abode," she said as she opened her arms to present her brand-new town house.

"Wow," was all I could say.

The gray brick-stone home looked just as captivating inside. The white and gray interior décor was elegant. With dark gray hardwood flooring, a crystal chandelier in the front hall, and tall windows with sheer white curtains—it was chic. On the powder gray sofa, near silver glass end tables, were plush pillows. I looked up at the light-colored paintings and contemporary pictures on the wall.

How can she afford this? I wondered, though I was not bold enough to ask. I went with the less nosy alternative.

"Do you have roommates?"

"Yes, I have two. Sophie and Monica. They both stay upstairs, and my room is in the basement."

"Okay, nice!"

"Let me give you a brief tour," she said as she showed me around.

Their kitchen reminded me of those kitchens in the magazines. The white marble countertop and breakfast bar looked spotless.

"Does anyone cook in this kitchen?"

"Yes, we use it all the time. Sophie does a lot of baking." She pointed at the fancy mixer at the side of the counter. It was also gray.

"Wow, everything is spotless."

"Yeah, we're all pretty meticulous. Now, I shall take you to my fortress," she said as she led me downstairs.

The basement held a little sitting area and her bedroom. Amid the white and brown décor the first thing that caught my eye was the African mask on the wall, right above the brown sofa. In one corner were framed pictures of different indigenous African people—from Kenya, I suspected. The first photo was of two tall men with colorful beads around their necks and colorful beaded headbands, with feathers that stood tall.

"My mom got me those photos from Kenya," she said.

"Oh yeah, my dad mentioned that your mother travels to African countries for work."

"Yes, of course. My mom is an African studies professor."

"Impressive."

She led me to her bedroom, which was also amazing. Staying true to the white and gray theme upstairs, she had an elegant silver and gray poster bed with white sheets and a white duvet.

"I love your home décor. The gray and white is such a good color scheme. Who came up with it?"

"Sophie and I mostly. It's nice, clean, and simple."

"There is nothing simple about this house."

"Oh, it's okay," Paige said, waving away my compliment.

"We'll be studying in the sitting area," she said as she pointed to the sofa. On each side stood wooden end tables with drawers.

"They extend so you can put your laptop and textbooks on them. We can also use the coffee table, of course. I have a lot of school supplies. Some are in the drawers of the end tables."

"Sounds good."

"I can order pizza, unless you have any other suggestions."

"Pizza is fine," I said. "But please, let me chip in."

She gave me a look of the senior in charge. "Absolutely not!"

I took a seat on the sofa and began taking my books out.

"Want anything to drink?" Paige asked from upstairs.

"Water, thank you."

Shortly thereafter, Paige came downstairs with two bottles of water. We cracked open our books and got to work. I liked to make notecards to facilitate my studying, and sure enough, I found packs of notecards in the drawer of my end table.

We were deep in studying when we heard the front door open. The hum of classical violins did not drown out the sound of the footsteps upstairs.

"That must be Monica," Paige said.

"Hello, Paigey-poo!" came a voice from upstairs.

"I'm down here!" Paige yelled.

Then we heard footsteps descending the stairs. Not long after, a tall white girl with long brown hair appeared.

"Is this the mentee?" Monica asked as she hugged Paige and then came over to hug me.

"Yes. Foma, this is Monica, and Monica, this is Foma."

"Nice to meet you!" Monica said.

Ding-dong, the doorbell rang, and Paige stood up.

"That must be the pizza; I'll be right back," she said as she and Monica headed upstairs.

After we ate, Paige took me home.

"Let me know if you need me for anything or if you wanna have another study session," she said as I got out of the car.

"Thank you, Paige, I'm so grateful to have you here."

Again, Paige waved away my compliment. "It's my pleasure. Greet your parents for me," Paige said as I shut the door.

Watching her car speed away, I couldn't help but hope that some of Paige would rub off on me. She was so together: she had academic success, was well-respected on campus and had an elegant town house and a fancy car, and seemed to get along with her roommates. Papa was right in recommending that I stick by Paige. I was lucky to have her as a source of support.

That evening at our ASA meeting, the members voted me in as secretary and Ife, parliamentarian. I beamed at my fellow ASA members when my position became official. For the first time since coming to America, I felt pride in being African. Although I had mastered how to talk without an African accent, with my ASA family I could let my African accent free without the annoyance of people asking where I was from.

Most of the members of ASA were born in America, but they claimed their African heritage proudly. This impressed me. Nothing annoyed me more than when American-born Africans turned their backs on their heritage.

The next day, Ife and I were in a group study room at the library, studying for our chemistry quiz, when a tall guy walked by. Passersby could see in through the glass walls.

"Oh, Kunle!" Ife said as she waved at a tall, buff guy with neatly cut hair and a deep brown skin tone.

He peered into our room and opened the door.

"What up, little sis?" he asked as he hugged Ife. Then he glanced my way and smiled. "Who is this?"

"Kunle, this is my friend Foma."

"Ife and Foma, how lovely. What're you ladies studying?" He lifted the opened cover of Ife's textbook. "Ugh, chemistry." He twisted his face in disgust. "I'll stick with political science."

"We have a quiz tomorrow," Ife informed him.

"The two doctors to be! I am sure your parents are proud o. Look at the way the two of you are just here studying."

His eyes pierced me. He furrowed his brows as though he was trying to place me.

"Where are you from?" he asked me.

"Cameroon. And you?"

"Ahh, I knew you were one of us. I am from Naija. Can you not tell?" he asked, feigning annoyance.

"I am sorry o, I don't like to assume," I said in an African accent, imitating his.

"It is well, I won't hold it against you."

"What're you doing here?" Ife asked.

He looked hurt. "Why? Can I not come and say hello? Is my presence disturbing you?"

"No-o. I was just wondering what you were doing in the library," Ife said, pointing to his hand, which held a sheaf of flyers.

"I do actually visit the library from time to time for academic purposes. But today I'm here to hang up these flyers." He gave one to each of us.

"What's it for?"

"Have you heard about the Elijah Barnett shooting? We're marching on Monday and having a Town Hall meeting on Tuesday to discuss it."

A few nights earlier, Elijah, a local teenager, had been jogging in his neighborhood when a member of a neighborhood watch, "fearing" that Elijah was up to no good, followed him. After an altercation the man shot Elijah three times in the back, killing him.

"Thank you, Kunle. I would love to join, but I have lab at that time on Monday," I told him.

"I don't know the facts of the case, so I don't know for sure if I will participate," Ife responded.

"You don't know the facts? We already know what this is about. That coward saw a black kid jogging in the suburbs and just assumed that he was up to no good," Kunle said.

"How do you know that for sure?" Ife asked.

Kunle's tone was firm but calm. "You need to open your eyes to what's going on around you. They don't respect us. We are suffering out here, and black people like you who choose to not see that are part of the problem."

"Okay, so now I'm the problem? All I said was that I don't have all the facts. And tell me, how are you suffering?"

"Coming from a successful family cannot protect us. Elijah's parents are successful too, and that means nothing. This is all they see," he said, pointing at his skin.

"Hey, all I am saying is that I can't say that man killed Elijah because he was black if I don't have the facts to prove it."

Kunle shook his head. "Well, I gave you the flyer. If you can join, we would appreciate it. Have a good one, ladies."

"Bye," Ife said curtly.

"Enjoy the rest of your day," I said. He gave me a lingering look before he walked away.

Her frown changed after he was gone. "I think he likes you."

"What?" I asked, pretending that I did not also get that impression.

"Did you not see the way he was looking at you?"

"No." I played coy.

"But I don't understand what struggles he has had. His father works for the Nigerian government, and his mother is a vice president at a bank here in the U.S. You should see their house."

"You've been there before?" I asked her.

"Yeah. My mom is friends with his mother, and he and my brother are best friends. Ever since he started at this college, all he talks about now is race or racism. That is why he left ASA o. He left his people to join BSA because he said ASA does not like to talk about real issues." Ife put air quotes around the words "real issues."

"Okay, I see."

"He tried to convince me not to join ASA, but I'll do what I want."

"What year is he?"

"He's a senior."

The butterflies in my stomach settled. If he was a senior, he couldn't be interested in me, a freshman. Even if he was, he would be graduating soon. I kept telling myself excuses until I could finally concentrate on the chemistry page in front of me.

CHAPTER FIVE

Kara's bed was empty when I woke up. This was the third morning in a row that I woke up to find her bed empty. I assumed she spent the night with Thomas. I hoped that this would be a frequent occurrence.

As I left my room, my mind was on the bacon, egg, and cheese breakfast sandwich sold at my favorite fast-food restaurant at Sterling. I had a biology quiz that morning, and I had my note-cards in my backpack to review the material while I ate breakfast. I felt my chemistry quiz from the week prior had gone all right, but I couldn't be certain until we got our grades back.

My phone vibrated as I walked to the stairs. "Good morning, my love," Nana Ola said on the other end of the phone. Her voice lifted my spirit.

"Where are you, Nana Ola?" I asked her. I could hear the wind blowing on her end.

"I'm outside, sitting in the veranda. How is school?"

"Everything at school is fine. I like it so far."

"How is that your friend...eh...?"

"Michelle. She is doing fine. How's everyone over there?" I changed the conversation hurriedly, before Nana Ola could ask me if I had had the talk with Michelle.

"Humph. Everything is fine o. But Susana is always disturbing me. 'Ma, do you want this?' 'Ma, do you want that?'" Nana Ola said, imitating Susana's drawly, nasally tone.

"But, Nana, she is just looking out for you to make sure you're doing okay," I managed between my laughter.

"Yes, I know, but she is treating me like I'm a child," Nana Ola muttered in a loud whisper.

Just then I heard Susana's nasally drawl in the background. "Ma, where are you?"

"Osh!" Nana Ola exclaimed. "Now she has found me and will begin disturbing me again!"

I had just gone down a flight of stairs, and I stood at the bottom of the first flight, shaking with laughter. I was laughing so hard I got stomach cramps. I bent down to hold my knees for support.

"Be nice, Ma," I said in Susana's nasally drawl. We both laughed. I missed her so much. I longed to be back in her village. My last visit to see her had been wonderful.

"I am always nice. She should stop treating me like a child o. You seem like you are out of breath. What are you doing?"

"I'm just going down the stairs. I'm headed to class."

"Okay, o. I was just calling to greet you."

As I walked out of the building, I saw the shuttle approaching.

"Okay, Nana. I will call you sometime this week."

On the noisy shuttle, laughter still shivered in my chest. I didn't want to look like a crazy person, so I covered my face with my hands as I let out the last bit of laughter. Laughter formed the basis of my relationship with Nana Ola, and I missed watching the dynamic between Nana Ola and Susana. Their battles had been epic.

I still remembered Nana Ola's house in Buea, the one she lived in with Pa Ola, her husband and Mama's father, before he passed away. As long as I could remember, I spent most of my summers at that house when we still lived in Cameroon. Nana Ola was the

unofficial mayor of the area—everyone knew her, and her home
was open to many. She had one of the biggest homes in the neighborhood—the lime green home with tan canopy brick pillars that
surrounded it, and a reddish-brown roof. Her home had many
bedrooms and two living quarters for her house help.

I can still smell the mouthwatering scent of the grilling food
coming from the stations of the different vendors in that town.
Near the bus stop, metal bars held up the zinc roof of the grill site.
Inside, grill metal sheets were distributed throughout the space,
forming a right angle. Men perspired as they flipped over *suya*
meat on long metal skewers. The light post, headlights of vehicles,
and the light coming from the grill spaces illuminated the area.

Beside the grilling site, women sat on plastic crates, tending
to their roasting corn and fish on the small grills before them. Their
heads were tied in a variety of styles with *ankara* cloth, and they
wore t-shirts and wrapped ankara print loincloths around their
waists. Another group of women would fry *puff puff* and *accra*
banana in the large black pots on top of their outdoor stoves—
large rocks encircling a firewood-lit fire. Some women would stir
beans, which I ate with puff puff. They would talk to each other
and laugh, only silencing their chatter when customers came to
make their purchases.

Makossa music permeated the air, coming from the vehicles
on the road and the motorcycles called *benzikins*—the cheapest
form of transportation for those who did not want to pay for a taxi.
The city was alive with people talking and little children running
around while their mothers cooked.

"Come with me, my dear. Let's buy suya meat and fish,"
Nana Ola would say.

"And puff puff," I always reminded her.

"Of course, and puff puff, my dear."

"Mami, good evening," the women would greet Nana Ola
as we walked to the station where Nana Ola preferred to buy her
grilled fish.

Nana Ola always stopped to talk to each woman who greeted her. Seeing the admiration on their faces when they spoke to Nana Ola made me feel proud to be her granddaughter. Nana Ola seemed to know everybody. She asked about their children and spouses, which brought pleasure to their faces; this important woman cared about them.

Nana Ola was in fact an important woman. Although Pa Ola had been a learned man with a European law degree, Nana Ola with only a high school level education was a jurist in her own right. When people had disputes in her neighborhood, they came to her. They trusted her judgment. Thanks to my grandmother's notoriety, I was treated very well. When I played outside with friends from the neighborhood, people gave me things just because they recognized me as her granddaughter.

"Is Mama Nanadou your grandmother?" they'd ask.

"Yes, auntie," or "Yes, uncle," I'd reply proudly.

"Okay, come and take," they'd say, as they gave me anything from candy to fruit. Some even called me to go to their homes to eat with their children.

These types of things were common in Cameroon. Young children like myself called almost everyone older than us auntie or uncle. We trusted people, until they gave us a reason not to. Because we regarded almost everyone as a distant relative in the Cameroonian culture, we often lacked reason not to trust each other. The saying "it takes a village to raise a child" could not have rung truer in Cameroon.

I also got to know Susana. On my first day at Nana Ola's house the summer after Susana moved in with Nana Ola, my grandmother had told me all about her.

"That girl is truly a village girl. On her first day here, I showed her how to turn on the faucet in the kitchen and the bathroom. You should have seen the way her eyes bulged when she saw water streaming out. When she felt that the water was warm, she jumped and asked, 'Nah who di boil wata?'" Nana Ola said, imitating

Susana's nasally voice and her Kamtok—Cameroonian pidgin English. We laughed as we lay down on Nana Ola's veranda, above blankets she laid out on that cool June Buea night. This was one of my favorite things to do with Nana Ola—lie out on the veranda with her at night while she told me stories.

Nana Ola called Susana a village girl because Susana grew up in a small country town, and growing up, she did not have exposure to some of the most basic things, like having a faucet or bathroom inside the house. That's why, when she felt the hot water coming from the faucet, she assumed that someone must have been boiling the water and filtering it through.

One day that summer, Nana Ola had to go to visit a woman who had just given birth. She told me I could not go with her because she would be away too long. I could sense that Nana Ola was tired of me tagging along everywhere she went, so I let her go without fussing.

While she was gone, a group of neighborhood girls came with the extension cords they used for jump rope—they had taped several extension cords together to create a thick rope. I agreed to join them because jumping rope was my favorite activity. I was a fantastic rope jumper. I could do tricks when I jumped rope, and liking to show off, I did my best trick of bending down low and coming back up as I jumped.

We were jumping by the concrete veranda and my leg got caught in the opening between the taped extension cords, and off I went, falling headfirst to the veranda. I felt the worst pain of my life. I rolled on the ground crying, blood gushing down my face. The girls went running for Susana, who was inside the house.

"Ma mami!" Susana exclaimed when she saw me.

She ran around frantic, not knowing what to do. In the throes of the fiery hot pain I felt, I yelled for Susana to get something to wrap my head. Even I knew that much. Susana yelled for the girls to go call Nana Ola while she ran inside to get me something to wrap my head with.

After what felt like forever, even though I was certain it was just about half an hour, Nana Ola's red car zoomed into the compound, and they carried me to a neighborhood clinic. It was in a small house. I remember lying on the mattress on the long table while the doctor examined my cut and gave me medicine before suturing the four-inch gash on my forehead.

For days, I had the worst headache of my life. Mama and Papa told me it was time to go home, and they would come get me. I refused. I had another week left with Nana Ola, and I had no intentions of cutting my summer break short, like they had done the year prior. So, each night that week, I slept with Nana Ola because she could not bear to be away from me.

"I left you in the house and see what happened?" she moaned as she lay beside me.

She told me folk tales every time I asked, and she had Susana kill a chicken so that she could make me "special soup."

As the days went by, I watched as the cut healed. I was amazed by how the doctor had closed the long wound on my forehead to the point that the skin was sealed and healing nicely.

When I returned home that summer, I told Mama and Papa that I wanted to become a doctor.

In my biology lab that evening, we dissected a rabbit. I winced as I tore into its tough skin. I fought the instinct to reach for my forehead, to make sure that the cut from ten years ago was still nicely healed. I knew dissecting would be the toughest part of practicing medicine, so I had talked myself up to it before my lab.

"You can do this!" I told myself.

The largest animal I had ever dissected was a frog in high school biology. It was no match for this large rabbit before me.

When I got out of lab, I spotted a small gathering of students. On the shuttle, I overheard details of the march from a group of black students talking about the news helicopter that followed the marchers' movements.

Kara was not in the room when I got back, but I could tell that she had been there earlier. Strewn on her bed were clothes that had not been there that morning.

After taking my shower, I tuned the television to the ten o'clock local news. A few minutes later, I saw images of protesting students. They chanted, "Justice! When do we want it? Now!" and "Justice! When do we need it? Now!"

When the newscaster mentioned the Town Hall meeting was to take place on campus the following day, I decided I would go.

If nothing else, I would be obeying my grandmother's love for justice.

CHAPTER SIX

I persuaded Ife to go to the Town Hall meeting with me. Michelle said she was busy, of course.

The meeting was more crowded than I had expected. It was open to the community at large, which explained the diversity of the attendees. Three professors from the African American Studies Department were panelist members. The event began with the display of a big noose on the overhead projector right behind the panelists' table. I and many others in the room gasped.

After the noose, an image of Elijah Barnett's tenth-grade yearbook picture, taken just months prior, was displayed on the large screen. He was smiling, without a clue that just months later, a grown man would gun him down because he saw him as a "threat."

During the event, the professors gave powerful responses to the questions asked. The ones they gave to the last question gave me goosebumps.

"When people ask me, why do black people always talk about race? I tell them it is because society reminds us of our race every day. Elijah got his reminder when that man stopped him because he saw the color of his skin and assumed that Elijah was up to no good. Now, where is little Elijah? In a morgue somewhere. This is real life, folks. We are under threat every day," Professor Bonds said.

In her response, Professor Sharon Davies recounted seeing a bumper sticker that read, "Had I known, I would've have picked my own cotton." "This is what we deal with every day. I too wish they had picked their own cotton. But now we are here, and this is our home, so deal with it. The only way for us to fix the race issue in America is to acknowledge it exists and speak out against it."

After the panelist segment was over, Kunle came on stage to conclude the event.

"Thank you, everyone, for coming out today. We really appreciate your support. To all the other black organizations on campus: we need to come together to target these race issues. We are all blacks in America; it doesn't matter where you are from originally. This message is specifically for the African Student Association and the Caribbean Student Association," he said.

"That stupid boy, did he have to call us out like that?" Ife huffed.

At our next ASA meeting, Gillian said Kunle had reached out and wanted the ASA and BSA to co-sponsor an event regarding the rift between African and African American students on campus.

I knew what he was talking about. Africans and African Americans had a tendency to look down on one another.

When Gillian asked if we agreed that there was a rift, most of us raised our hands and we agreed to co-sponsor the event. They voted me as lead organizer from the ASA. I hardly minded, since that gave me a chance to talk to Kunle again.

The following week, we met in the downstairs lobby of my dorm. He was serious and all about business. After the way he had looked at me the first time we met, I expected him to be flirty. I had even worn jeans that hugged my hips in just the right way and a tight top that teased some cleavage. He did not seem to notice.

After we agreed on the layout of the event, I asked him squarely, "Why are you so into talking about race stuff?"

"Because I am black."

"I am too, but you're more passionate than most people I know. Why is that?"

"Remember what Professor Davies said at the Town Hall? The only way we can end racism is to acknowledge it and speak against it."

"That's true."

"Besides, you must care. I heard you were the only one from ASA advocating for this event. Why is that?"

"I'll be honest. When I was younger, some African Americans teased me for being African, and I also saw how some African adults around me looked down on African Americans. It shouldn't be like that. We are all black."

"Interesting."

"Were you not teased for being African?"

"Yes, of course," Kunle said. "I came when I was twelve, and I went to an inner-city school because they had a good magnet program. But the black boys in my class called me 'black monkey' and would tell me to go back to Africa. They were terrible! My dark skin did not help. A friend of mine was African, but he didn't get teased nearly as much as I did because he was light-skinned."

"I'm sorry about that. I went through something similar. In Cameroon, I never gave the color of my skin a second thought, but in America, I overheard a black classmate say that he wouldn't date me because even though I was pretty, I was dark-skinned and that he doesn't 'do' dark-skinned girls. Like what did that even mean? We were only like eleven years old, and I had no interest in him."

"Slavery and colonialism have done a number on our people. It's all self-hate and lack of self-respect. It is sad how early it starts. How old were you when you came?"

"I was ten," I said. "How long were you teased for?"

"The teasing stopped after my growth spurt. At six feet, two inches, I was big enough to beat their behinds, and they knew it. Then I started playing football and basketball, and everyone wanted to be my friend because I was good."

I ignored him bragging on himself. "It is funny how being good at sports can change things in America."

We both chuckled. "As I started making friends with African Americans in high school, I understood why they made fun of me. Africa gets a bad rep in American media. The media portrays us as destitute and starving, and blacks here don't want to be associated with that. Likewise, it portrays African Americans as criminals and thugs, and our African parents assume it is true."

"This event will be powerful, Kunle. Thank you for thinking of it."

"No problem."

As we headed out of the room, Kunle asked, "So, would you like to grab dinner sometime?"

A wave of heat rushed to my cheeks. Not sure if he was asking me out, I responded, "Yeah, sure. Ife and I usually eat at the dining hall. You're more than welcome to join us anytime you want."

Kunle frowned, presumably because I had included Ife. "Have a good night, Foma. We can touch base again in the coming week about the event."

And like that, he was gone.

His story about being teased for being African brought back a stinging memory. I had met Michelle on the first day of sixth grade at Harris Middle School. In the cafeteria at lunchtime, I looked around. I didn't know where to sit. I saw a familiar face, and I remembered the girl's name was Michelle. I had three classes with her. She had asked to borrow my pencil sharpener in math class. I was sure she would recognize me.

"Hi, can I sit here?" I asked her. She was sitting at a table with six other black girls.

"Yeah, sure," she said cheerfully. "What's your name again?"

"Foma. And you're Michelle, right?"

"Yes."

Michelle introduced me to the other girls seated at the lunch table.

"Where are you from? You have an accent," Michelle asked.

"I am from Cameroon."

"Where is that?"

"It is a country in Africa," I said.

Out of nowhere a boy seated right behind us blurted out, "You from Africa?" He had a light brown complexion and an Afro.

"Yes," I replied.

"African booty scratcher!" he mocked, and the boys seated at his table laughed. The laughter encouraged him. "Go back to Africa, you African booty scratcher."

I froze.

"Shut up, Jamaal!" Michelle said to him.

I sat there looking petrified.

"Sorry about him, he's so ignorant."

Then the Africa questions began.

"Did you live in a hut in Africa?" one girl asked.

"What did y'all wear?" another wanted to know.

"Did you have lions as pets?"

I couldn't take any more. "I'm feeling sick, I gotta go."

I got up and hurried to the exit. I dumped my food in the trashcan and went straight to the bathroom. I stayed in a stall until the bell rang. Lunch period was over. I checked my class schedule and made the lonely walk to my next class.

The rest of the school day was a blur. I couldn't wait to get home. As soon as I walked through the door that afternoon, Mama called out, "Foma, how was your first day of school?"

Tears rolled down my eyes as I told Mama about Jamaal.

"Dear, don't worry about that foolish boy."

"But, Mama, he embarrassed me in front of everyone."

"Foma, dear, he was just being silly. People will forget about it by tomorrow, if they haven't already."

So, yes, I knew what Kunle meant.

⌒

Later that evening, I went downstairs to let Michelle into my building. A few hours earlier, she had texted me to say she was coming.

"I feel like I haven't seen you in ages," I said as I opened the door for her.

"Yeah, I know. How've you been? What's been happening?"

"Same ole. You know Kunle, right?"

"Do I? Mr. Tall, Dark, and Sexy from BSA?"

"Yup, that's the one."

"Why do you ask?"

"We just had a meeting. We're planning the Bridging the Gap event that BSA and ASA are co-sponsoring."

"Oh, I didn't know."

"I thought you were a part of BSA."

"I'm a general member, not a board member."

"Okay. Anywho, I think Kunle just asked me out on a date."

"What?"

"Yeah, after the meeting, he asked me if I wanted to grab dinner sometime."

"What did you say?"

I cringed. "I invited him to join Ife and me for dinner."

Michelle's frown confirmed how idiotic my answer was. "You friend-zoned him?"

"I didn't mean to. I didn't know what to say."

"Argh, Foma."

We were upstairs in my room when Kara, Shannon, and Casey walked in.

"Hello," Kara said. Her friends said nothing.

"Hi," I responded.

Michelle stared at them.

"He said he doesn't want to hang out tonight," Kara complained to her friends, obviously continuing a former conversation.

"Did he say why?" Casey asked.

"What's going on?" Jessica asked as she peered into the room. Her lower half was still in the bathroom.

"Thomas doesn't want to hang out with Kara tonight," Shannon said.

Jessica walked by Michelle and me and stood in front of her friends, not giving us the time of day.

The strained situation didn't last for long. When Kara and her friends left, Michelle said immediately, "I see what you were talking about. They all seem bratty."

"Oh my gosh, I'm glad it's not just me."

"Forget them. How was that Town Hall meeting?"

"It was intense, but good."

"What made it intense?"

"They started off the event with the image of a noose on the projector."

"Oh, yeah, that does sound intense. So, what is this Bridging the Gap event going to be about?"

"The divide between Africans and African Americans on campus."

"Do you feel like there's a divide?"

"Yeah...don't you? Well, it is a little different with you because your dad is Jamaican and your mom is white. You're not really African American."

She protested, "Yes, I am African American."

"Not in the traditional sense you're not. From my understanding, African Americans are the descendants of slaves in America."

"Oh, I've just always called myself African American."

"I know, people don't really think about that, but I have no choice but to think about it."

"Why is that?"

"When I came to America, my accent gave away that I was African. But when I lost my accent, people started referring to me as African American. That confused me, so I looked it up. African American is not a skin color, it's a culture."

"Oh, yeah? I never thought about it."

"People like me can't afford not to think about it. I went through a lot because I was African, so I'm just sensitive about cultures and titles. Don't you remember Jamaal calling me an African booty scratcher in the sixth grade?"

"No, not really," she said. "That was so long ago."

"Yes, it was, but I remember because I'm still mortified by it."

"I think I vaguely remember," she said casually. Then she clapped her hands. "So, I've been meaning to ask: are you interested in going with me to New York City next month?"

"What for?"

"A few of the girls from SAWP are in NYC for college, and we've been planning a reunion. I mentioned that you're also interested in writing, and they said you can come."

She had hit a sore spot. "Interested in writing? If it wasn't for me, you would've never known about SAWP." Once I had started, I couldn't stop. I said what I had been holding in for months. "I was the writer in this friendship. You never once told me you were interested in writing until after you went behind my back and applied for it. Don't make it seem like you thought of it all on your own."

Michelle's mouth dropped open. "I didn't go behind your back."

"When I told you about the opportunity, you never once said you were interested. Then you went and applied without saying a word to me."

"That's because I didn't think I was going to get in."

"So, you don't see how you were wrong for applying without telling me?"

"No, I don't. The application was open for anybody. You're only mad because I got to go and you didn't. Stop being dramatic, Foma."

It didn't help that she was partly right. "I am not being dramatic. I am also not mad that you got to go. I just don't like how you went about it."

"You can't tell me you're not jealous because I won that award and money." She rose to her feet. "I've been sensing that you're not happy for me. I get it, that's why you're picking this fight."

I didn't like having to look up at her. "No one is jealous of you. I thought you would understand where I'm coming from, but you're too self-absorbed to think about anyone else's feelings but your own."

"You know what, Foma, I am tired of you playing victim. You always feel that someone is doing something to you. I had the opportunity to go and I took it."

"No one is playing the victim. You're my best friend and you hurt me. If you can't see that, I have to question this friendship."

"You're always playing the victim. Like bringing up that whole Jamaal thing from the sixth grade. Get over it! It was middle school. We all got picked on!"

"Whatever, Michelle. Like I said, you're too self-absorbed to consider my feelings. You were the 'it' girl in grade school. You can never understand what I'm talking about."

By now we were shouting at each other. "You know what, I'm not doing this with you. I'm out of here." Michelle stormed out.

"Bye," I yelled after her.

I stood there fuming. Yet I was disappointed in how I'd approached it. I hadn't expected our talk to end in a fight. I had every right to be upset with her, and she was wrong about middle school. I wasn't playing the victim, I kept repeating to myself. She was born and raised in the United States. She could never understand how isolating it is to not just move to a new country, but a new continent, and for people to tease you because of where you came from.

I covered my hands over my face. Michelle and I had had disagreements before, but it had never ended in a screaming match. She was one of the few friends I had on campus, and I had hoped to maintain my cool and approach the situation delicately. However, now I wasn't sure if we would ever speak to each other again.

CHAPTER SEVEN

I was walking back to my dorm from class when I heard someone call my name. I turned around and saw Paige and her
roommate Monica. They were walking with a short blonde
girl I did not recognize.

Paige's bouncy curls concealed most of the left side of her
fair face. She was wearing her school ambassador polo and slacks.
She towered over her blonde friend, who stood to her left. "This
is Dawn. We're heading over to Sterling. You wanna have lunch
with us?"

Soon I was sitting with them, burger and fries before me. I
was more of a spectator than a participant in their conversation.
At first, Dawn and Monica asked me brief biographical questions,
but they were now talking as though I was not there. I didn't
mind. Paige was one of the few black people I knew with mostly
white friends, and I was interested in observing her relationship
with them.

In high school, a girl on the field hockey team, Niecy, had all
white friends, and she was the only black girl on the team. Out
of curiosity, I used to watch her and her white friends. The same
girls who didn't give me the time of day rushed to talk with Niecy
when they saw her.

Unlike Paige, however, Niecy was a dark-skinned black girl
like me. While it was easy to reconcile how someone as fair-skinned

as Paige could innocuously fit in with an all-white friend group, it puzzled me how Niecy fit in with those preppy white girls.

Niecy only spoke to her white friends. On my first day of school at St. Joseph Academy, I approached her because we were the only two black students in my homeroom. After throwing a cool greeting my way, she walked away and began talking to her white friends. I did not initiate contact with her again after that day.

"She's an Oreo," Michelle commented that night when I told her about it.

"What does that mean?"

"She is white on the inside but black on the outside," she had responded.

Thinking of Michelle made me angry. I hadn't spoken to her since our fight. I knew she was waiting for me to reach out first, like I always did, but that was not happening this time.

After we finished eating, Paige's friends left, and Paige and I walked out together.

"Where're you headed?" Paige asked me.

"Back to my dorm."

"There's a party this Saturday at one of the frat houses. You should come with me."

"Um. I would love to go, but there's this party at Sterling this Saturday."

"Oh. What party is that?"

"The multicultural programming board is hosting it."

She frowned. "Yeah, the MPB. I always wanted to go to one of those parties."

"It is not too late. You can come with me and my friends." I knew she would not accept.

"No, that's okay. I'm a senior now. My time for those parties has long passed."

"Okay, let me know if you change your mind."

We hugged and parted ways.

Because Michelle and I were still not talking, I went to the party with Ife and Neema.

The morning of the party, I slept in. It was almost noon when I dragged myself out of bed. Ife texted saying she and Neema were headed to our meet-up spot. The thought of waffles made my stomach growl.

As soon as I stepped into the bathroom, I saw my light green towel on the floor, a puddle of someone's dirty bath water under it. The drain in the shower was always clogging. I stood there trying to understand why it was my towel on the floor.

I heard someone fiddling with the doorknob to our room, so I turned as Kara walked in.

"Kara, who put my towel on the bathroom floor?"

"I did," she responded.

"Why?"

"The shower overflowed and someone didn't bother to put a towel down."

"Why did you use my towel, though?"

"I needed something quick."

"Why didn't you use the towels hanging on the bar in the bathroom?"

"I didn't know who they belonged to."

"But you used mine, knowing it belonged to me. Did you use your own towels?"

She hesitated. "Yes," she said finally.

I walked over to her towel hamper between our wardrobes. I didn't see a single wet towel.

"They are all dry."

"Well, I just grabbed the first towel I saw," she said defensively.

"You should've used yours. I hope you're planning on washing my towel and putting it back where you found it."

She gave me a dirty look and left the room. I stood there in awe.

"Are you okay?" Neema asked when she and Ife found me sitting on a bench scowling. I was still livid from Kara using my towel.

"No, I am pissed."

"What happened?" Ife asked.

I explained everything.

"That your roommate is so disrespectful," Ife said. She sometimes spoke in an African accent when she was annoyed.

"Yeah, she is," Neema said. "If I were you, I would've thrown her towels down right next to yours."

While we ate, I complained about my rooming situation in general. She was constantly monopolizing our room, and I was sick of the lack of respect and consideration.

"You can stay in my room for the rest of the day," Ife offered. "Let's get your clothes after brunch. You can get dressed for the party in my room."

"Thank you, Ife."

The party was just what I needed. Ife, Neema, and I danced the night away in the dimly lit room. I spotted Michelle, and she gave me a dirty look but said nothing. I knew she thought I would have apologized by then, but I still had no intention of apologizing.

The night was almost over when someone grabbed my hand. I turned around and I found myself face to face with Kunle. He was grinning at me.

"What's up?"

I felt a rush. "Hi."

"How are you doing tonight?" he asked as he entangled his hand with mine.

"I'm doing good. How are you?"

We were now facing each other. I could smell his cologne and sweat. I looked up at him, and butterflies filled my stomach. He was looking into my eyes. Thanks to the shots I had taken at Ife's room and adrenaline from a night of dancing, I was bold enough to match his stare.

A slow song filled the room. The DJ was wrapping up the party. Kunle leaned back against the wall and pulled me close, until I was leaning against his body. He raised my right hand and spun me around. My back was now to him.

"Dance with me," he whispered in my ear.

We danced to several slow songs before the lights finally came on.

I was now back to being my usual shy self. "See you later," I said to him as I tried to flee to Ife.

"Nope, not so fast," Kunle said teasingly.

He pulled me in for a hug. He smelled so good. When I tried to pull back, we were face to face, and then before I knew it, his soft lips touched mine. Now I really wanted to run away.

"See you later," he said, and then just like that, he was gone.

Ife and Neema came running over. "Oh, my gosh, Foma! Don't tell me you and big-head are now a thing," Ife cried.

I didn't respond because I didn't know what we were.

CHAPTER EIGHT

That Monday morning, I wore my best outfit, a black blouse and jeans, both very flattering to my figure. I had butterflies in my stomach all day as I counted down the hours until four o'clock, when Kunle and I planned to meet to set up the Bridging the Gap event.

I began walking over to Sterling twenty minutes early. In the empty room, I put my things down on an empty chair at the front of the room. For what was probably the thousandth time, I thought about that Saturday night. The way Kunle pulled me to him and held me.

Kunle's voice shook me out of my daydreaming. I turned to see him walking toward me.

"No African time for you, huh?" he asked.

I chuckled. African time was a stigma that followed us because our events usually started hours after the invitation time. I'm not sure if people purposely came late because they "knew" no one would be there on time, or if they just lost track of time.

"Not today," I said.

As he came near, I froze. He had a grin on his face.

"I can't get a hug?"

"Bring it in," I said, trying to maintain my cool.

We hugged, and before I could pull away, he kissed me. I kissed him back, but abruptly he pulled away and began organizing the chairs. I stood there awkwardly, then decided to join in. I didn't know what to make of this thing between us. He was the first guy I had ever kissed, and I had always imagined my first kiss being with a boyfriend. However, here Kunle was, kissing me casually. Did that mean we were in a relationship? We had never even been on a date and I hadn't given him permission to initiate the first kiss. Now, because I hadn't protested to the first kiss, he thought he could kiss me anytime he wanted. I decided I would ask questions the next time he kissed me.

When the room was all set up, we went through the flow of the event, and by five, people began streaming into the room.

As planned, Kunle started the event by asking if there was a rift between the African and African American community. Not surprising, more than half of the attendees raised their hands.

"For those of you who raised your hands, who would like to explain why they think there is a rift between our two communities?" I asked.

"Africans think they're better than us," Krystal said.

"Can you elaborate?" Kunle asked.

"It's hard to explain. I just get that vibe," she clarified.

"Who else gets that vibe, and can anyone articulate it?" I asked.

"I do," Trina, the secretary of BSA, said. "I've noticed that Africans on our campus don't get involved in racial issues. They didn't join us in our march to protest Elijah Barnett's killing, and I don't remember seeing any ASA members at the Town Hall."

"Trina, I was there," I responded, "but I understand what you're saying. To the Africans in the room, how do you respond to what Krystal and Trina have said?"

"I don't think we feel we are better than African Americans," Chad began. "I think it's the other way around. In grade school, African Americans bullied many of my African cousins and friends who immigrated to America at young ages. These experiences stay with people, which is why many of the Africans I know prefer to stick with each other on campus. I was born here, so things were a little easier on me."

"I agree with Chad's point," Gillian put in. "I also have to add that some Africans don't get involved in quote-unquote black issues because we have different views on life. Most of our parents are immigrants; they came to this country to make a good living so they can take care of their families. They raised us to be successful and not bother ourselves with race issues."

"The problem with that, Gillian, is," Rhonda responded, "Africans are black just like us, and are not immune from racism. You may not care about casual racism, but you saw what happened to Elijah Barnett. Elijah could be your brother. That's why we call racism out. You can only end racism if you speak out against it. I bet most of you will end up staying in America. If you do, there is a strong possibility that some racist jerk may harm you or your family for no reason but the fact that you are black. Racists don't care where you come from."

"That's a good point, Rhonda," Jacob said. "Many of us are staying in America long-term. However, I don't think we can ever feel the same pain that y'all feel about racial issues because despite the racism, the circumstances here are still better than what awaits us in our respective countries. America provides us opportunities that we wouldn't have otherwise."

"Exactly," Jerome said. "My parents came here because even with an education, they couldn't find good jobs in Nigeria. When they got here, they worked hard and went to school and they've done very well for themselves. My parents have expressly told me to work hard and not worry about racism."

"Also," Kunle said, "I must point out that in Africa, people don't think of white people negatively. When people in African countries think about whites and white countries, they think about wealth, educational opportunities, and economic advancement. Yes, when Africans come to America, they face racism. However, I think many Africans in our parents' generation feel an indebtedness to whites for allowing them into their countries to take advantage of these opportunities."

"I agree with Kunle," I said. "In Africa, we looked at white people as saviors. Most people in Africa want to live in a 'white country,' so it is hard for us to see white people as oppressors. Also, personally, growing up, my parents made it seem like there is a high percentage of poverty amongst African Americans because y'all don't take advantage of the opportunities this country has to offer. That...y'all feel entitled. Who wants to respond to that?"

That caused an uproar, and Larissa was first to raise her hand.

"We have every right to feel entitled. Our ancestors built this country for free, and we've never gotten our just respect or compensation. Instead, after slavery, they terrorized us and killed us. When we tried to build ourselves up, they burned down Black Wall Street in Tulsa, and so many other black businesses. Just so y'all know; you wouldn't have all these opportunities if it wasn't for us fighting against racism."

"Exactly!" Deana agreed. "We got absolutely nothing for our ancestors' labor. Where are our forty acres and a mule? We are living in poverty because they didn't want us to succeed. We didn't get opportunities that white Americans got. Instead, they created the ghettos for us. Ever heard of redlining? Our men couldn't get decent jobs, and somehow drugs and liquor found their way in our neighborhoods."

"Yeah," Kim added, "Foreign business owners have a monopoly in the hood. Arabic people sell us their liquor, the Chinese sell us their food, and the Koreans sell us their hair. What do they all have in common? They don't respect black people."

"Not just that, but it's hard to find a grocery store in the hood. All you see are corner stores. Kids in the hood grow up with limited access to fresh foods. Those things matter," Rhonda chimed in.

"Have any of you thought about opening up businesses in the hood, then? I say, if you don't like something, try to fix it," Jerome said.

No one had a response.

"Just to play devil's advocate, do African Americans hold any blame because a greater number of African Americans live in poverty compared to whites?" Kunle asked.

"I don't think so," Larissa responded. "Let's not forget that most white people in America have the wealth they have because of our ancestors' free labor. Even worse, when slavery ended, the government instituted the 1862 Compensated Emancipated Act, which compensated white slave masters three hundred dollars for each freed slave. Our ancestors got nothing. To say white people got a head start would be an understatement. We now have to battle unfair policing, which has left many of our black men in prison, working slave wages all for the benefit of private corporations owned by who? White people."

"Wow, that was powerful, Larissa," I said. "Thank you for that information. No one is denying how bad racism has been. However, would y'all say that things are getting better or that they're still the same?"

"I think some things have improved, but mostly, things are still the same. They've replaced overt racism with institutional racism, which is harder to call out," Leticia responded.

"The reason I ask this is that many Africans have come to America and found success. Very few Africans live in poverty in America. So, if there's this big conspiracy to keep black people down, how come Africans have been successful?" I asked.

There was silence.

"I believe it is because the Africans who come to America are educated people who lack the resources we have in America. Most African immigrants succeed because they're usually the best of their African societies," Larissa said.

"I am so happy to be a part of this conversation. I am learning a lot," Gillian said, "but one thing I have been wondering, knowing the history of America, why are African Americans still so dependent on white people? Just the other day, an African American friend was complaining about the white companies not making foundation to match her skin tone. Is that racist, though? I suggested that she create her own shade of foundation."

"Gillian, Africans do the same thing. Whenever there's a conflict in an African country, you see African people calling on the United States and European countries to help," Kunle said.

"What I'm getting from this conversation is that us black people need to fix our own problems," Jerome said.

"Good observation, Jerome. Now that we've aired our grievances, how do we move forward?" I asked.

"We have to stop having preconceived notions about each other. Instead of making judgments, we should talk to one another and learn the other's culture."

"I really enjoyed this discussion," Ife said. "We should have more events like this. Thank you for putting this event together, Kunle and Foma."

Kunle and I wrapped up the event. I looked on with pride as the African and African Americans students engaged each other in conversation.

I was getting the room back in order when Kunle and Larissa approached me.

"Have you met Larissa?" he asked.

"No, I haven't."

"Well, Foma, meet Larissa, and Larissa, meet Foma."

Long box braids trailed down her back. She was short, shapely, and pretty, with fair skin and perfectly arched eyebrows. Larissa looked me over from head to toe. My hand remained in the air, unshaken. I put it down.

"This event was solid," Larissa grumbled.

"Thank you," I said awkwardly.

Larissa looked at Kunle, then back at me, and left the room. She intimidated me. I assumed she and Kunle were close since they led BSA together.

"Don't be offended. She's like that with new people," Kunle assured me.

"Um, okay."

"So," he began.

"So?"

"Let's try this again: Would you like to get dinner sometime?"

"Sure, where do you have in mind?"

"That's more like it. What are your plans for Thursday night?"

I smiled. "As far as I know, I have nothing planned."

"Okay, good. I'll text you the details when I figure them out."

"Sounds good."

When we exited the room, we found Ife and Neema standing outside. They were both beaming at us.

"What're you smiling at?" Kunle teased Ife.

"You tell me," Ife replied.

"Okay, Foma, I'll be in touch," Kunle said.

I watched as he walked down the hall and then down the steps. As soon as he was out of view, Ife and Neema hugged me in excitement.

"So, are you two a couple now?" Ife asked.

"I don't know what we are. He asked me out to dinner this Thursday."

Both girls squealed. "Foma, Kunle is a nice guy. I wouldn't lie to you. As you know, he is one of my brother's best friends," Ife assured me.

"Yes, I know," I replied.

"We're going to help you get dressed. Knowing Kunle, he's gonna plan something special for this date."

I wished I could time travel to Thursday at that very moment. He had given me the confidence that I needed without me even having to ask. He liked me and I liked him.

CHAPTER NINE

The rest of my week was a countdown to Thursday night.

On Wednesday afternoon when I walked into our room, anger replaced my dreamlike mood. First, I noticed my rug, which I kept at the foot of my bed to protect my feet from the cold floor, was now in the hallway. Kara had not asked for my permission to move my rug. Also, without a heads-up, she had pinned a cloth to the part of our room that divided our hallway from the part of the room with our bed and the rest of our furniture.

After I parted my way through the cloth, I saw she had reorganized our room and placed our trashcan right by the head of my bed, where my pillow lay. I was livid. I moved the trashcan to a neutral location and returned my rug where it belonged. Even though she had moved her larger rug toward my side of the bed, it was still at least a foot away from my bed, guaranteeing that I would feel the cold floor every morning.

Later that evening, I was in deep sleep when suddenly I felt the weight of something being pulled from under me. I was facing the wall, and I turned to see that Kara had yanked my rug from beneath the two side posts of my bed that were holding it down.

"What in the world!"

My rug in her hand, she challenged me with her glare.

"Why'd you do that? Put my rug back!" I yelled at her.

"No, I put it there because I need something to stand on when

I get dressed in the morning. The floor is usually cold," she said.

"I don't care why you put it there. That is my rug, and it belongs wherever I put it."

"It makes little sense there. You already have my rug by your bed, so it defeats the purpose."

"No, your rug covers the majority of your side, while I'm left with the cold floor still," I said. "Give me my rug. I need it back where I put it."

"Well, I put it here and that is where it is staying."

I reached for my rug, but she pulled back.

"Let go of my rug."

"No, I will put it where I like."

"I don't care what you like. This rug does not belong to you." I pulled some more, but she tugged back.

I retreated because I knew that I was on the brink of getting physical with her. I knew if things got physical, she would run off crying, and her white tears would render me a bully. The smirk on her face let me know that she too understood this.

First thing Thursday morning, I knocked on our resident assistant's door, and told him about the previous night's incident.

"Can you come back in a few hours?" Andrew asked me, looking around the hall.

I suspected this would happen. He was the one who had taught Kara and her crew to smoke marijuana in the bathroom without getting caught. How could I expect him to be impartial?

I walked away, knowing I wouldn't go back. I was taking this matter to Sarah, the hall director.

I left for class that morning without being able to get ahold of her. However, when I came back to my dorm that afternoon, I found her in her office. When I explained the situation to her, including the incident with the towel, Sarah was furious.

"That's unacceptable. Have you spoken to Andrew about this?"

"Yes, I have. He hasn't been any help."

"I see. Well, Foma, we don't tolerate such disrespectful behavior. Don't worry, I'll talk to Kara and get this situation squared away."

"Thank you, Sarah."

"I'll let you know when I speak with her. In the meantime, put your rug wherever you please. It is your property."

As promised, that evening Ife asked me to come to her room so she could help me get ready for my date with Kunle. He said he was going to pick me up at seven.

No African time, he added in his message.

The night before, Kunle texted that I should get dressed up. Dissatisfied with my wardrobe, Ife gave me one of her dresses to wear.

"Foma, you have the wardrobe of a librarian," she mocked.

So, there I was, in a red dress with a plunging neckline. I borrowed a safety pin from Neema, because I didn't want to overexpose my chest. The dress hugged me in the right places, tastefully accentuating my backside.

"When he sees you, his mouth is gonna drop to the floor," Neema said.

"I hope so."

Kunle came to pick me up in his black luxury vehicle. As I approached, he got out and walked around to open my door.

He hugged me and whispered in my ear, "You look great."

"Thank you," I said. "You look good too. And you smell good."

He was wearing a cashmere sweater, slacks, and dress shoes. I saw studs in his ears.

The restaurant was only fifteen minutes away from campus. When we walked in, I felt like a kid playing grown-up. Kunle confirmed our reservation.

"Follow me," the hostess said, and Kunle paused so I could

walk ahead of him. As he trailed behind me, I was happy I had worn the dress.

At the table, Kunle pulled out my chair.

"You can get whatever you want," he said as I looked over the menu.

"How come you're not looking at the menu? Do you already know what you're getting?"

"Yup, I've been here many times. I always get the same thing."

"What is that?"

"Surf and turf."

"Surf and turf?" I mocked. I thought he was joking.

"Steak and lobster."

"Oh." I felt embarrassed for not recognizing the name. "I'll get that, then."

I put aside my menu, and there was a bout of silence before he asked:

"How was your day?"

"It was all right," I said a touch sharply. "Yours?"

He saw through my response. "What happened?"

I explained everything. As I spoke, he studied me.

"Have you seen your roommate since your talk with your hall director?"

"Nope."

"My advice to you would be, don't back down. You should have a direct talk with her and let her know that she cannot keep disrespecting you. The hall director can only do so much."

He meant well, but the whole discussion was killing the mood. "I don't wanna talk about her anymore."

Just then the server arrived with a basketful of bread and seasoned olive oil for dipping. He took our orders before disappearing again.

The food was phenomenal, as was the conversation. Throughout dinner, I stared at his smooth deep dark chocolate skin and pearly white teeth. He was so handsome. I told him about my family, that we came to the United States because Papa was admitted to a medical program that prepared him for licensing as a doctor. I explained that Mama recently got her nursing degree.

Kunle also told me about his family. He had an older brother named Kofi. He and his brother had initially come to America to live with his aunt when they were twelve and fourteen, respectively. His mother joined them a few years later, but his father, who was a geophysicist with the Nigerian government, had remained in Nigeria for work, but visited several times a year.

When Kunle dropped me off that night, he squeezed my lap when I tried to get out of the car.

"I got you," he said. He exited the car and came to open my door.

I felt like I was in a romance movie. When he hugged me tight, I breathed in his scent. When we separated, he kissed me. He watched me as I walked away. I teased him with the subtle swaying of my hips as I walked.

Back at my dorm room, I was relieved to find Kara was not there. I got undressed, washed my face, and got in bed.

I was still in a sleepy haze when I reached for my vibrating phone. I checked it to see Paige was calling me. I rubbed my eyes and looked again.

"Hello. Paige…?"

"Foma." Paige's voice was shaky. I heard noises in the background. "I need your help, Foma."

"What's going on, Paige?"

"Something has happened, and I didn't know who else to call. Please, I need help." Paige was crying.

"Everything okay? What can I do to help?"

"Can I come to your dorm?"

"Sure, Paige."

Twenty minutes later, I got a text from Paige saying that she was outside.

I gasped when I saw her. Her face was red and her eyes, puffy.

"Paige, what happened?" I asked as I slipped into the car.

"Oh, Foma," she wept, "I said no."

"Paige honey, you said no to what?"

"Foma, he raped me!"

"What? Who raped you?"

Paige shook her head. She didn't want to tell. I sat there, hugging her, allowing her to cry on my shoulder. I allowed her to talk at her own pace, until the entire ugly story came out.

CHAPTER TEN

Paige spent the night in my dorm room. I broke my silence with Kara when I told her Paige was going through a hard time and asked if Kara could spend the night with Thomas or her other friends. She obliged.

That night Paige told me everything. She had been at a frat house with Dawn, her short blonde friend I had met the week before. The football team was throwing a party there. Dawn was a cheerleader and her boyfriend, Ray Palmer, was our star football player. Dawn left the party early because she wasn't feeling well, and Paige stayed. Jamie, the guy she was seeing casually, was also at the party, but at some point they got separated.

"Ray saw I was alone and came up to me. He saw my cup was empty, so he got me something to drink. As I drank, I felt woozy. Ray held my hand and pulled me upstairs, saying Jamie was there and was looking for me.

"When we got upstairs, there was no Jamie. It was just Ray and me in a room. I reached for the doorknob to leave, but Ray rushed in front of me and blocked my exit.

"I asked him to let me go, but he wouldn't move," Paige said between sobs. "I panicked and began pushing him away, but he led me to the bed and pushed me down."

Paige hid her face in my pillow. I sat patiently, waiting for her to continue.

"After he pushed me to the bed, he climbed on top of me, clasped my wrists above my head with one hand, and kissed my neck, saying, 'I've always wanted to do this.' I was squirming, trying to kick him, you know where, but I could barely move. He is really strong."

I rubbed her back as she spoke.

"I froze when he lifted my skirt. Foma, I swear I didn't want it. I didn't want any of it!" she cried hysterically.

Instincts told me to hug her, and when I did, her crying eased.

"I lay there, staring at the clock above the dresser. The clock said it only lasted a few minutes, but those were the longest minutes of my life. I watched as the second hand of the clock moved. Yuck! I can still feel him inside me. Then he started panting and sweating and it was over.

"He collapsed on top of me and whispered, 'That was so good.' Then he kissed my forehead before he pulled his pants up. I watched him leave the room, but I just lay there, unable to move. I just watched the clock."

I was still rubbing her back. "Are you going to report him?"

"I don't know. What about Dawn? She is one of my closest friends."

"Paige, you're the victim. Ray did this to you. You can't let him get away with it."

"Foma. I just wanna sleep."

I lay down beside her, still rubbing her back.

The sun was out when I woke up. I could hear her sobbing quietly. When I rubbed her back, she turned to face me. Her pale face was flushed. Smudged black makeup outlined her puffy eyes. Her long curly hair was unruly.

"How are you feeling?"

"I'm all right."

"Do you need anything?"

"What time is your class?"

I checked my phone. It was just after six. "It's at eight, but don't worry about that."

"I don't want you missing class because of me."

"Oh, please, I'm worried about you. Can I get you anything?"

"No."

We lay down in silence until just after seven, when Kara opened our room door and peeked her head inside. I nodded, and she came in. Paige was facing the wall so Kara couldn't see her face.

Kara quietly grabbed her clothes and went into the bathroom.

"I need to get out of here so you can start your day," Paige said.

"My top priority is making sure you're all right. I think we should tell somebody. Your parents...campus security? If you want to, of course. Just know this is not your fault."

Paige was silent until finally she said, "Let's go to campus security."

"How can I help you?" an officer asked when we walked into the office. His badge read, Carter.

"Can we speak to a female officer?" I asked.

"Just a sec." Officer Carter got up and went into the back room.

Paige and I sat down in the waiting area. Minutes later, he was back.

"Officer Smith is not here yet, but can I help you?"

I wasn't comfortable talking to him right there even though there was no one else in the room.

"We're here to report a crime. Can we go somewhere more private?" I asked.

Paige sat quietly as I spoke. In just a matter of hours, our roles had switched. I was now her protector.

"Okay...follow me."

He led us into a drab office with a desk and three chairs. He sat behind the desk, and we sat in the chairs in front of him. "So, ladies, how can I help you?"

I frowned. "We'd like to report a rape."

"Who was raped?"

"My friend here was raped."

He reached to his side and pulled out a pen and notepad. His thick eyebrows furrowed. He was an older gentleman. His hair was shaved low, and his fleshy nose was light pink.

"Ma'am, is this true? Were you raped?"

Paige opened her mouth to speak, but no words came out. She cleared her throat and fidgeted in her seat. Her voice cracked when she said, "Yes, I was."

"Okay. First things first. Tell me your name."

Officer Carter jotted down her name before asking her to explain what happened. Paige described the situation but named no names.

"What's this fella's name?" Officer Carter asked.

Paige stared at the wall.

"Ma'am, it's best that you tell me his name so we can investigate your claim."

Finally, Paige whispered, "Ray Palmer."

"What was that?" Officer Carter asked, leaning in to hear.

Paige was silent, until she finally said out loud, "Ray Palmer."

Officer Carter swallowed hard and raised an eyebrow. "Ray Palmer? The football player?"

"Yes."

Officer Carter fell silent for long moments. I shifted in my seat. Paige studied her hands.

"Just so I'm clear, you said that Ray Palmer, the school's star football player, drugged your drink, led you to a room, and raped you?"

Paige would not respond, so I spoke for her. "Yes, you wrote it down. That's what she said."

Officer Carter cleared his throat and closed his notepad. He studied us so hard, I got uncomfortable. Before I could ask him about the next steps, we heard a light knock at the door.

Officer Carter got up and opened the door. Closing it behind him, he slipped out into the hall. From where I sat, I could hear him speaking softly to someone outside the door. Then the door opened. A middle-aged brunette woman with her hair gathered in a bun at the nape of her neck entered the room.

"Good morning, ladies. I'm Officer Smith. Can you please tell me what happened?"

Paige told her story again, while Officer Smith took notes. The empathy on her face as she wrote relaxed me.

"Did you shower after the incident?"

"No," Paige sobbed.

"I'll be right back. I'm going to arrange for you to go to the hospital to get a rape kit." Officer Smith stood, and as she passed, she comforted Paige with a touch of her shoulder.

When the security officer left the room, Paige began crying hysterically.

"Paige, honey, I think you should call your mom."

"I am so embarrassed. I should've never followed him up there."

"Oh, Paige. This is not your fault. Your parents will understand that."

As I consoled Paige, Officer Smith came back into the room. She asked us to follow her.

Once outside, she and Paige spoke for a few minutes, and then Officer Smith asked if I needed a ride.

I told her I didn't, and I hugged Paige before leaving the building.

I went straight to my chemistry class. Ife looked at me with concern when I sat down next to her. I was over fifteen minutes late. I hadn't responded to her text about going together to class that morning.

I took notes as the professor spoke, but my mind wandered. I hoped Paige had already told her parents what happened.

"How was your date? Is that why you missed bio?" Ife asked as soon as the professor dismissed class.

"The date went well. No, I didn't miss class because of Kunle. I had other things to do."

"Are you okay?"

"Yes, I am fine."

Ife was chatty as we walked to English class. She had an audition for On Pitch, one of our school's a cappella groups. She was an aspiring singer, though only in college because her Nigerian mother and father did not support the idea of a music career. Little did they know they were footing the bill for her musical aspirations.

"They pay for my voice coach and studio sessions, and don't even know it," Ife had told me during the first week of school.

"How do you manage that?"

"I inflate textbook costs and other school fees, and use the leftover money for my music."

"You're bold."

"It's a win-win situation. They get to say their daughter is in college pursuing medicine, and I get a head start in my music career. I have no other choice. I only have four years to make it big because I am not going to anybody's medical school."

"They're going to freak out when they find out you don't want to become a doctor."

"For now, what they don't know won't hurt them," Ife responded.

After English class, I told Ife I couldn't join her and Neema for lunch on Main Street. Instead, I went to Sterling and ordered a to-go burger meal. On the shuttle back to my dorm, I called Paige. She did not respond. Hours later, as I lay in bed unable to move, she texted me saying she was fine and with her mother. I breathed a sigh of relief, but I knew there would be harder days ahead.

CHAPTER ELEVEN

I got up early on Saturday morning. Kara was still sleeping, and she was not alone. I squinted and made out another figure in her bed. I assumed it was Thomas.

In the lobby across from our room, I turned one of the plush chairs around to face the tall windows. I studied the view of other reddish-brown dorm buildings. Most on our campus were still asleep.

As I sat, I tried to make sense of the past two days. On just one night, I had both the best and worst experiences of my life. I breathed in as I tried to recall the scent of Kunle's cologne, but then images of Paige's puffy face came to mind. "Poor Paige," I whispered to myself.

Hours later, I was jolted awake by the explosion of someone laughing hysterically. My floor mates were up. I had nodded off on the chair.

That afternoon, I was in my room organizing my desk. Kara and her posse were taking up most of the space.

I was fixing a thumbtack that secured my small bulletin board to the wall when Mark said, "You're not supposed to use thumbtacks on the wall."

"And you're not supposed to use illegal drugs, but yet you

still do," I responded. I was in no mood for his rules. This was the same guy who smoked marijuana in our bathroom.

He had no reply.

Kara and her group resumed their conversation. I listened in and out to what they were saying as I packed my schoolbags with textbooks I needed for my study session with Ife.

"Yo, my friend Tim just told me that Ray Palmer was arrested," Thomas said.

I froze.

"Arrested for what?" Mark asked.

"I don't know. Oh snap, someone else is texting me."

"Man, Ray better play this season. Our team sucks without him," said Mark.

"He got arrested for rape," Thomas said, still looking down at his phone.

"I don't believe it."

"You know Tim and Cody live right by Ray. They wouldn't lie."

"Why would Ray want to rape anybody? He's with Dawn, and she's like the perfect girl."

"I know, right?"

"Mark!" Shannon yelled. "That statement is wrong on so many levels."

"Yeah, his girlfriend being pretty means nothing," Jennifer interjected.

"You guys are dogs for saying that," Shannon said.

"Woof, woof, woof," Thomas and Mark barked.

I couldn't take their joking any longer, and I rushed out of the room.

The plan was for Ife and me to study together, but we spent the day watching junk television.

We were on our seventh episode of our favorite reality show when Kunle texted me, asking if I wanted to go out.

"Kunle wants us to go to the movies tonight," I told Ife.

"Say yes! You've got nothing else to do."

"Good point."

"So, are you gonna tell me what's going on?" Ife asked.

"What're you talking about?"

"You haven't been the same since I saw you on Thursday, right before your date with Kunle."

I shied away from her insinuation. "Why do you say that?"

"I can just tell that your mind is elsewhere. Besides, this is the first time I've heard you say you don't feel like studying."

I laughed. "Am I that much of a nerd? I'm just worried about something. No big deal."

"Did Kunle treat you right during your date?" Ife was studying my face.

"Yes, don't worry, Kunle was the perfect gentleman."

Ife looked like she was going to say something, but she held back.

After a few more hours of watching television, I got up. I had to get ready for my date with Kunle.

"Do you need me to dress you again?" Ife asked.

"No, ma'am, I've got this one."

In my room, I threw on a pair of jeans and a yellow dress shirt. I took a moment to admire how my dark skin glowed under my yellow shirt.

"Just like a bar of chocolate," I said to myself as I jelled down the fuzzy hairs that stuck out from within my braids, secured in a bun at the top of my head.

When I stepped outside, the cold September air ambushed my face. I brought my white scarf up to my nose. As I turned the corner, I saw Kunle standing by the passenger's-side door, waiting. He grinned when he saw me. I floated toward him, and he pulled me close and kissed me. I closed my eyes, enjoying his sweet kisses.

He opened the door for me and I got inside. We made small talk in the ten-minute ride to the theater.

At the movies, I declined his offer to buy popcorn. He did have some candy in his pocket and he promised to share.

Thoughts of Paige filled my mind as I tried to pay attention to the movie. It was an action-comedy, and I feigned amusement each time Kunle smiled at me, motioning at the movie screen. As hard as I tried, I could not focus.

After the movie, Kunle and I went to a restaurant. In our booth, he slid into the seat across from me.

"Are you all right?" Kunle asked, concerned.

"Yes, I'm fine," I said, more cheerful than I felt.

"How are classes going?"

"They're going all right. I did well on my first few quizzes and my English paper, but there's always room for improvement."

"I'm glad to hear that. It's best to start and end strong. Many of my friends are trying to pull up their grades, but it's senior year and too late for that."

"I have no choice. Before I started school, my dad and I mapped out the GPA I need to have in order to be competitive for top medical school programs. I have no room for failure."

Kunle chuckled. "That sounds so much like an African parent. Have you always wanted to be a doctor?"

"Yes, as long as I can remember."

"Okay, good. Just make sure of that. There's nothing worse than majoring in something you don't like to please someone else."

"Absolutely. I wanna become a doctor for sure."

"Okay, Dr. Fotabeng. That has a magnificent ring to it, by the way."

"That sounds like someone is addressing my dad," I said as I giggled.

"Okay, well, how about Ms. Dr. Fotabeng?" he joked.

His smile revealed perfectly straight, pearly white teeth. He was so handsome. It felt surreal that I was on a date with someone so good-looking.

"That sounds better. Have you always wanted to major in political science and black American studies?"

"No. I came in as an engineering major."

"What changed your mind?"

"I realized that I only wanted to be an engineer because it sounded nice and my parents thought it was a great idea."

"Why political science and black American studies?"

"I've always been interested in politics, and I want to know more about the socioeconomic struggles of black people in America. If I'm going to be a great civil rights lawyer, knowing that history is very important."

"Civil rights lawyer—that's impressive."

"I want to fight for the under-represented. The American legal system has dealt black people a poor hand, and I want to help fix it. We should all be treated equally under the law. My goal is to open a small firm after law school."

"You have it all planned out, don't you?"

"That I do."

I wanted to kiss him right then, but I wasn't bold enough.

Later that evening, when Kunle pulled up to the curb by my dorm, I waited impatiently as he got out and walked around to open my door. I wanted to be in his presence as much as possible, and I was sad the night was over.

After he opened my door, he extended his hand. I held onto it as he guided me out of the car. As I stood up fully, he pulled me in close. I could hear his heartbeat as we joined in a warm embrace. When I looked up at him, he planted a kiss on my lips.

CHAPTER TWELVE

Somehow, word got around that Paige was Ray Palmer's accuser. Our campus was abuzz with rumors of what happened. Paige's and Ray's high profiles on campus only exacerbated things. I heard some say that Paige accused Ray of rape to retaliate against Dawn over a petty dispute. Others said that she seduced Ray to make Jamie jealous. Because I knew the truth, these rumors frustrated me, and I scolded Ife when she repeated them to me.

"Just because Paige is your mentor does not mean she is incapable of doing wrong," Ife lectured as we left our last class, "unless you know something that we don't."

"Ife, you can't believe everything you hear."

"What do you know?" Ife asked.

I was defensive of Paige. "I have nothing to share. I'm just saying that people make up all kinds of wild stories."

"Okay, you don't have to tell me."

"Tell you what?"

"You know something, I can tell. But I'm going to drop it. It's none of my business, anyway."

After a weekend of reality television and my date with Kunle, I knew I had to focus on my schoolwork, but I daydreamed instead. As I sat in a cubicle overlooking the lawn in front of the library, I recalled how soft Kunle's lips had felt against mine. When I closed my eyes and focused, I conjured up the scent of his cologne.

My phone vibrated. It was a text from Kunle. Just when I had been thinking about him. He said he was a few minutes away. I tried to finish the chapter I was reading before he showed up, but I kept glancing out the window until I spotted him coming.

Kunle wore khakis and a zip-up sweater. He walked with confidence and purpose. I had only a page left in the chapter. I reread the same paragraph several times before giving up.

I felt a tap on my shoulder. "Foma." Kunle's deep voice was mellow.

I turned around to face him. "Hi, Kunle."

"Get up and give me a hug."

I stood up gladly. I closed my eyes and inhaled as he held me close. As we pulled apart, he kissed my lips softly.

"Working hard or hardly working?" he asked.

"Hardly working."

"You looked focused when I got here."

"I was pretending," I said.

"No need to pretend with me. I won't distract you, though. I'm actually here to work."

"What're you working on?"

"I am studying for the LSATs."

"Is that the exam to get into law school?"

"That's the one."

After a much more productive three hours, we were both ready to leave. I accepted Kunle's offer to grab fast food. I wanted to be with him as much as possible.

Kara and her posse were lounging in our room when I got back that night. Despite our brief interaction when Paige came over, we were still not speaking. My unwashed towel still lay on the bathroom floor. I resolved to not say one word to her until she washed and dried my towel. When I walked past our hall, I was satisfied at least that my rug had not been moved from the foot of my bed.

Someone cleared their throat when I stepped into the room, and silence fell over the room. I didn't bother saying hi, and neither did anyone else. I got my stuff and went into the bathroom. Still, I pressed an ear against the wall when someone started talking.

"You two are still not talking?" Casey asked.

"Nope," Kara responded.

"That's wild. All over a towel."

"I'm not washing it," Kara said.

That must have elicited some nods, because all I heard was silence.

"Anyway," Casey began again, "what I was saying was, why would Ray Palmer need to rape her? Dawn is gorgeous."

"Yeah, Paige is definitely no Dawn," Shannon said.

I stood there, waiting to hear what Jessica had to say. She and Paige had the same features, except Paige wore her hair in natural curls and Jessica ironed hers bone straight. Jessica said nothing.

It amazed me how Shannon's tune had changed now that Paige was the suspected victim. Before, she had berated Mark for suggesting that Ray could not have committed the rape.

Our room was empty when I returned from the shower. I went to my desk and opened a mid-sized cardboard box from my mother. I pulled out a tall water bottle filled with the small tasty groundnuts that only Cameroonian soil could produce. I unscrewed the bottle cap, tilted my head back, and raised the bottle to my mouth. I closed my eyes, enjoying every slightly salty bite.

I reached into the box and pulled out a Ziploc bag filled with small four-sided pieces of *chin chin*. I munched on the sweet, fried, crispy dough. I inhaled the scent of nutmeg. I realized it wasn't too late to call Mama to thank her.

"Good evening, Papa."

"Foma. How are you?" I could hear the news playing in the background.

"I am fine. How are you and Mama doing?"

"We are okay. How is school?"

"School is fine, Papa."

"That's good."

"Where is Mama?"

"I think she is taking a shower."

Papa and I made small talk for a few more minutes. Before we hung up, I told him to tell Mama that I would call her again later. I was glad to be away at college but I missed my family.

In my last summer with Nana Ola before coming to the United States, I was disappointed that I was not going to be returning to the house in Buea, but instead going to the village. I was going to miss my friends in the old neighborhood. Nana Ola said I would make new ones at her home in the village. I was not convinced because the village children were different from the ones in the city—they were too serious for my liking, and always seemed to have too many responsibilities, like helping with their parents' farms or accompanying their mothers to the market.

In the end, my summer at the village had been my best one yet, special thanks to Auntie Lulu, my mother's younger sister, and her husband, Uncle Gerald.

Uncle Gerald was a white man. When I heard they were coming to visit, I was beside myself. I was looking forward to seeing my first white man in person. The only white man I knew of was Santa Claus, and as much as Papa and Mama tried to make me believe in Father Christmas, as they called him, I found it hard to believe that he could have ever come to visit our house without me hearing him.

I had seen a white woman in person, though. Her name was Madam Cecil. She was a Belgian woman who financed the rebuilding of our school. A year prior, she had visited our school to officiate over the opening of our new building by cutting the ceremonial ribbon. The pupils stood in several lines, observing this woman with very pale skin and red patches on her face and arms. Her nose was thin and its tip extended out to a point. On this day, she wore a t-shirt and tied an ankara cloth around her waist, like the other Cameroonian women. She even wore an ankara head-tie that engulfed most of her orange-reddish colored hair. I watched in amusement as Mr. Bertrand and the other teachers fawned over her and grinned from ear-to-ear when she paid them attention.

Auntie Lulu and Uncle Gerald made their appearance on Saturday. I remembered because people had come to Nana Ola's house in their best Sunday outfits. Even Susana in our own home had on her Sunday's best.

Throughout the day, people filtered in and out of Nana Ola's house, each time disappointed that the guests had yet to arrive. They couldn't have cared less to see Auntie Lulu; they wanted to see her white husband. Seeing everyone's excitement, I too dressed up, eager for the arrival of our special guest—the white man from Germany.

Auntie Lulu and Uncle Gerald arrived just before the sun went down. He was tall and pink. People, hearing of the arrival, showed up at Nana Ola's compound in droves. They just stared at Uncle Gerald. He had on clear-rimmed bifocal glasses, and his face was pink, but his arms were a light tan color. He barely spoke English, and Auntie Lulu spoke little German. I looked on in awe as they communicated with hand signals and Uncle Gerald's very broken English. He was a calm man, and it was funny to see him with my extremely outgoing auntie with the larger than life personality.

Uncle Gerald and Auntie Lulu met a few years prior, when he was in Cameroon on business; he worked for a German company that had interests in Cameroon. They were married within months of their meeting, and when he returned to Germany, he took Auntie Lulu back with him.

"I am just coming from seeing your mother," Auntie Lulu said when she hugged me. "She told me to greet you, and that she misses you."

Auntie Lulu and Uncle Gerald's short-lived visit provided me with more laughter than I could have imagined. I was an early riser, and I enjoyed looking out my window at the happenings on our compound early in the morning. Usually, I would see Peter sweeping the red clay dirt at the front of the house with a broomstick, tending to the garden, or another of his morning chores. I loved watching him walk—people with bowed legs fascinated me.

This morning I saw Uncle Gerald. He was very tall, taller than all the Cameroonian men I knew. He was wearing very short shorts, with his sleeveless shirt tucked into them, and he wore a blue head band. He had on clunky sneakers, and he was running in place. I laughed because I wasn't sure what he was doing. Yet I was also captivated.

I laughed as he jumped, separating his legs and waving his hands in the air. Wilfred, the gateman, was watching in puzzlement. Uncle Gerald cupped one hand in the other and extended each hand to the opposite side, moving his body along. He bent down to touch his toes; the tip of his fingers went only slightly below his knees. Finally, he ran toward Wilfred, who was befuddled. Uncle Gerald motioned for Wilfred to open the gate, while he ran in place. Wilfred obliged. Uncle Gerald went sprinting out the gate, and Wilfred stood to watch, with his hands over his head, displaying his astonishment.

Hours later, Uncle Gerald was all people could talk about—the white man wearing the funny clothes and running on the road as though a wild animal was chasing him.

In Cameroon, the adults I knew didn't exercise; exercising was the way of life. You exercised when you walked to the market, worked on your farm, or walked to a neighbor's house to discuss. Some homes in the village didn't even have running water. The residents had to go to the well to fetch water to bathe and cook food—fetching water was another form of exercise. Nana Ola had running water in her house, thankfully.

Later that day, the conversation between Auntie Lulu and her childhood friend who still lived in the village convinced me that her husband Gerald was indeed an odd man. Auntie Lulu and her friend were out in the veranda, talking in the evening. Uncle Gerald was in their room, lying near the fan. Auntie Lulu had been complaining that they needed a fan in their room because it was too hot for Uncle Gerald, so Nana Ola had sent Peter and Wilfred to the nearest market to buy a fan. Peter now did all the driving in Nana Ola's household. I sat in Nana Ola's living room, listening to their conversation. The front door was open to let in fresh air.

"When we were in Cameroon, before we left for Germany, I knew he liked animals, but sistah, his obsession with animals is too much for me. He kisses the dog and likes the dog to sleep in the bed with us. Ah ah, what kind of thing is that? This type of thing, I have never seen."

"Ah, Lulu, I know how you like to exaggerate, I am sure it is not that bad."

"I am not lying o. The dog stays in the house with us. When we sit down to eat, the dog sits down to eat his own food. He has special food that they buy from the market. I swear to you, I am not lying."

Her friend laughed, just as I did too—only quietly, as not to give myself away.

"That is ridiculous. For a dog? I cannot believe that."

"I told you, I am not lying, it is true. In Germany, a dog is part of the family, they treat them like they are children."

"Ah Lulu, you are really telling me something today o."

"I cannot lie to you. And when I found a way to ask if the dog can sleep outside, he got so mad. Can you imagine? All day I follow behind it sweeping the floor because all it does is shed and shit. When he comes home and sees that I put the dog in the backyard by himself, he becomes so mad! He expects me to walk the dog too, two times a day."

Auntie Lulu was right, I thought, as I sat at my desk laughing to myself. My laughter stopped when I heard screaming coming from Shannon and Jessica's room. I opened the bathroom door and listened to hear what was going on.

"They're not pressing charges against Ray Palmer," I heard Shannon scream with happiness. "Let's go tell Kara."

My heart sank. I texted Paige asking if everything was okay.

I checked my phone several times that night but heard nothing from her.

Early the next morning, I woke up to my phone vibrating.

"Paige?" I whispered.

"Foma, I'm sorry for calling so early. I really need someone to talk to. Someone I can trust."

"Sure, Paige. Give me a second." I hurried out of our room and went to the lobby for privacy, taking a blanket with me.

"What's going on, Paige?"

"Did you hear? They're not pressing charges against him."

"Yes, I heard someone say that."

"Someone? Who? People are talking about it?"

I bit my lip. I struggled to find the right thing to say to calm her. "I've heard some whispers here and there."

"Oh, my gosh. I don't think I can show my face on that campus again."

"Paige, you're the victim. Remember that."

"Foma, I'm happy that you're one of the few people who thinks so."

"What do you mean?"

"Almost all my friends have stopped talking to me."

"What? Why is that?"

"Ray told Dawn that I made everything up, and now she's turned everyone against me. Even my roommates are giving me the cold shoulder. They think I lied about this whole situation. That I am jealous of Dawn and Ray's relationship or that I seduced Ray to make Jaime jealous. It's all ridiculous."

Those were the same rumors I had heard. "That all sounds silly," I said.

"He raped me, Foma."

"I know he did, Paige. Where are you?"

"I'm home now with my mom."

"Good. Do you know why they released him so soon?"

"Ray told the police we had consensual sex after I seduced him. The cops say they don't know who to believe. Officer Smith is the only one who had my back, but she got in trouble after she arrested Ray. They say she didn't have probable cause to arrest him."

"What about the rape kit?"

"They're saying it is not enough to prove I was raped."

"I am praying you get justice, Paige."

"I doubt it. Ray's parents are connected. They've invested a lot of money in this town, including the school."

"But your parents are also successful."

"I know. My mom has been using her connections to call people to put pressure on the prosecutor's office to charge Ray. She is really upset right now."

"Let's be optimistic that everything will work out."

She didn't respond to that but instead said, "Thanks for picking up, Foma."

"Any time."

"You know, you're my only friend right now."

"What happened with Monica?"

"We still talk, but it's awkward because she is also friends with Dawn. I want to trust her, but I feel that anything I tell her will get back to Dawn. Sophie, my other roommate, has stopped talking to me completely."

"Oh, Paige, I am always here for you. Have you heard from Jamie?"

"He texted me the morning after…you know, but I didn't respond because of everything that was happening. When I called him after Ray got arrested, he didn't pick up and I haven't heard from him since."

"Then he shouldn't be in your life."

"Exactly. Foma. Thank you for picking up. I'm going to let you go back to sleep."

"Please call me at any time."

CHAPTER THIRTEEN

"Stop trying to steal my friend away," Ife told Kunle when he joined us in the library.

"Who is the one doing the stealing?" Kunle asked. "I knew her first."

"Hey, you two, I'm sitting here and available for the both of you. But I'll tell you, it feels good to be wanted."

They both laughed. I was thankful for my blossoming friendship with the two of them. I still missed Michelle, but not enough to reach out first.

"I know you two usually eat together, but is it okay if I take Foma out to dinner?" Kunle asked Ife that Tuesday afternoon.

"I suppose I can do without her at dinner."

This time Kunle took me to a Nigerian restaurant. As I sat in my chair, I found myself swaying from side to side, enjoying the Afrobeat tunes that filled the room.

As we ate, Kunle seemed unlike himself. Then, after platefuls of jollof, fried plantains, and suya, he announced, "This is long overdue, but I want to be clear. I am your boyfriend. There's no girl in my life but you."

I was happy to hear this announcement, even if it came out oddly. "Is there a question in there somewhere?"

"Would you like to be my girlfriend?" he asked with a smirk.

"Of course," I said, and we leaned over the table between us and sealed it with a kiss.

"Phew, I wasn't sure what you'd say," he said.

I was crazy about him. How could he not know that?

A few days after we confirmed our relationship, Kunle invited me to attend a poetry jam with him. He knew I loved to write and that I enjoyed poetry.

When we arrived at the crowded coffee shop, he ushered me right to the front of the stage. His friend Marcus was organizing the event and had saved us seats. The host of the show and an up-and-coming poet, Mya Shanti, was speaking with Marcus to the side of the stage.

Minutes later, the lights dimmed low, and Mya got on stage.

"Good evening, y'all. I'm glad to see your faces tonight. I have a feeling we're going to have a splendid night. Snap your fingers if you are."

Finger snaps resounded in the room.

"Okay, thank you. I'm glad to hear that. I call this first poem, 'I Am.' Let me hear those finger snaps."

We snapped our fingers.

I am the girl with the hair that extends to the sky
I am the girl with the hair of wool like the Messiah

I am the girl with skin that glistens in the sun
I am the girl with the womb from which humankind began

I am what I define myself to be
You cannot define me; I am simply me.
You cannot educate me; I already know my history.

I am who I am; I stand up tall because that is who I am.
I am who I am; I raise my head up high because that is who I am.

I am who I am, your words cannot hurt me.
I am who I am, you have no power over me.
I am who I am, your prejudice does not consume me.
I am who I am, who I am is just me.

Several finger snaps later, Kunle and I looked at each other, both impressed with the way Mya had delivered the poem.

A less experienced poet was next in line. We gave him finger snaps for encouragement, but we could tell he was nervous. Halfway through, I was ready for Mya to recite another poem.

For her next poem, titled, "Who Do You Think You Are," she gave a remarkable performance. Her voice boomed as she recited it.

Who do you think you are to believe you can offend me?
Who do you think you are to think you can degrade me?
Who do you think you are to think I need your respect?
Who do you think you are to think I need your approval?

Who do I think I am to refuse to acknowledge who I am?
Who do I think I am to believe you can offend me?
Who do I think I am to think you can degrade me?
Who do I think I am to think of you so highly that I feel
I need your respect?
Who do I think I am to think I need your approval?

Who do I think I am to refuse to acknowledge who I am?
I am Mya Shanti, proud and black is who I am!

Her recitation of the poem gave me chills. When she finished, I snapped my fingers with all the energy I could muster. The snaps resounded all around me. A girl at the back of the room yelled, "You better say it, girl!"

The next man who popped onstage was smiling as he said, "Hello, my name is Lamar, and this is my first time doing this."

We gave finger snaps to let Lamar know that we were there to support him.

"Thanks, guys. I named this poem 'Listen, Son,' based on the talk my father had with me when I was just ten years old."

I was ten years old when my father told me, son, I need to educate you.
I know you are just ten, but you are tall son,
You need to understand how some people see you.

You can no longer think like a boy son,
When you leave the house, do not take that water gun.
I know it is green and that green is your favorite color,
But you must understand that your blackness overshadows that green color.

You need to be aware that people fear you, son,
Please do not let the sharpness in my tone as I say these words scare you.
But you must understand that as your father I love you.
When you leave the house, I am afraid we will lose you.

Because of your black skin some people see you as dangerous.
Because of your black skin you will seldom be viewed as a victim.
Son, because of your black skin, people will assume you are the aggressor.

Because of your black skin I felt it was important to have this talk with you.
When your mother and I adopted you, we could never imagine that we would have to have this talk with you.

I know because of our white skin we can never understand all the struggles you will face.
But please understand that our love for you transcends any race.
Our love for you has compelled us to acknowledge the flaws within this human race.

We erupted in applause, clapping and shouting. We had all forgotten to snap. Lamar asked his parents to stand up, and we watched as a white couple seated in the middle of the shop rose.

The last poem of the night was Mya's poem "Victim No Longer."

We have an accepted system of hierarchy in our society.
The whites supersede the Asians, the Asians supersede the white
Hispanics and the white Hispanics supersede the blacks.

The blacks are the common enemy of all,
And upon the backs of the blacks, all the evils of our society fall.

The blacks are the victims,
The blacks are the oppressed,
The blacks are dispensable,
The blacks are the marginalized,
The blacks are the unintelligent,
The blacks are the destitute,
The blacks are just good at being black.

This system works because the blacks agree with it.
The system works because we the blacks feed into it.

It is time that we stop playing victim.
It is time that we realize that victim, oppressed, dispensable,
marginalized, unintelligent, destitute is what they expect us to be, but
that we are not.
It is time that we change our story,
Because black is beautiful indeed.

At the end, Mya informed us that she would be signing books after the showcase. Kunle and I got in line. We each planned on buying a copy.

As we stood, I noticed a head of bone-straight, long, dark, silky hair. I recognized the dark green sweater dress. She was standing several people ahead of us. The girl turned and we made eye contact—it was Jessica. I gaped. She looked away swiftly.

I strained to see who she was with. I gulped—she was with a black guy.

"Wow," I whispered.

"What?"

"That's my suite mate. I don't think I've mentioned her to you. She looks black, but she gets offended when people ask if she is black. She says she is just Hispanic. I'm surprised to see her here with a black guy."

"That sounds tragic."

"It's annoying."

We were still in line when Marcus approached us. "Hey, what's up?"

"Thanks for saving us the spots, brother. The event was fantastic; my girl and I enjoyed it."

Hearing Kunle call me his girl made me smile.

"How are you doing?" Marcus asked me, a twinkle in his eye.

"I'm fine, thank you. Nice to meet you, Marcus."

"The pleasure is all mine. Why are y'all standing in line? Kunle, you know I can hook you up, right?"

"We're good, man, those seats were enough."

"How about we get something to eat after this? I have my young cousin with me. He loves poetry."

"Okay, yeah, sure, man."

Some minutes later, Jessica and her date walked toward us, signed books in hand. Jessica and I made eye contact, and she approached me, feigning surprise.

"Foma," she called.

"Hi, Jessica," I said flatly.

Kunle and her date did the handshake-hug thing that guys do.

"You two know each other?" I asked Kunle.

"Yeah, Chris is in BSA. Chris, meet my girl, Foma."

"Hey, what's up, I'm Chris." Chris held out his hand and I shook it.

"All right, man, I'll catch up with you later," Chris said to Kunle as he and Jessica walked away.

Shortly after we got our books signed, Marcus was ready to go, and we headed to a local pizza place.

"Thank you again, Marcus, for organizing such a powerful event," I said as we waited for our pizza slices.

"You're very welcome," he said. "It's nice to finally meet the girl who has had my man so occupied."

I blushed.

"Hmm, smells good," Marcus' cousin said.

My mouth salivated when the waitress placed my two large slices of pepperoni pizza in front of me. It was still hot to the touch, so I waited impatiently. I didn't want to burn my tongue.

"Did y'all hear about that black girl who said Ray Palmer raped her?" Marcus asked in between chews.

I froze, but Kunle responded. "Yeah, Paige. I've worked on a few projects with her."

"Watch him get away with it," Marcus said. "They already released him from jail without pressing charges. I don't see this ending good."

"Man, we can't let that happen. I've been monitoring the situation."

"We? You ever seen Paige hanging around any black folks? That is what she gets for not being around her kind. I've never seen her with any brothas."

"A black person having mostly white friends does not justify rape," I said.

Kunle was in full support. "Yeah, man. You've got a real messed-up way of thinking. She is a sista. If something happens to her, it happens to all of us. You have a sister. Wouldn't you want people to stand up for her if she were in Paige's position? Would it matter that she mostly had white friends?"

"I'm just saying. That girl acted like she was above black people. Now that they hurt her, why should we have to run to her aid?"

"United we rise, divided we fall," Kunle said firmly.

Marcus said nothing else.

I beamed at Kunle. I knew I liked him, but I learned something new about him that night.

When he dropped me off, I touched his arm when he was about to exit the vehicle to open my door.

"Regarding that conversation about Paige, I wanna to tell you something."

"Okay, what's up?"

"Paige is my mentor."

"Is she?"

"Yes. She came to me after she was raped."

I went on to detail what had happened, leading to Paige visiting my dorm that early Friday morning. When I finished, Kunle looked ahead, deep in thought.

"We can't stand for this. We will raise hell to make sure that Ray gets arrested again and that he pays for his crime this time," he said finally.

"What'll you do?"

"The same thing we did for Elijah. Protest to bring about justice."

"You think that'll work?"

"Do we have another choice?"

The following morning, I was in the bathroom, getting ready to meet Ife to head to class, when Jessica came in.

After we greeted each other, she started talking about how

great the poetry jam was. We both agreed that the twist with Lamar's parents being white was impeccable.

Speaking of his white parents, I commented on how uncomfortable the white establishment owners looked during some poems, especially during "The Oppressor."

"What about me? I was uncomfortable," Jessica commented.

I looked at her, confused. "Why were you uncomfortable?"

"I'm not black. I know I'm multicultural, but I'm not black, and I felt uncomfortable about what she was saying."

"But you are also not white," I said. "She said nothing about Hispanics."

"I still felt uncomfortable because I'm not black."

Her denials struck me as very disingenuous. "Then what race are you?"

"My family is Dominican and Cuban. That's why I said I'm multicultural."

"There are black Dominicans and Cubans, though. Being Dominican and Cuban does not make you not black."

"Well, I'm telling you I'm not."

I pointed out the obvious. "You're also not white."

"Neither are you."

"Yes, I know I'm not white. I'm black and proud of it. But you don't have to be condescending when you say you're not black."

"I have never been condescending toward you or any black person."

I looked at her in disbelief. "Whatever."

"I think I know what this is about. You're just mad I have a black boyfriend. I'm tired of jealous black girls like you who have a problem with interracial dating."

"No one cares about your relationship," I scoffed. "For it to be interracial dating, it has to be between people of different races."

Jessica scowled at me. "I don't need to prove anything to you. I am Dominican and Cuban, and that is that."

This wasn't going anywhere, and I sighed. "You know what, you can identify with whatever you want. All I'm saying is, be respectful to me when you make your comments about your ethnicity."

"I have been nothing but polite to you."

"I don't care about your politeness. Just show me the same respect I show you."

"I've shown you nothing but respect. There are racists all around you, but you choose to only pick on me."

"What are you talking about?"

"I should be the last one accused of being racist around here. I am done with this conversation."

"As am I," I responded.

She stormed out of the bathroom. *Well,* I thought as I picked up my toothbrush, *at least I got it out. Now it can't bug me anymore.*

CHAPTER FOURTEEN

"Dear, when was the last time you spoke to your Nana Ola?" Mama asked me during our call that evening. "Maybe a week ago, why?"

"How did she sound when you spoke with her? What did she say?"

"She sounded the same as always, I suppose. She mostly complained about Susana. Why are you asking, Mama?"

"Oh, Foma. Susana called me this morning and told me that your grandmother is not doing well. She has been hiding so much from us, I was not sure if she told you something. I know how close the two of you are."

I became alarmed. "No, Mama. I know nothing. What has she been hiding?"

"She has been coughing up blood. They took her to the hospital yesterday. She has also been complaining of stomach pains. She has not been eating. Susana caught her hiding food."

"Mama, is she okay?" I was now in a state of full-blown panic.

"My dear. That's why I was calling you. I just booked a flight to Cameroon. I am traveling to see her on Tuesday. Your Uncle Paul is en route to the village as we speak, but I want to see her and make sure she is all right."

"Mama," I decided instantly, "I will come home this weekend."

"Dear, please, if it is going to inconvenience you and your studies, don't. I just wanted to make sure you knew what was happening."

"I'm going to come. Can you pick me up tomorrow?"

"Sure, dear. Text me to let me know what time. I am off tomorrow, so I will be around."

When I got off the phone, I was relieved that Kunle was coming to pick me up. I needed something to distract me from what was happening with Nana Ola. He and I were having dinner at his place. He told me he was an excellent cook, and I was looking forward to deciding for myself.

I acted cheerful when I saw Kunle.

"How was your day?" he asked once we were seated in his car.

"It was fine," I said. I did not want to share what was happening with Nana Ola. "How was yours?"

"It was going okay, until I saw Ray Palmer at Sterling sitting in a booth with all his friends, acting like he didn't just rape a girl."

"What? They let him back on campus?"

"That's what it looks like. We are not going to take this lying down."

"Who's we?"

"Me, Larissa, and the other members of BSA. We need to get ASA involved with this too. He needs to know there're consequences for what he did."

"What exactly is the plan?"

"We're still figuring that out."

Kunle lived with two roommates in a town house just outside of campus. When I walked into the place, the orderliness surprised me.

"For guys, y'all keep your place tidy."

"I'm not sure how to take that comment. Do I look like a slob to you?"

I chuckled. "Not at all." I reached in my bag and pulled out a Ziploc bag of chin chin.

"I have something for you," I said, waving the bag in the air.

"For me? Thank you," he said as he hugged me.

"There's more…" I handed him a bag of fried groundnuts.

"Why are you spoiling me like this?"

"I just want to share my snacks with you. My mom sent them."

"If I haven't told you before, you're awesome."

I beamed as he enveloped me in his arms again.

I followed him to his kitchen, where he put the chin chin and peanuts in a cabinet. He guided me to have a seat while he prepared the meal.

"Who taught you how to cook?" I asked as he dipped a thinly sliced piece of ripe plantain into hot oil.

"My mom. She was adamant that my brother and I be able to feed ourselves."

"Wow, that's very interesting. My mom was all about me being able to 'cook for my husband.'"

We both laughed. "Oh no! My mom is a career woman, and she didn't want us to be like our father, who doesn't do 'domestic work.' We had a house girl who did most of the cooking and cleaning. My mom cooked occasionally, though. Food always tasted better when she made it."

I could imagine him as a young boy, standing by his mother, learning how to cook.

"Okay. I hope you do your mom proud with your jollof. We both know that Cameroon jollof is the best, but because I respect you, I will eat this Nigerian jollof that you're preparing."

"So, you have jokes today, huh?"

"No jokes, just facts."

Half an hour later, when I ate my first spoonful of jollof, I was

impressed. Kunle was an excellent cook; the jollof was phenomenal. He laughed when I nodded my approval.

After dinner, we sat on the sofa, watching a sports drama. I
was not a fan of the show, but sitting on his sofa with my head on
his chest and his arms wrapped around me felt good.

My mind drifted, though. It was hard not to think about Nana
Ola, as hard as I tried. My grandmother was strong. *She will make
it out of this okay,* I convinced myself.

"Pennies for your thoughts."

I looked up at him and felt my cheeks flush.

"A penny for yours," I said.

He raised my chin and kissed me. It was a soft kiss. I wanted
more, so I kissed him back. We kissed passionately. He kissed my
neck. As we kissed, he shifted his body to lay me down. When he
got on top of me, enjoyment turned to panic; I felt suffocated. He
started touching my body with his right hand. Then his left hand
moved up and held my chin. He directed my face to his and we
kissed again. I was now uncomfortable, but I didn't know what
to do. With his left hand, he lifted my wrists above my head and
held on tightly. I squirmed to get loose.

"Stop," I said, panting, but he continued. Now my heart was
racing. I thought of Paige. I felt my body come out of me and
watched as Kunle continued to kiss me, while his left hand still
gripped my wrists. My chest got heavy.

"Stop," I yelled.

Kunle looked at me, startled. He didn't move. I wiggled my
hands free, pushed him off me, and sat up.

"Whoa, what just happened? Are you okay?" he asked as
he got off his knees and sat down next to me. I flinched when he
tried to touch me.

"Did you not hear me say stop?"

"Foma, I did, which is why I stopped."

"No, you didn't. The first time I said stop, you kept going."

"I didn't hear."

"But I said it."

We sat there silent for what felt like a long time.

"Would you like me to take you back to your dorm?"

"Yes, I think that's a good idea."

When Kunle dropped me off, I expected him to get out of the car to open my door. He did not.

"Have a good night" was all he said as I got out of the car.

The drive had been awkward. For ten minutes we sat side by side, not saying a word. We let the radio host do all the talking.

I felt terrible as I climbed the stairs to the fifth floor. Part of me was angry at myself as I questioned whether I overreacted. The other part resolved that he had been overly aggressive. By the time I made it to my floor, I was certain that he had not meant to hurt me.

I was mortified that I had shown my inexperience with intimacy. Yet as I washed my face in the bathroom, I changed my mind. Kunle had been overly forceful. His grip around my wrists was so tight I felt uncomfortable. That was the same thing that Ray Palmer did to Paige.

As I lay in bed, I changed my mind once again. Maybe I was hypersensitive because of what was going on with Paige. I wanted to text him to let him know that I was not accusing him of anything, but I decided against it.

CHAPTER FIFTEEN

Mama picked me up early the following morning. I was looking forward to getting away from campus for a few days. My body felt tense. I felt uneasy about Nana Ola's medical condition and my relationship with Kunle.

"Are you okay?" Mama asked when we got on the highway.

"Yes, Mama. I'm just worried about Nana Ola. Can we call her?"

"Yes, dear. Uncle Paul should be with her now. We will call them when we get home."

A wave of nostalgia overcame me when Mama turned onto our street. Our tan two-story, five-bedroom house that Mama and Papa purchased when I started high school was just as I had left it. The grass was full and green, thanks to our gardener, Angelo, and my car was still parked by the curb near our house.

Papa's car was missing from our garage. When I opened our garage door and stepped into our house, I smiled.

"Are you hungry?" Mama asked as she pressed the button to bring down the garage gate.

"Yes, Mama."

"Okay. How about I make you Cameroon pancake and eggs?"

"That sounds fine, Mama," I said as I went into the laundry room. I had brought my dirty laundry with me. I didn't like using the laundry room in my building.

After I started the cycle, I went upstairs to my room. It looked neater than I had left it. Only Mama could make my bed so skillfully. I jumped on it and lay there, thinking about Nana Ola and Kunle. Not wanting to wallow in self-pity, I went downstairs to help Mama in the kitchen.

She was pouring the pancake batter into the pan when I walked in. The batter was just like I liked it, nice and runny, which is best when you are making thin, crepe-like Cameroon pancakes.

"How is school?" Mama asked.

"School is going all right."

"And Michelle and Paige?"

I paused before responding. Michelle and I were no longer friends, and Paige had just been raped. Talking about Michelle would just make me upset all over again about her betrayal as well as the role Mama and Papa played in my missed opportunity. Word had already spread about Paige. Mama would likely find out soon.

"Mama, Paige is going through a hard time right now."

"Why? What happened?"

"She accused one of the football players of raping her," I said.

"Oh, my goodness. Is she all right?"

"I hope so."

"Papa God! She is such a nice girl, not like some of these loose girls you see walking around. Foma, you should be careful in that university, o."

"Mama, even if she was 'loose,' it still would not excuse her being raped."

"You know what I am saying, Foma. Girls who behave like they are open to anything should not be surprised when a man thinks he can have his way with them."

"No man should ever feel it is okay to engage with a woman's body without her permission."

"You know what I am saying, Foma," Mama scolded. "How are you yourself doing at that school? I hope you are being careful."

I didn't care to think about the situation with Kunle any longer. Before I started college, Mama had told me to focus on school and not boys. "Boys will come later," she had said. However, here I was, just a month into college and already with a boyfriend, a senior at that.

"Yes, Mama, I am being careful. When can we call Nana Ola?"

"We'll call after we eat breakfast. Just sit down, my dear, no need to help me. I miss cooking for you."

We were sitting at the kitchen dinette, eating breakfast, when we heard the garage gate open. I listened out for the jingling of keys. Papa always spun his key ring around his finger when he stepped out of the car. Then we heard the garage door open, followed by the sound of the gate descending. The sound of the jingling keys got closer.

"My daughter is home," Papa said as he smiled at me.

"Welcome, Papa," I said as he came over and kissed the top of my head.

Mama and Papa smiled at each other sheepishly. After all these years they sometimes still behaved like a shy schoolboy and girl around each other.

⌒

They met at the University of Buea. Papa was twenty-four years old, and Mama, twenty. Papa was enrolled in the pre-med program, and Mama was studying law.

They were two people from two different worlds who found each other. Mama's father, Pa Ola, was a successful lawyer in Buea who had attended a top university in Britain, where he received his master's in law degree. Pa Ola did not approve of Papa. He forbade his daughter from seeing the "poor man with no family."

When we were in Cameroon, Papa told me the story of how he lost his family. He had started helping his father at their family farm when he was just five years old. His mother convinced his father to enroll him in school when he was eleven. For him to attend school, he had to get up at four o'clock in the morning every day to work the farm before running to school three hours later.

He ran because he didn't want to be late; the school was an hour's walk away. Being late was not an option for Papa. The teacher only allowed twenty-five students at a time, and Papa didn't like learning from outside. The school was a small mud house with a thatched roof. Papa showed me the picture. It didn't look like a school at all; my school in Yaoundé was the only Cameroon school I knew. We had a wide compound with many buildings, and a grass field in the middle of the compound where the boys played soccer.

The school lasted only a half day; the teacher dismissed the students by 11:30. After dismissal, Papa would run back to the farm, hoping to get there by noon. That was when his family took a break from work to have lunch. Because he missed breakfast, by lunchtime he was famished. He told me that sometimes, away from his father's watchful eye, his mother slipped food into his pocket in the morning when he went off to work the farm. He whispered even when he made this revelation years later.

After Papa learned all he could from the teacher, he found an upper-level school. His father refused to pay for the school, and it was a three-hour walk from his father's farm. Papa already knew how to measure and calculate, so his father didn't see the value in him getting more education.

Papa did not want to be a farmer. Since British missionaries had come to his village and opened a small hospital, Papa wanted to be a medical doctor. This desire only strengthened when they treated his ear infection. Risking coming home to an angry husband, his mother had taken him to the hospital because the herbs the local herbalist gave them were not working fast enough. Papa's father did not believe in western medicine. Yet within days of visiting the hospital, Papa's earache was cured.

Seeing that his dream of becoming a doctor was slipping away, Papa began strategizing ways to attend school. When he heard his father's elder brother, Uncle Pius, was coming for his grandmother's funeral, he factored his uncle in his plans.

His father and uncle did not get along because Uncle Pius left the village at a young age, leaving Papa's father to inherit and work the farm. His father saw his brother's desertion as a betrayal to the family. The two of them were the only sons, so Papa's father was left with the responsibility; traditions dictated that their six sisters could not inherit the farm from their father.

The animosity was so thick between the two brothers that Papa's father prohibited him from stepping foot on his land. His uncle stayed with neighbors. On the night before Uncle Pius's departure, Papa begged to go to the city with him. Papa heard that there were great opportunities in Bamenda. His mother supported his decision. She admired the white people who visited their village, and the thought of her son being like one of them thrilled her.

His uncle agreed after Papa promised to work with him in his construction business and fund his own education. When Papa told his father, in a fit of rage, his father chased him out of his compound with a piece of firewood. He told him to go and not come back. Papa left with only the clothes on his back.

In Bamenda, Papa worked and went to school. At fifteen years old, he only had a third-grade education. He worked hard to catch up, and by eighteen he had a ninth-grade proficiency. He started school at the University of Buea when he was twenty-two years old. Considering all the adversity he had overcome, he refused to give up on marrying Mama.

Auntie Lulu and Uncle Paul called Papa "Mr. Never Give Up." After each time Pa Ola refused to give Mama's hand in marriage, Papa kept coming back. The third time, Pa Ola chased him out of the house with a gun, yelling, "You want to marry my daughter? Where is your family? How are you going to pay the bride price? How can you insult me and my daughter like that? Do I look like a common man to you? Do you think we are a common family?"

Weeks later, Papa returned, a few bills in hand. He explained to Pa Ola that the bills might not amount to much, but that he was going to become a medical doctor and provide Mama with a life far beyond what he could ever conceive. And again Pa Ola chased him out of the house.

After their graduation, my two defiant parents got married without Pa Ola's permission.

Papa was twenty-six years old and Mama, twenty-two. After their wedding, they moved to Bamenda because Papa had secured a job there. Mama, unable to find work as a lawyer, worked as a typist. She could have found a legal job if she sought help from her father, but she knew any favor from Pa Ola would be contingent on her leaving Papa.

Mama got pregnant with me within a year of their marriage. Because her pregnancy was high-risk, she left her job and became a stay-at-home wife. Mama remained that way until we moved to the United States.

When I was seven years old, Papa obtained a higher-paying position at a hospital in Yaoundé, and enrolled in university courses that facilitated his acceptance to the medical program in the United States. Eight years later, here we were, living the American dream. I was certain Pa Ola would be proud had he still been alive.

After we finished breakfast, Papa went to the den, where he grew disgusting-looking things in red plastic cups—he was a true scientist.

I cleared the table while Mama dialed Uncle Paul's number. Mama handed over the phone once it started ringing. I made small talk with Uncle Paul, eager for him to give the phone to Nana Ola.

"Hello, Nana Ola."

"Fomanju, my baby. How are you?"

"I am fine. How are you?"

"I am doing wonderful, dear," she said, clearly lying. It hurt me to hear the pain in her voice as she spoke.

"Nana Ola, please, get well for me. I don't want to lose you. Mama said they took you to the hospital. I beg you, please do all you can to get well soon."

"Foma, my dear. Do not worry about your old grandmother. Why are you at home and not at school?"

"I came to spend the weekend with Mama and Papa."

"I'm happy to hear that. You are a thoughtful girl," Nana Ola said, before breaking out in a fit of coughs.

Her crackling cough burned my ears. In that moment I knew my grandmother was very ill.

"Nana Ola. Please get some rest, we will talk to you later," I said. I gave Mama the phone.

When Mama took the phone, she began speaking in our dialect. I knew she was talking to Uncle Paul because she kept saying, "*ndo*"—a term of respect reserved for greeting an elder brother.

During times like these, I regretted not knowing our Nweh dialect. Growing up in Cameroon, we lived in cities, where either English or French were the predominant languages. To make matters worse, Mama and Papa only spoke to me in English, so I never learned our dialect.

I went upstairs telling myself I would read for class, yet knowing I would lie on my bed thinking about how my life was falling apart.

CHAPTER SIXTEEN

The ride back to school Sunday evening was awkward. Mama and I barely said a word to each other. She was still upset from our fight that afternoon.

It all started after Mama told me she had just spoken to Michelle's mother, who told her about Michelle's $10,000 award.

"I'm so proud of Michelle. That is a lot of money," Mama said as we ate at the dining room table.

"That could've been me, but you and Papa blocked my chance."

"But, Foma, that program was not in line with your decision to become a doctor."

"So? Michelle wants to become a psychiatrist, but her parents still let her go. That opportunity only comes once in a lifetime. I would've worked with Esther Collins, Mama!"

"You already had the internship at the hospital. Didn't you say you enjoyed it?" Papa asked.

"Yes, Papa. I enjoyed it because I had no other choice. You and Mama forced me to go."

"Foma, we spoke about it and came to an agreement."

"That's not how I remember it, Mama. You and Papa sat me down and told me you would not support my decision to travel to California, and that I was throwing my future away by not taking the internship."

My father said mildly, "That is because the hospital job was a great opportunity for you."

"Papa, you and Mama are always lecturing me about opportunities. Just because I want to become a doctor does not mean I cannot take advantage of unrelated opportunities. Life in America is limitless. I can be a doctor who writes poetry or even novels. I don't always have to choose. Yes, I love science, but I also love writing."

"But Dr. Osei told me that Sylvia learned a lot from that same internship. Look at her now, at the country's top medical program. Foma, your mother and I just want the best for you."

I was sick of being compared to her. "Sylvia Osei this, Sylvia Osei that. Papa, I am not Sylvia Osei, and I don't want to be Sylvia Osei. I want to be me, Fomanju Fotabeng," I yelled.

"Foma, mind the way you talk to us. You are still our child. We never said we want you to be like Sylvia. We are just trying to help you pursue your dreams."

"Yeah, only the dreams you approve of. I am my own person and I know what is best for me. Papa, remember how bad it felt when your father did not support you getting an education? Or when Pa Ola would not allow you to marry Mama? You fought for what you wanted. Allow me to do the same for myself."

"Foma, that is not the same thing," Mama said.

"Yes, it is."

"Everything we do is because we want the best for you," Mama said. "Foma, you are our only child; we won't have another chance to get things right."

"I shouldn't have to suffer because you couldn't have any more children. That is not my fault."

Mama winced in shock. She got up slowly, patted her stomach, and left the room.

"Mama, I did not mean to…" I began, but she didn't turn around.

"Look what you have done," Papa said as he spiked a roll of ekwang with his fork.

"Papa, you know I didn't mean to offend her. I was just making my point."

"Young lady, let me never hear you talk to us in that manner again."

Before I could respond, Papa also got up, leaving me alone at the table.

Coming back home was stirring up all sorts of memories for me. Mama had suffered a stillbirth when I was eight years old. One afternoon after school, I got home to find a note on our door telling me to go to Auntie Ngozie's house; she was Mama's friend.

At her house, I felt uneasy because Auntie Ngozie was being very gentle with me. That was not her nature. She allowed me to choose what I wanted to eat, and sent Ben, her youngest son, to the store to buy orange soda. Ben came back with three bottles. I got an entire bottle to myself while Auntie Ngozie and the boys shared two bottles between the four of them. The boys glared at me as I drank.

When I asked Auntie Ngozie where my parents were, she told me not to worry. Her tone was soft, but the look she gave me discouraged more questions.

After hours of waiting for my parents, I fell asleep and woke up to Papa tapping my leg.

"Papa, what is happening?" I asked him as I stood up.

"Foma, let us go home."

I knew it was late because except for the lit kerosene lamp that stood on the floor beside me, all the lights in the house were off.

Outside, I saw Auntie Ngozie leaning into the passenger-side window of Uncle David's car. He was Mama's cousin, and he occasionally allowed Papa to borrow his car. As we approached, I saw Mama in the car.

Auntie Ngozie directed me to the back seat when I tried to talk to Mama. When I waved at her, Mama gave me a sly smile.

"Mama, what happened?"

"Foma, leave your mother alone."

Papa got in on the driver's side and started the car. Auntie Ngozie backed away.

"How was school, dear?" Mama asked.

"School was fine, but why won't anyone tell me what happened?"

"You will know soon enough," Papa scolded.

When we arrived at home, Papa helped Mama out of the car. He supported her as she walked into the house.

I could not sleep that night because my mind was running wild. The following morning when I saw Mama, I gasped.

"What happened to the baby?" I asked.

"We lost the baby, Foma."

I noticed her eyes were puffy, and that she had deep dark circles around her eyes. While I was sad, I knew that Mama needed me to be strong for her, so I didn't cry.

Five years ago, I found out more about what happened to Mama when I had absentmindedly asked her why I didn't have siblings. Surprisingly, she had been candid with me.

"When I was pregnant," she explained, "there was something else growing with your baby brother. It grew until it suffocated him."

"What thing?" I asked.

"Tumors called fibroids. I did not even know I had it. When we lost him, the doctor told me that the fibroids had grown so much that they had to take out my uterus. That means I cannot have any more children."

I went to comfort my mother as tears streamed down her face.

That was the day I decided that as a doctor, I would specialize in obstetrics and gynecology.

It pained me that my thoughtless words hurt Mama. It hurt even more that she didn't want to accept my apology. When I tried to apologize, she said, "Don't worry, dear." I could tell she was still upset.

"Have a safe flight to Cameroon," I said as I got out of the car.

"Thank you, Foma. I will call you before I leave."

When I got to the front door of my dorm and turned to wave at Mama, she was already gone.

Back in my room, I placed my neatly folded clothes in my drawer and hung the rest in my wardrobe. I checked my phone—still nothing from Kunle. I wondered if he was waiting for me to contact him first. Maybe he was through with me. But we were boyfriend and girlfriend now. Didn't he have to contact me to break up with me? We had just had a fight, not a breakup.

I thought about texting him to ask him how his weekend had gone, but I didn't want to pretend that night had not happened. In my state of indecision, I threw my phone on my bed.

It didn't stay still long. I was in the bathroom, brushing my teeth, when I heard it vibrating. I sighed when I saw Paige's name, only because I was hoping it was Kunle.

"Paige, how are you?" I asked.

"Foma, I'm so sorry for not getting back to you earlier."

"Please, don't apologize. I know you have a lot going on. How are you?"

"I am trying to stay in good spirits, but everything is coming apart. My friends are not talking to me, except for Monica, but she's being iffy. I don't think she believes me. Nobody believes me."

"Paige, I believe you, and many others do as well. They've told me."

"You've been talking to people about me?"

"No!" I assured her. "I haven't been telling people about you. No one knows that you told me anything. I just mean from what

I heard from people in passing." I had told Kunle, but she didn't need to know that.

"Everything I've worked for is coming apart. For the past three years I have done everything right. I have been an exceptional student, I have done my best to represent the school well as an ambassador, and I even let them use my face to promote diversity. Now I feel like I have nothing to show for it all."

"Paige, you have many supporters. I am sure the school supports you. Things will work themselves out."

"If the school supports me, how come they're allowing Ray to walk around campus? A family friend called my mother and told her that her son saw Ray at Sterling."

"I know, Paige, I heard about that. It is not right. Did someone bring this to the school's attention?"

"My mom definitely did. I heard her yelling in the phone last week."

"Okay, good."

"Foma, don't get creeped out by what I'm about to ask you. I promise, I'm not planning on doing anything crazy but do you ever think about not being in this world?"

"What?"

"I mean, about the afterlife. Like what would become of you if you left this world."

"Um, Paige, honey. Are you sure you're all right?"

"Yes, Foma. I am fine. I've just been doing a lot of thinking. I'm not planning anything. The thing is, I don't understand why God allows bad things to happen to good people. Why do children get cancer? You know."

"I think everything happens for a reason. Sometimes, God allows bad things to happen to good people because he is preparing them for something great."

"I know you're just trying to be supportive, but I don't see how anything great can come out of this situation. Foma, I can't sleep because all I can think about is how he bound my wrists. His grip was so tight, Foma. And then the smell—he reeked of booze. I can still taste the alcohol and sourness in his mouth. I didn't remember this before, but he belched when he was kissing my cheeks. I can still smell it. I can't sleep without taking sleeping pills, and I wake up in the middle of the night, drenched in sweat. I've screamed in my sleep several times."

As I sat there listening to her, I asked myself if the experience I had with Kunle was comparable. I wanted so badly to ask Paige about my situation with Kunle, but I knew it wasn't a good idea. I would have to handle that situation myself.

I woke up to find my pillow vibrating right beneath my face. Sluggishly, I felt for my phone. It was still dark outside; I knew it was not my alarm. My eyes half-closed, I looked at my phone and saw Papa was calling me. It was 3:23 a.m. My eyes welled up with tears because I knew what Papa would tell me when I picked up the phone.

CHAPTER SEVENTEEN

My body felt limp as I sat on the chair in the lobby.

"Foma, your grandmother has passed away." Papa's words echoed in my ears.

I declined his offer to come pick me up. I sat in the lobby for the rest of the night. I watched out the window as dawn broke. I was watching when the sun made its appearance. I replayed my conversation with Nana Ola over and over in my head.

I had heard the defeat in her voice when I spoke to her on Saturday. I tried to ignore it but it had been there.

"Why did you give up, Nana Ola?" I whispered. Then remembering the crackling sound of her cough, I shuddered.

I didn't know what we would do without Nana Ola. Mama was now an orphan. The people who brought her into this world were no longer. When Papa called, he said Mama was in no state to talk on the phone.

"Why didn't you stay, Nana Ola?" I whispered.

She had been impatient to leave. She told Mama she wanted her freedom and that being in America was suffocating her. Now she was gone forever, and I felt like her death was suffocating me.

The image that came up when I thought of Nana Ola was of the day we picked her up from the airport. Her high cheekbones were sunken, she was almost totally gray, and she was in a wheelchair. She had looked so small. I learned she suffered from lung disease. Everyone assumed that it stemmed from her years of smoking cigarettes—a conventional African grandmother, Nana Ola was not.

⌣⟶

When she was young, she had been a gorgeous woman. I still remembered her black and white photographs displayed in our home in Yaoundé. Someone told me that Pa Ola eloped with her to London because he did not want to risk leaving her behind and then coming back to find her married off to someone else.

During one of our many chats that summer, Nana Ola told me she felt Mama running off and marrying Papa without their approval was the universe's cruel joke on her.

"Foma, what goes up must come down," she told me.

Her stories about London were also captivating. She told stories so vividly.

"I had never seen anything like that in my life. The buildings were so tall, the roads were rife with vehicles, which they drove on smooth roads. I watched in awe at the hurried pace of the people walking down the concrete streets, on a mission. That was London!

"I had some of the most horrid experiences of my life there, and also the absolute best. We lived in a small room. It was so small, I could stretch out my hand from the cot where we slept and touch our small stove. While your grandfather attended school, I stayed home, alone."

Nana Ola told me about the many days she spent crying in their small apartment because Pa Ola was always gone, and she had no friends. The white women she encountered at the market were cordial, but she understood that she could never permeate the barrier between them.

"Foma, people complain that hell is hot, but my time in England convinced me I would rather be hot in hell than feel the cold that I felt in that place."

⌣⟶

Now my grandmother was gone, off to the afterlife, and all I could do was sit there, thinking of the good times I had with her. I had to use the bathroom, but the thought of getting up was too taxing. When I couldn't hold it anymore, I rushed to our bathroom.

I moped over to my bed. Kara was up by then, lying in bed and staring at her phone. She looked over at me.

"Are you okay?" she asked. We had not spoken in days, so I looked at her in shock, not sure if I just imagined her talking.

"Foma, are you okay?" she repeated.

"Not really. I found out early this morning that my grandmother died."

"Oh, no, Foma, I am so sorry. Do you need help with anything? Can I get you something?"

"That's nice of you, Kara, but no, I don't need anything, thank you," I said as I climbed in my bed. My entire body ached.

"I'm about to head off to class, but please, just text me if you need anything."

"Okay," I mumbled.

I was still in bed when Mama called me. "My mother is gone," she wept.

I sat on my bed, heaving as tears pooled down my face.

"Foma, do you need to come home?"

"No, I don't, Mama," I managed. I wanted to mourn Nana Ola in my own space. I could already hear people in the background; visitors were at our house consoling Mama.

"Who is there with you?" Mama asked.

"Nobody right now. I am in my room by myself."

"Where is Michelle?"

"She is probably in class."

"Will she come see you?"

"Mama, I don't know."

"You need someone to be with you."

"I'm fine, Mama. Are you still going to Cameroon tomorrow?"

"Yes, dear. I will leave early in the morning."

"Okay. Are Papa and I going to go too?"

"Yes, your father is searching for tickets as we speak. Oh Foma, what are we going to do without our Nana Ola?"

I did not know how to respond. I could not imagine going back to Cameroon and not seeing Nana Ola.

Not long after I got off the phone with Mama, Ife texted me asking why I had missed two classes. I told her my grandmother just died. She offered to come to my dorm right away. I told her she could come after class.

Hours later, Michelle called. "Foma, your mom told my mom about Nana Ola. I am so sorry. I'm coming over."

"Okay," I said. Despite what had happened, I needed my best friend.

I was still in bed when Michelle texted to say she was downstairs. I went to let her in.

"Hi, Foma, how are you doing?" Michelle asked as she hugged me.

"I'm maintaining."

"I'm so sorry about Nana Ola. I know how much you loved her. When I saw her this past summer, she looked fine."

"Yeah, I can't believe this," I said. I could not hold the tears back. Before I knew it, I was sobbing on Michelle's shoulders. No matter what rift had formed between us, she was the person I trusted the most.

When we got upstairs, Michelle and I lay on my bed and reminisced about Nana Ola. She remembered the time Nana Ola gave us an example of how they used to dance back in her day. We recollected watching in awe as my petite grandmother swayed her hips from side to side and even spun around.

"Your grandmother was amazing," Michelle said.

"I know."

I was grateful to have had a worldly grandmother—one with whom I could communicate on a deep level. Most of my African age mates could not communicate with their grandmothers because they did not speak the tribal dialects and their grandmothers could not speak English. Over the years, Nana Ola had imparted a lot of wisdom—what she lacked in formal education, she made up for with eventful life experiences. She had traveled all over Europe and Africa with Pa Ola.

Thinking back on that dance lesson brought fresh tears to my eyes, and Michelle consoled me. I cried ugly tears in her arms. I felt like my heart was being pulled from out of me.

Michelle stayed for a few hours, but then she had to leave for an afternoon class.

Shortly after her departure, Ife called to say she was coming up. I dragged myself out of bed to let her in. Although our buildings were separate, the hall between our back staircases connected us. I went to open the door to my side of the building to let her in.

"How are you feeling?" she asked.

"I'm in shock."

Ife and I sat on my bed. The television was on from earlier, when I turned it on during Michelle's visit. A daytime soap was playing. While we gazed at the television, my mind was somewhere else.

"I told Kunle about your grandmother passing," Ife said suddenly.

"What?"

"Kunle, I said I told him about your grandmother."

"Oh, did you?"

"Yes." Ife studied me suspiciously. "I thought you told him already, so when he asked about you, I mentioned it."

"Oh."

"What's going on?"

"Nothing, why?"

"I don't know, I was just asking."

I was happy when she said nothing further. I didn't want to discuss Kunle. I checked my phone: still nothing from him.

He knew my grandmother had passed away, and he had yet to contact me.

Ife stayed with me for half an hour. When Papa called, I told Ife it was okay for her to leave.

"I'm just checking to see how you are doing," he said.

"You're at work?" I asked in disbelief. I heard hospital sounds in the background.

"Yes, unfortunately, I had to come here because a patient of mine had an emergency. Don't worry, your mother has many people in the house caring for her."

"Auntie Rubi and the others?" I asked.

"Yes."

"Well, Papa, I will let you go. Just know I am doing fine and my friends came to see me."

"Okay. Please let me know if you want to come home. Also, I will let you know when I book our flights. Speak to the people at your school and tell them what's happening so you can take time off."

"I will, after you tell me the travel dates. Also, how long do you expect us to be gone for?"

"At least a week and a half."

Thirty minutes after I got off the phone with Papa, I picked up my vibrating phone. Kunle was calling. My heart jumped. I stared at the pulsating phone in my hand, not sure whether I should answer the call.

"Hey," Kunle said hesitantly.

"Hi."

"I heard about your grandmother. I am so sorry."

"Thanks for calling."

"Um...how are you feeling?"

"I'm doing all right. I've had better days."

"Again...I am so sorry. Let me know if you need anything."

I didn't know what to say. It hurt me that he had not taken the time to actually come see me. After all, wasn't he my boyfriend?

Did he not know how important Nana Ola was to me? I suppose he probably didn't because we had just started dating, and Nana Ola only came up a few times. Even so, I expected more than just an awkward phone call. Were the shoe on the other foot, I would've at least attempted to see him.

"Thanks for calling, Kunle."

After I got off the phone, I texted Paige to let her know what was going on and that I would be traveling to Cameroon shortly.

I cried myself to sleep afterward. I mourned my grand-mother—and what I thought was the end of my relationship with Kunle.

CHAPTER EIGHTEEN

When Papa and I stepped off the plane on that brisk afternoon, a feeling of nostalgia came rushing at me. After eight years I had returned home. We flew in to the city of Douala, where we would stay at Uncle Folemji's house for a few days before our drive to the village. Uncle Folemji was Papa's cousin, Great Uncle Pius's son.

We arrived at Uncle Folemji's house to find a crowd waiting for us. In awe, I hugged Edward, Uncle Folemji's son. He was only four years old when I left Cameroon, and now he was a big boy, taller than his father.

A feast and the arms of unfamiliar—at least to me—uncles and aunties awaited us.

"Foma, you are a woman now, ma mami! Look how pretty you look, just like your mother," an aunt said.

Everyone kept calling Papa "American doctor." There was so much hoopla! While I wished we had had time to rest before this elaborate gathering, I understood the excitement. We had not been back to Cameroon since we left.

No one allowed us to lift a finger for anything. They served our food and brought us a bowl of water to wash our hands. I felt awkward when an auntie picked up my plate and cup when I finished eating. Their hospitality felt excessive even if it was endearing.

As some younger people left for their relative homes later that night, they had expectant looks on their faces. I was surprised when Papa took money out of his wallet and gave some to each person. The looks of delight that filled their faces were priceless.

In Uncle Folemji's compound were the main house and quarters for the house help. Uncle Folemji, Auntie Linda, and Edward occupied two of the five bedrooms in the main house. They had set up the other two for Papa and myself.

I got up the following morning to the sound of Grenadine knocking on my door asking whether I wanted to eat breakfast. I assumed she was the house girl. When I got to the dining room, I saw familiar faces, but mostly new ones. More people came to see us.

"Future doctor!" Uncle Folemji exclaimed when I walked into the room.

I cringed when he said this because everyone turned to look at me. The guests came to greet me.

"Hello auntie," said a man who I was certain was around my age, or older.

I found it funny how although I was young, a lot of the older people were treating me as their senior. I spoke with Papa about this and he said that it was because in our culture, people who were perceived as being wealthy received a lot of respect even if they were young.

After I ate breakfast, Auntie Linda asked, "Why don't you escort Grenadine to the market?"

I guessed Grenadine was my age or older. At first I thought she was maybe sixteen years old because of her small stature; however, her demeanor was more mature. I went to my room to freshen up. Papa and Uncle Folemji had already gone out into the city to run errands.

When I came out of my room, I went to the kitchen, but

Grenadine was not there. I walked outside to the back of the house to her quarter.

I walked past the washroom; I observed a brand-new washer and dryer in the room. They also had a dishwasher in the kitchen. Uncle Folemji was wealthy by Cameroon standards. Papa said he had a good job with the government. I was almost at the door of Grenadine's quarter when I saw Auntie Linda.

"Foma, why are you people still here? Where is Grenadine?"

"I'm not sure. I went into my room and came back, and I can't find her."

"That stupid girl," Auntie Linda said, before yelling, "Grenadine!"

"Yes, Mama, I am coming," Grenadine said as she ran outside.

"What were you doing there? Didn't I ask you to go to the market?" Auntie Linda barked. I jerked, taken aback by the venom in her tone.

Grenadine's hands shook as she gave me one of the shopping bags in her hand.

"Foma is not going to carry a shopping bag. Do you think she is a bush girl like you?" Auntie Linda scolded. Grenadine put her head down.

In all the time I had known Auntie Linda, I had not known her to be so cruel. I looked at Grenadine with sympathy.

As we began our walk to the gate, Grenadine told me the market was a thirty-minute walk from the house. I was happy that it was not too hot outside. At the gate, the gateman stood stiffly and addressed us.

"Good afternoon Madams," he said, with a playful bow as he took his hat off. I could not ignore the longing look he gave Grenadine.

Once we stepped out of the gate, it surprised me to see that there were many people out in the street, also walking. This was something I rarely saw in America because people usually took the bus or drove.

As we walked to the market, I asked Grenadine about her relationship with Auntie Linda. "Why does she speak to you that way?"

Grenadine opened her mouth to say something but stopped herself.

"You can tell me. I won't say anything to her."

"I am very grateful that Papa took me in. You see, my mother died giving birth to me and my father wanted nothing to do with me. So, his mother came and took me from his compound. I was happy to go. His three wives were so wicked, they never wanted to give me food. Thank God for my grandmother who rescued me, but she has nothing. That is why she sent me to live with Papa; he is my mother's elder brother."

I gaped at this revelation. I had just assumed that she was the house girl, not Uncle Folemji's niece.

"Oh Grenadine, I am so sorry to hear that," I told her. "But just because they are giving you a place to live doesn't mean that she should speak to you in that way. Don't let her speak to you like that."

"Do I have a choice? I have nowhere else to go. I need to stay here and help them so they can help my grandmother. He gives her money every month. She has gotten so old and she has glaucoma. It is very difficult for her to work. She depends on their support."

"Yes, but how can you stand it when she speaks to you like that?"

"I told you, I have no choice. This is not America. We do not have the freedom that you have there."

My heart broke for her, she was such a sweet girl. I had known Auntie Linda to be a gentle, soft-spoken woman; this new side of her shocked me.

We walked in silence for a while. It dismayed me that the city I once saw as grand now looked small and flimsy. The waste lined up at a corner seemed to grow as we approached the outdoor market. Also, the path was muddy because of rain that had fallen the night before. There was no pavement to shield us from the rich reddish soil that clung to the bottom of our shoes. Certain areas of Cameroon, such as the area where the airport was located, were more modern, with tall buildings. But I was still in a third world country. At least, the jovial looks on the faces of the vendors and shoppers were welcoming.

"I was sorry to hear about your grandmother," Grenadine blurted, breaking the silence.

"Thank you, we all miss her so much."

At the market, people, cars, and motorcycles surrounded us, as did many tents.

"Fresh, fresh groundnut," I heard a woman yell from a tent.

I told Grenadine I wanted to go over to buy a bag of boiled groundnut. I had not had them in so long. Grenadine followed me.

"Let me do the talking," she said. "They will know you are a foreigner and charge us more if they hear you talk."

"Doesn't she already have a sale price for the groundnut?"

Grenadine laughed. "No-o, she will tell you a high price so you can negotiate down. Let me take care of the negotiation."

I stood back and watched as Grenadine walked to the woman's tent and haggled on the price.

As Grenadine reached into the coin purse tied in the wrapper she wore around her waist and pulled out some money, the lady asked, pointing at me, "Na who dat?"

"Na ma sistah, from America." Grenadine beamed with pride.

When the lady heard the word America, she smiled and waved at me excitedly.

"Hello, how are you?" she asked in what I thought was her most American accent.

"Hello, madam, I dei fine," I responded, trying to make my pidgin sound as authentic as theirs.

Both women laughed at my attempt.

"Here you go, coconut sweet for my American friend," said the lady as she handed me a bag of grated and sweetened coconuts.

She placed her hands behind her back and swayed a little as she looked at me with a big grin on her face.

She grabbed my hand to stop me when I reached for my wallet.

"No dear, jus take am," she said as she smiled on.

There was no way I was going to accept a gift from this lady. Despite her protest, I reached for my wallet again. This time she did not stop me. I pulled out a few bills and squeezed them into her hands. Her willingness to give me something for free because I lived in America saddened me, especially since I was certain her family relied on her sales for their survival.

"Aye! Thank you, thank you," she said as she jumped in excitement.

We proceeded to other tents, and Grenadine made the purchases she needed. We were exiting the market when we heard music playing. I looked over to see where the music was coming from and saw a crowd gathering. As we approached, I peeked through the crowd of people and saw children dancing in front of a booth that sold CDs and other electronics. Makossa music wafted through the air, and the children were dancing their behinds off. The look of joy on their faces was one that I had not seen since I left Cameroon eight years prior. People were cheering them on.

Twenty minutes later when we exited the market, I was sure of one thing. Life's joys did not always come from the material things that hard work and success provide. Those children had so little, as reflected by the tattered clothing they wore, and yet they had such joy deep within.

By four o'clock the next morning, we hit the road, headed to the village. Uncle Folemji was driving, and it pleased me that Auntie Linda was not joining us. Then I felt bad that Grenadine was stuck with her. Before I left, I gave Grenadine a few items—clothing, shoes, a purse, jewelry, and a few bills.

"Aye, thank you sistah!" she exclaimed.

"No problem, I wish you all the best," I responded.

As we approached Nana Ola's compound, I saw a large bill-board advertising her funeral. I felt an ache in my heart because this billboard so close to her home solidified that she was no longer.

The nostalgia I felt was overwhelming. Everything looked the same as the last time I was there. As we stood before Nana Ola's gate, I saw a slender figure with bowed legs approach. I squinted to make out who it was. It was Peter, Nana Ola's house boy.

Peter waved at us before he opened the gate. Uncle Folemji proceeded into the compound.

"Foma, wow, you are a big girl now," Peter said admiringly. "Last time you were here, you were so small. Now look at you."

As Peter and I hugged, Mama came running outside. At first I didn't recognize her because her luscious long hair was gone. Following tradition, she had cut her hair to mourn Nana Ola's passing. Fortunately for me, as a granddaughter, no one expected me to do the same.

After we said our greetings, Mama informed us that there was a cry-die going on in the living room and that we should take the back entrance into the house. Papa and Uncle Folemji stayed outside, while Mama led me to the kitchen.

"Foma!" Susana exclaimed in her irritatingly nasal voice. "Na how na?"

"Good morning, Susana, I am fine. How are you?" I said, suppressing the temptation to reply in pidgin.

We hugged, and Susana attended to the pot on the stove. There was much to do in the kitchen. Different ingredients were scattered everywhere.

"I'll be right back," Mama said as she left the room.

I stood by the counter awkwardly, watching Susana as she cooked. Beads of sweat covered her caramel brown face as she stirred a large pot of chicken stew on the white gas stove. A large pot of fufu sat on the floor, on top of a folded cardboard box, and a thick, long wooden spoon pierced the center of the fufu.

I looked around at my grandmother's kitchen. Everything

was the same as I had left it nine years prior, except that it was not as clean as I had remembered. Nana Ola was a stickler for cleanliness.

I studied the tan walls and dark wood cabinets. The white sink and tile floor. Nine years ago, this kitchen had seemed massive. I was still looking around when two light-skinned children peeked through the white door that separated the kitchen from the rest of the house. I recognized those children!

"Leo, Nana," I called. They ran, and the door closed behind them. Those were my aunt Lulu's children from Germany.

Within seconds, Auntie Lulu appeared, Mama standing behind her. She was holding Leo and Nana's hands, preventing them from running.

"Foma, my sweetheart!"

"Auntie Lulu!"

"How are you, my baby? Long time."

"I am fine, Auntie. It is good to see you." I relaxed when Auntie Lulu turned around to Leo and Nana. The last time I saw Auntie Lulu, she pinched my chest in a room full of people and commented on how fast I was growing.

"Leo, Nana, say hello to your cousin Foma," Auntie Lulu instructed her children. Mama was holding their hands tightly.

"Hello," they both said in the cutest accent.

Before I could respond, they wormed out of Mama's hands and ran away.

As I was making small talk with Auntie Lulu, Mama sat on a short step stool and began pounding the hot fufu in the pot—I could see vapor rising as she pounded. Minutes later, a group of five middle-aged women entered the kitchen with large plaid shopping bags in their hands. When I extended my hand to greet them, they ignored it.

"Dear, young girls in our culture do not extend their hands to elders," the first auntie said. I dropped my hand to my side, and the auntie gave me a hug. The other four women hugged me, each asking if I remembered them. I smiled out of politeness—I did not, but I was hesitant to say so.

I watched as the newcomers removed containers of cooked food and plastic bags filled with foodstuff from their blue plaid shopping bags. Within minutes, young Susana went from the woman in charge to the fetch girl, as she ran around finding pots, spoons, and other things the women needed as they cooked.

I heard wailing coming from Nana Ola's living room. The bereft grandmothers were in full force, grieving Nana Ola's death. Since my arrival, I had stayed in the kitchen, in a corner, listening to the women as they cooked. When the kitchen got too hot, I went outside.

I smiled when a cool breeze hit my face. I strolled to the veranda where Papa and the uncles sat. They were commenting on how people who live in the village all their lives are the healthiest people on earth because they have an active lifestyle and eat the freshest of foods. In so many words, they seemed to be blaming Nana Ola and Pa Ola's deaths on their overexposure to the modern world of cigarettes and alcohol. Then the conversation moved to Africans they knew who had gone abroad and contracted cancer.

When the conversation got too morbid for my liking, I took a walk around the compound, inhaling the fresh air that surrounded me. As I walked, I saw a group of young men enter the house with drums in hand and the blue and white *nchen* cloths tied around their waists.

Not long after, now back to my seat on the veranda, I heard singing and drum playing coming from inside the house.

"They are playing music?" I asked Papa in surprise.

"Yes. The cry-die is not just for mourning. It is also for celebrating life," he explained.

Celebration of life, I thought as I sat there more at peace than I had expected to feel so soon after my grandmother's passing. I peered into the living room, where the grandmas sat, their heads in their hands. Some sat on Nana Ola's antique chairs and sofas with the dark wood legs and the tan flower-patterned cushions, while others sat on the also flower-patterned tan rug with burgundy trim. The young men had set up their drums at the corner of the room, in the same place where those four children had knelt about nine years prior, during my last summer with Nana Ola before we left for the United States.

On that day, a woman had come to this very house with her four children to discuss the case of the missing meat; she needed help finding the duplicitous culprit.

"Ma, I was cooking soup when I heard my baby crying in the house. As the soup was almost ready, I removed it from the fire and put it on the ground. I ran into the house to tend to my crying baby, and when I came back, I noticed that there were two pieces of meat missing from the pot."

"Mm hmm," my grandmother said as she followed along.

"I knew that I put eight pieces of meat in that pot: two for my husband, two for myself, and one for each of my four older children here. I asked each one if they took the meat and they all refused. One of them or maybe even all of them are lying. I have come to you because I want answers."

"My daughter, thank you for coming to me to address this matter," Nana Ola said, then she directed her attention to the children. They looked up at her from where they knelt with bewilderment in their eyes. I knew that the children in the area were afraid of Nana Ola—they called her the "woman god."

"Now, which one of you took the meat?" Nana Ola asked the four children who knelt before her.

"I will ask just once again, who took the meat from the pot?" Still nothing.

Nana Ola suddenly clasped her hands behind her neck as she wailed in agony, "Juju is coming, he knows the person who took the meat, he is coming for you. Run! Run! I cannot save you, run!"

The youngest of the four sprinted out of the room, and the other three cried in fear—the oldest must have been twelve years old, and the youngest around eight years old.

"And there, we have our thief," Nana Ola said.

I could tell she was trying to suppress her laughter. She knew what I had come to discover about the children in that village— they were very gullible. She looked at me sternly when I busted out in a fit of laughter; her trick was working, and she did not want me to spoil it.

Juju was our name for a monster. During village occasions, the juju would come out, standing at least eight feet tall with the help of wooden stilts. Its face was concealed by a sometimes-colorful mask. It wore a tall headdress, and a long, flowy dress, made of the dark blue and white nchen fabric of our Lebang chiefdom—one of the nine that made up the Nweh tribe. The first time I saw the juju, I had been scared out of my mind, but I was wise enough to know that he would not come out for a matter so trivial.

As I thought about celebrating Nana Ola's life, I felt that this incident embodied all that she was: a woman who, despite her sometimes-tough exterior, was welcoming to others and whom others sought when they needed help. Nana Ola could have admonished this woman for bringing such a trivial matter to her doorstep, yet she indulged the situation and weeded out the culprit—even if it was just a rambunctious eight-year-old. So, as the drums beat, my spirits lifted as I reminisced about the colorful life of my grandmother.

The following day, we walked to the burial site to lay Nana Ola's body to rest. The family members who had been at the house the day before were back, and the celebration of Nana Ola's life continued with more singing and dancing. After hours of celebration, Nana Ola's pastor delivered the eulogy, and we laid Nana Ola to rest beside the gravesites of the parents who had disowned her half a century prior after she ran off with Pa Ola. She refused to be buried near Pa Ola, after he betrayed her by having five wives besides her, and producing ten children in those marriages. In Cameroon, polygamy was perfectly legal. Nana Ola only found out about these other marriages after he died and the women came to collect their share of their husband's estate. I came to find out later that her altercation with these women inspired Nana Ola's move from her home in Buea to the village.

I was holding up fine until her casket began descending into the ground. At that moment something inside me wailed. The pressure in my chest was so deep that I fell to the ground heaving, as it became final that my best friend and the one who knew me best in the world was gone forever. She was the only one to whom I could speak candidly, with full confidence that she would not judge or chastise me. As Nana Ola's body went down into the ground, it felt like she was taking a piece of me with her.

I was still rolling on the ground when I felt two hands on either shoulder. I looked up and saw Mama and Papa holding onto me. Their grip was strong. I wept in my mother's arms. I remembered little else from that day. I was shocked when someone told me that Papa carried me on his back from the grave site to Nana Ola's house.

The following morning when I woke up, I had a headache. I frightened myself when I looked in the mirror beside the bed. My eyes were red and puffy. Mama came into the room.

"Foma, are you all right?"

"Yes, Mama."

"How did you sleep?"

"I slept okay."

Mama sat beside me on the bed. "Dear, your father and I were worried about you yesterday."

I said nothing.

"I understand how close you and your grandmother were, but Foma, I want you to know that your father and I love you so much. We only want the best for you. Now with your grandmother passing, please don't feel you are alone. We support you in everything you do. Never be afraid to tell us anything. Do you understand?"

"Yes, Mama. I understand."

"Okay, take this. Your Nana Ola left this for you."

I waited for Mama to leave the room before I unfolded the lined paper. I recognized my grandmother's meticulous cursive handwriting.

My daughter, the day I held you in my arms for the very first time, I knew that you would grow to become someone special. As I have watched you flourish before my very eyes, there is no doubt in my mind that you will be a light to many. You are strong beyond what you know. Please stop doubting this. Be sure of yourself and don't be afraid to stand up for what you believe is right. This life is not promised to anyone, so make sure that every day of your life, you live with courage, for it is the most important thing in this life. Courage allows you to fight for what you believe and face any consequences doing so may bring. Say what you want and do what you want so long as it is not coming from a place of malice. Most important, don't worry about anyone else's opinion. Once you apply these things to your life, my daughter, I assure you, you will have the only happiness that matters—that which comes from within.

Love, Your One and Only Nana Ola

CHAPTER NINETEEN

After Nana Ola's burial, we stayed in the village for several more days. Mama and her siblings had many affairs to tend to with Nana Ola's passing. I spent most of my time strolling along the peaceful village dirt roads, remembering the last time I was there.

During my strolls, I thought about Kunle, and the disappointment I felt about the downward spiral our relationship had taken. I also thought about Paige. The last I had heard from her, she said she was doing okay. In fact, she seemed more concerned about how I was coping with Nana Ola's passing.

"She is at peace, I am sure of it," Paige had said.

While her words were comforting, they made me feel uneasy because just a week prior, she had asked me about the afterlife. I wished I could call or text her to see how things were going. However, we were in Cameroon and I couldn't use my cellphone to send international texts. Even if I could, I dared not because I was certain the bill would be outrageously high. Besides, my phone died and I could not find the proper outlet converter to charge it.

By the last day of our stay in the village, I was eager to return to my life in the United States. I felt the week and a half was just what I needed to gain some mental clarity.

Mama, Auntie Lulu, her children, and I left the village together to visit Auntie Efa and Uncle David in Yaoundé. Auntie

Efa was one of my favorite aunties when I lived in Cameroon, and I looked forward to seeing her.

Mama was especially happy to see her because after many years of barrenness, she now had a baby boy. In a few days, Papa and Uncle Folemji would pick Mama and I up so we could ride back to Douala together so Uncle Folemji could drop us off at the airport. Papa and Uncle Folemji were staying behind because Papa was volunteering his services at a local hospital. They dropped us off at a bus station.

We boarded the bus early in the morning. Still tired from all the festivities, I fell asleep as soon as the bus began moving.

The bumpiness of the road woke me up. I was happy to have a window seat as I looked out, observing the city. There were vendors outside selling fruit and groundnuts; some people were selling out of carts while others carried their food items in baskets balanced on their heads with the help of a cloth twisted in the shape of a halo. It fascinated me to see how the baskets remained steady on their heads without support from their hands even when they walked.

Cars filled the road, and the sound of the city permeated the air.

"Fresh groundnut!" I heard a woman yell.

I also heard cars honking and people talking in elevated tones. Some were calling out the items they were selling, while others were just discussing with their neighbors. There were tented booths lined up on both sides of the road, in which a variety of foods were sold, from fresh fruit to roasted fish.

I noticed the children who stood alongside the road displaying their goods to the passengers of the vehicles, hoping to make a sale. Because of the congestion, the bus was moving at a slow pace. A few bus passengers pulled their windows down and called for the children to bring snacks over.

"Madame, I want the groundnut. How much for the groundnut?" one passenger yelled.

The children who were selling the foodstuffs looked rough. One boy wore a dingy brown holey t-shirt that looked like it had once been white but was discolored from excessive use. Also, he wore trousers too small for his long skinny legs, and sandals that looked worn down. I wondered if these children went to school. I pitied them, and I was grateful that in my childhood, I had been a child, not burdened by the responsibilities of adults.

Uncle David came to pick us up at the bus station. I didn't recognize him at first because of how much he had aged. Gray hairs now held his once black hair hostage.

"The American and German express. How are you people today?" he asked as he hugged us.

Per usual, Leo and Nana stayed back, looking uneasy. They didn't like meeting new people. I felt they were going through a bit of culture shock too. From what Auntie Lulu had said, there were few black people where they lived in Germany, so I was certain it must have been strange for them to be in a country of nothing but black people.

A few nights prior, I overheard Mama and Auntie Lulu talking about the bullying Leo faced at his school.

"Those children in that school, heh, they keep disturbing my boy. He is the only black boy, so he is their target. Luckily, things have gotten better; we gave him permission to fight back. The school has been complaining that he is now beating those boys. That is their problem. When they were bullying my son, those people said that is just what children do. Now that roles have reversed, they are complaining."

"Lulu, you shouldn't tell your son to fight in school."

"Sistah, even you should know that people will keep attacking you if you do not stand up for yourself. Those children were relentless. His father even went to the school to talk to their teacher several times, but they did nothing. Everything is better now. My boy has learned to defend himself."

It was a short drive to Uncle David's house. I looked around, perplexed when we pulled into the driveway of a house smaller than that I had remembered. I was certain my memory was not failing me.

Uncle David had been one of my wealthier uncles in Cam–eroon. From what I remembered, he had a big house. I was even surprised when he had picked us up in the same car from years ago, the one Papa often borrowed.

I squinted as I saw a woman come to the door. She looked like Auntie Efa, and she was carrying a baby boy. However, the Auntie Efa I remembered had dark brown skin just like mine. As we got closer, I realized that it was Auntie Efa. I gulped hard. My beautiful auntie had transformed herself to a chalky light-skinned person. After I hugged her, I tried not to stare. I didn't know what to make of this new version of my auntie. Her new complexion dulled her beauty.

"Aye, Efa!" Mama yelled as she hurried to her, seemingly oblivious about the change to my auntie.

"Sistah! Welcome o!" The two women did a side hug, since Auntie Efa was holding the baby.

"My goodness, is this baby Joshua? What a handsome boy," Mama said as she took the baby and hugged him. He gripped the inch of hair on her head. Mama winced as she tried to pry his hand away.

"I say, Efa, this your son is strong o," Mama commented when she was finally free from baby Joshua's grip. He was smiling as though it had all been a game to him. Drool was smudged around his puffy, dimpled, dark brown cheeks.

"Big boy," Auntie Lulu gushed over Joshua. Leo and Nana stood by either side of their mother, observing everything.

"Foma. How are you my girl?" new Auntie Efa asked.

"I am fine, Auntie," I said, trying not to stare.

A few hours after our arrival, Leo and Nana were fast asleep.

They were jetlagged. Before they fell asleep, Auntie Lulu gave them their German meal. She had brought a lot of dry German foods because Leo and Nana refused to eat African food.

Auntie Efa prepared *ndolé*, boiled yam, and baked chicken for us. She proudly proclaimed that she killed a fresh chicken in anticipation of our visit.

I winced as I recalled images of a headless fowl running around the backyard of Nana Ola's home in Buea, after Susana had cut its head off so Nana Ola could make my "special soup" following the jump rope fiasco that left me with stitches on my forehead.

"We are so happy that Efa is finally a mother. What a beautiful boy you have!" cooed Auntie Lulu.

"Thank you, sistah. After all what we have gone through, we are truly blessed."

"Oh yes, I am so sorry," Mama said.

"No, sistah, we are doing fine. The one that should be sorry is me. I am so sorry about your mother. You know how much I loved my auntie. If it wasn't for our financial situation, we would have gone to her funeral."

Mama turned to Uncle David. "It's not good that you did not tell us about your financial situation. We could have helped you."

"No problem, sistah. We are doing better now. My job is tough but I am managing. Never in my wildest dreams did I think I would be working as a bricklayer, but here I am," Uncle David said.

"Yes, you have always been a hardworking man. I am glad you all are in a good place now," Mama said.

"We are in a good place o. The one thing I can say is that being a poor man really shows you who your friends are. When I was making all the money, you should have seen the friends I had. You know, Rebecca," Uncle David said to Mama.

"Yes, I know. You people's house was the party house. Every weekend, pah-tee, pah-tee."

"Those were the days, but now I am happy to just be a family man. That life was too much to handle. Those people sucked me dry of my money. Then when I lost my job and started telling them about my financial problems, you should have seen how fast they disappeared from my corner."

"That's how people are o," Auntie Lulu said. "When things are going good, they are all around you, but the moment you start to fall, you find that they won't be there to catch you."

"I am telling you. To think I used to call those people friends. Foma, be very careful about the people you invite into your life. People can be wicked. When they show you who they are, believe them the first time. These were people who would borrow money and never pay me back, and I would forgive their debt. But the moment I was without, they just ran. Ahhh shhh! These past years have shown me something."

"All is well o, all is well. You now have your miracle baby!" Auntie Lulu responded.

"Yes, it has been all worth it because I have such an amazing wife."

Auntie Efa beamed as she looked down at her plate.

"My saving grace was that I bought land in Nkongsamba that I sold at a profit. Foma, can you believe your auntie began planting fruits and vegetables to go sell at the market to help support us? A woman as beautiful as she is, she stuck by me. I am sure that most of these other beautiful women here in Cameroon would have just left, but she stuck by me," he said as he smiled at his wife.

"You people stop that thing," Auntie Lulu said. "All these years and you are still doing lovey-dovey."

"What can I say, I am just a lucky man. I have been thinking; maybe my misfortune was also my blessing. For twelve years we tried to conceive, but no luck. Then after I become a poor man, we finally succeed."

"Maybe it was all that drinking you were doing in your rich days," Mama said.

She and Auntie Lulu threw their heads back in laughter.

"Efa, you know your husband. He used to drink that palm wine and beer too much."

Auntie Efa joined in the laughter.

"A beg, please, leave my man alone!" she finally said.

"You see? She also stands up for me. You people, I have changed my life o. Do I even have money to waste on beer? I tell you, being poor really helps you appreciate life."

"Sometimes it is not all about money," Auntie Efa said.

"Hmm, you people are crazy o. Me? I like money o," Auntie Lulu replied.

This time I joined them in their laughter.

"All is well. I am happy with what I have. My husband has been doing very well by us."

A while after we finished eating, we cleared the table. Uncle David excused himself to go to sleep. He had to wake up early the following morning for work.

Later that night, Aunties Efa and Lulu, Mama, and I stayed up talking in the living room. This new privilege of joining the women in these types of talks made me feel like a grownup.

"It wasn't just friends o, who turned on us, it was also family," Auntie Efa whispered. She often spoke with her hands, and I tried not to stare at the dark knuckles of her hands, which gave away her true complexion.

"Your auntie tried to convince my husband I was a witch and that it was me who was causing all this misfortune for him. 'What kind of woman cannot bear children?' they would say. Can you imagine? His mother even went as far as to try to find him a girl from the village. She thought if he married and impregnated the girl, she would save him from my 'charms' and that he would get his job back!

"But my husband was not having it! He told his mother that under no circumstances was he going to take another wife. But did that stop her? No-o, she brought the girl into my house. I sent that girl running back to wherever she came from."

"Nah wow o," Mama said, "that auntie of mine is too much!"

"Sistah, I am telling you. But when I was pregnant with Joshua, I told David not to tell her until I was far along and ready to give birth because I was afraid I would miscarry and add more fuel to her fire. Ma sistah, when she came to visit us after he was born, you should have seen how she was at my every beck and call: 'My daughter, what do you need? Tell me anything and I will do it,'" Auntie Efa imitated her mother-in-law.

"Why yes," Mama said jokingly, "you gave her a bouncing baby boy...with a good grip," Mama said, as she massaged her scalp.

We all laughed.

"These our African mammies are too much," Auntie Lulu added.

Hearing Auntie Efa's story solidified my decision to become an obstetrician-gynecologist, if it was not already. I knew I was destined to help women like her and Mama, who faced fertility issues, bring life into this world. I had lost my brother and Auntie Efa had struggled from years of barrenness. Something had to be done, and I felt I was just the one to do it. As I sat there with these women I loved, I was already brainstorming different charities I could start to help advance women's health practices in Cameroon.

After spending a few days in Yaoundé, I was ready to go home. I tried not to think about all the schoolwork that was piling up. I was relieved when Papa and Uncle Folemji made it to Yaoundé safely and on time. Auntie Lulu, Leo, and Nana had left for Germany the day before. I tried not to be offended that my two cousins avoided me at all costs until their departure.

I wished that I could have grown up with my cousins; however, we were children of the diaspora, living in different lands because the one from which we came could not provide us with the life we desired. I hoped that I could help change this. I promised myself that I would do all I could to help develop the country that I would forever call home.

CHAPTER TWENTY

O ur flight back was brutal. From Cameroon, we had a lay-over in the Ivory Coast. Our two-hour layover turned into a ten-hour layover, after which we had an eighteen-hour flight back to Hartford.

As soon as we stepped off the plane, I checked my phone. I had been able to charge it at the airport during our layover. Ife's message loaded first. It was from two weeks prior. She had wished me a safe flight and asked when I was coming back.

My missed calls also loaded. My heart jumped when I saw a missed call from Kunle. He had left a voicemail. I was too afraid to listen to it right at that moment. I had a sinking feeling that he had called to break up with me. I reprimanded myself for caring. He had not been kind to me right before I left for Cameroon. It still hurt me that instead of coming to see me, he had taken the easy way out with an awkward phone call. I had never had a boyfriend before, but that did not sound like boyfriend behavior.

I shoved my phone in my coat pocket when Papa's friend's car pulled up to the curb, where we stood with our luggage. We'd had to buy an extra suitcase because family and friends had requested that we bring them back certain Cameroon foodstuffs that were not easily available in America.

Before we left Auntie Efa's house, Mama stuffed packs of dried fish, dry eru leaves, bitter leaf, dried snails, and bottles of

Cameroon fried peanuts into a pub green suitcase. I refused when Mama asked me to stuff crayfish and more dried fish in my suitcase. Although Cameroonian food was yummy, dried foodstuff had an unpleasant smell. Papa begrudgingly agreed to sacrifice space in his suitcase.

As soon as we got home, I went upstairs to my room and washed the airport and plane stench off my body. Clean and tired, I lay in my bed, phone in my hand. I texted Ife and Michelle back, but my mind was on Kunle and the voicemail.

"Hi, Foma. You should be in Cameroon by now, and I am sure you will not listen to this message until you get back. But… umm…I was just calling to say that I am sorry for everything that happened between us. You are a great girl and I want you in my life, even though my behavior has not shown that. I was standoffish toward you because I was embarrassed and upset that you'd think I'd purposely push myself on you. I am not that kind of guy. I respect women and I would never do anything to purposely hurt you. We can talk more once you get back, but I just wanted to get this off my chest. Okay. Talk to you later."

His message melted my heart to slush. Just hearing his voice warmed me. I still liked him, and I was happy that he was not breaking up with me. I texted him, letting him know I was back in the States and suggesting we meet soon to talk about everything.

The following morning, I woke up early, unpacked my luggage, and did laundry. Hours later, I heard Mama cooking in the kitchen. The sweet smell of fried plantains and eggs made its way up to my room. I went downstairs to help her.

I set the table, and before anyone could call him, Papa came downstairs. My parents and I sat down to eat breakfast. It felt like old times, and I was grateful. Although Cameroon was where my life began, the United States was now my home. The trip to Cameroon had shown me how fortunate I was, and I now understood why my parents pushed me to be successful in a stable and prestigious field.

"Dear, your father and I have been meaning to talk to you. That's why we wanted you to come back with us yesterday evening."

"Okay."

"We know how much Nana Ola meant to you. You two had an amazing bond. Your mother and I were happy that you had someone outside of us who could guide you as you came into your own. Now, with her passing, we want to let you know that you can talk to us about anything and we will listen. From now on, we want you to tell us when you feel we are being unreasonable...with respect, of course. I promise you we will listen and support you."

I looked at him in surprise.

"Are you two saying that from now on, you will no longer push me to do what you think is best for my life, but instead actually listen to what I have to say?"

"Yes, my dear, your parents are here for you. You are a woman now. Please come to us about anything without worry we will judge you or be angry with you. We are both in your corner. We trust you and we know we raised you right."

"I am happy to hear that, Mama, Papa. I understand that in Cameroon, things were tough and that having a prestigious degree, whether as a doctor, lawyer, or engineer, was the best chance for a good life. However, I assure you, Mama and Papa, that in America things are different. You saw how Michelle won $10,000 from entering a writing competition. We have so many avenues for success here. Singers, basketball players, actors, and even writers make millions of dollars."

I could see the concerned looks in their eyes.

"I am not saying I want to do those things. I am just saying that we are in a different country, and that I don't have to pigeonhole myself into one thing to be successful. Nonetheless, our journey to Cameroon has confirmed that the one thing I want the most is to become a doctor."

My parents beamed. I regretted not tricking them and saying that I wanted to drop out of school to become a full-time writer, just to see if they would be supportive, as they claimed.

"Foma, God blessed us with the honor of being your parents. Our one and only," Mama said.

"Mama, I did not mean to hurt you when I said it was not my fault I was an only child."

"Say no more, Foma, I know that."

I hugged my mother, and my father joined in.

When I got to campus, everything seemed to be just how I left it. Yet being back felt odd. I had changed in the past two weeks. I had developed a deeper understanding of myself and of what I wanted to accomplish in the next four years.

Our room was empty when I arrived late Sunday afternoon. I placed my things down and texted Ife to let her know I was in my room.

Minutes later, Ife texted asking me to let her into our building. I took my fob, walked to the hall that connected our two buildings, and let her in.

"Foma, I am so happy you are back!" Ife said as she hugged me.

"I'm glad to be back. How have you been?"

"No, the question is, how are you doing? You look refreshed!"

"Thank you. I am in a much better place than when I left here, that's for sure."

"You look it. I can't wait to hear all about Cameroon!"

Ife followed me to my room, where I continued to unpack while she sat on my bed.

"Have you spoken to Kunle?"

"Yeah, I let him know I was back. Why?"

"Nothing, just asking."

The uncertainty in her voice reminded me that I had a few questions of my own. "I have a random question to ask you."

"Okay, shoot."

"Do you know of any girls Kunle has dated in the past?"

"Umm, yeah, a few. Why do you ask?"

"Do you know if any of his relationships have ended in a bad way?"

"When you say bad way, what do you mean?"

"Nothing in particular. Just whatever comes to mind."

"Well, he and my brother are best friends, and my brother has never said anything bad to me about Kunle and past girlfriends. Why?"

"It's just that the last time he and I hung out, things kind of got a little crazy."

Ife pursed her lips. "What do you mean by crazy?"

"He kind of got carried away and I thought he was being a little forceful."

"Oh, no!"

"It could be all in my head, though, considering the whole Paige situation."

Right after I said Paige's name, I saw another look come over Ife's face.

"What is it?" I asked.

"Oh, Foma! So much has happened since you've been gone. But first, in terms of Kunle being forceful, what exactly happened?"

"We were making out when he pinned me down and held my wrists above my head while he was on me, kissing me and feeling me up. I told him to stop. I'm not sure if he heard, but he kept going until I pushed him off."

"Oh, no. That's not okay."

"He said he didn't hear me say stop the first time. Things have been tense between us since then. We are going to talk about it soon, though. After it happened, we didn't really talk until he called me about Nana Ola's passing."

"He didn't come see you?"

"Nope, and I am supposed to be his girlfriend. I don't know what's going on with us, Ife, but I will find out when we meet this week."

"I've never heard of Kunle being pushy with a girl or anything like that. I hope it was just a misunderstanding. I will ask around."

"Please o. Don't go telling people about our business."

"Of course not. I will ask my brother some general questions about Kunle and his dating history."

"On second thought, don't ask. I don't want to bring too much attention to this whole thing."

"Okay."

"I noticed your facial expression when I mentioned Paige. What's up with that?"

"You haven't heard?"

"No. Heard what?"

"So much has happened since you've been away."

"Spit it out!"

"Paige tried to commit suicide, but last I heard, she is doing better now and is in the hospital."

"What? Who told you?"

"The word just sort of spread around campus."

"That's crazy! I had no idea. I texted her when I got back, but I haven't heard back from her yet. That must be why. Oh, my gosh. I'm going to call her again."

"Yeah. It all happened after Ray was arrested again. The following day, word spread that a group of people went to her parents' house and spray painted the message, 'Lying black slut' on her gate and tied a noose there too."

I felt a chill run down my back. "This whole thing is ridiculous. If I doubted that racism existed, this just confirmed it."

"Is it because of racism or because some fools who are fans of Ray Palmer are upset that Paige got him arrested?"

I looked at Ife in disbelief, hoping she was joking. "The fact that they hung up a noose and called her not just a slut, but a black slut, makes it clear to me that it is about race. Did you not take history class?"

"I'm just saying, I think they did all that because Ray Palmer is a football player."

"Yes, but the two don't have to be mutually exclusive."

"Anyways. I'm just glad that the suicide attempt failed."

"Do you know how she did it?"

"No idea. I heard someone at her house found her and called the police, and they rushed her to the hospital."

"When did this happen?"

"About a week ago."

"Oh, my goodness. This is just not right at all!"

"Welcome back," Ife responded.

After Ife left, I called Paige. Someone with a raspy voice picked up the phone.

"Hello, can I please speak to Paige?"

"Foma?" the voice asked.

"Yes."

"Paige can't come to the phone right now. She's sleeping."

"Okay, I just wanted to see how she's doing."

"I'll tell her you called. Foma, I would like to thank you for being there for Paige. So many people have deserted her, but you have continued to be a loyal friend. Maybe you can come visit her sometime. I think your presence will really help brighten up her day."

"Absolutely, ma'am. Paige has been a great mentor and friend to me. I just want to make sure she is okay."

"Thank you, honey. Her father and I appreciate everything that you've done."

CHAPTER TWENTY-ONE

When I walked out to Kunle's car the following Monday evening, my stomach was in knots.

He got out on the driver's side and came to open my door. He extended his hands, and I felt an instant gravitational pull into his arms. He smelled good, and he looked debonair in his gray peacoat. When I looked up at him, he captivated me with his pearly white smile. He was so handsome.

"Again, I'm so sorry about your loss."

"Thank you."

"How was Cameroon?"

"It was great!"

"Is that right? I can't wait to hear all about it."

In the car, I told Kunle all about my experiences, and he listened intently. I told him about Mr. Njinkeng, Uncle Folemji's friend, who had recounted to me stories of his family members who had traveled to China and countries in Europe for better opportunities. According to him, they had all been dealt brutal blows of racism. "No matter where we go, people will not respect us until we can fix our own home. Can you blame them? No one respects beggars," he had said.

Kunle nodded his head in response. "It's true, the world doesn't respect black people because of the state of our African countries."

"That's so sad. What can we do about that?"

"I don't know," Kunle replied, which caught me off guard. I was certain he would have a more concrete answer.

"I'm figuring it out," I responded.

"Foma, trust me, I study African politics. There's so much corruption in African countries that I don't know where to even begin."

"Helping develop African countries is not limited to making political change."

Kunle had no reply to this.

He drove us to the restaurant where we had our first date.

I was happy the server seated us toward the back in an isolated corner. The room was dimly lit. It set the right mood for an intimate conversation.

Kunle ordered surf and turf, and he raised his eyebrows when I only ordered soup. And when the server left, I was silent, as was he. I had a habit of overtalking in tense situations, which is what I had done in the car. This time I left the talking to him. We needed to address the elephant in the room.

"So, I'm sure you heard my voicemail," he began.

"Yes, I did."

"I just want to apologize to you for the way I handled that situation. I could've reached out to you that weekend to talk things through, but to be honest with you, I was upset with you because I felt you were accusing me of something I did not do."

"Kunle, I wasn't trying to accuse you of anything. I just felt you were being too forceful."

"Let me finish, Foma. What I'm trying to say is that I let my ego get in the way, and I should've taken time out to understand things from your perspective. I'm older than you are and more experienced. I should've thought about that. I want to assure you I didn't intend to do anything to hurt you. I would never hurt you. I care about you a lot."

"I appreciate you seeing things from my perspective and apologizing. That is big of you."

"Yeah, like I said, I was wrong for not reaching out to you soon after it happened. I needed time to think about whether we were a match."

My heart sank. "A match?"

"Yes, like maybe we're on different levels of maturity."

I frowned. "I don't think I'm following, Kunle. Are you saying I'm immature?"

"No, no, no! I suppose the right word is…less experienced, you know, with intimacy."

"Okay, I guess that is true."

"I'm guessing you're a virgin, right?"

My face got hot. "Yes."

"And that's great. It's very admirable. Like I was saying, we're on different levels when it comes to intimacy."

"Can you handle that?"

"What do you mean?"

"Are you going to be able to handle being with a girl who is a virgin?"

"Foma, I like you for you. I couldn't care less whether you're a virgin."

"Okay, Kunle," I clarified, "because if we were to continue being a couple, I have to know that you won't feel slighted if I'm not ready to have sex anytime soon."

"Foma, like I said, I want to have you in my life, and I don't mind if we start by taking things slow."

"All right. I'm glad we're still together."

"Me too."

That evening when he dropped me off at my dorm, he got out of the car and helped me out. I stood there, with my back to his vehicle, and him standing in front of me. He stared down at me passionately. I stared back up at him, pretending I wasn't nervous.

"You're beautiful, Foma. That Cameroon sun has done wonders to your skin."

I blushed. I didn't know what to say. He touched my chin softly. I got goosebumps. He pulled my chin up, and I obliged. Then, in what felt like slow motion, he planted a soft kiss on my lips. I wanted more, but he pulled away quickly.

"That's enough for today," he said with a grin.

I swallowed hard.

"We're taking things slow, remember?" he teased.

"I suppose so."

"Have a good night, girlfriend."

"And you have a good night, boyfriend."

As I walked back to my dorm, I could feel his eyes on my backside, and I was happy I had worn my sexy leather jacket, even though it was cold outside. I did it for fashion, as Ife would say. I also did it so Kunle could see what he would be missing if he broke up with me.

When I got up on Tuesday morning, I was tired. After my date with Kunle, I showered and studied in the lobby until just after 2 a.m. I was desperately trying to catch up on all the readings and assignments I had missed. Even with Ife's well-organized notes, I had still fallen far behind.

My trip to Cameroon lit a fuse in me, and I was willing to do all it took to make sure I met my goal GPA that semester. I was not getting my education just for myself, but rather for the countless others in Cameroon who could benefit from the skills I learned. I wanted to prove true what Nana Ola said in her letter about me being a light to many.

I didn't tell Kunle, but at the airport, I had started researching how to start a non-profit in Cameroon, Our Women Create Our Future, that focused on women's health. I told Papa about it, and he was over the moon that I had thought of the idea. He was already brainstorming how he could use his doctor connections to help while I continued school. I think he was especially happy because this decision confirmed to him that becoming a doctor was still my main goal; I had no plans for an illustrious writing career—at least not just yet.

I was in biology make-up lab when I saw Paige's number flash over my phone. I slipped out of class to answer the call.

"Hi, Foma, this is Paige's mom," the raspy voice said.

"Hi, Mrs. Mitchell. How are you?"

"I'm doing just fine. How are you?"

"I'm doing well."

"I'm calling you because we would like you to come see Paige at the hospital, to help lift her spirits. Is that something you can do today? I know you're a student and I would hate to intrude on your education, but Paige has been down lately and I think seeing you will cheer her up."

"Yes, ma'am, I can do that. I don't drive, so I'd have to talk to my boyfriend to see if he can give me a ride. Is there an address?"

"Yes. I can text you the address."

"Okay, I will see if I can get a ride."

"Thank you, honey. I will let the nurses know that they can direct you to our room. I'll also send you the room number. I hope you can come."

"Okay, sounds good, Mrs. Mitchell."

"We'll be here all day and night, so you just let me know."

"Yes, Mrs. Mitchell, I'll text you."

I texted Kunle right away, asking him if he would be able to give me a ride to the hospital. He agreed.

On the way, Kunle mentioned that he, Larissa and other members of the BSA were planning a protest to ask the school to restrict Ray Palmer's movements on campus.

Recently, he had been spotted at the Sterling food court again, getting food with members of the football team. Kunle said Larissa was outraged.

I didn't know what to make of Larissa since the cold introduction she gave me at the Bridging the Gap event.

I was still in my thoughts when I heard Kunle ask, "So, that's a yes?"

"What are you talking about?"

"I said we're meeting tomorrow to make plans for the protest."

"Oh, yeah, what time?"

"I think six or so, but I'll let you know."

"Okay, that's fine."

At the hospital, Kunle spoke with the receptionist. After he explained why we had come, she told us to have a seat.

As we sat by each other, Kunle squeezed my knee.

"Thank you for agreeing to give me this ride."

"Not a problem. I'm just glad she has a great friend like you in her corner."

I smiled at him. "Thanks," I said. As we gazed at each other, he winked at me.

Finally, the lady signaled Kunle to the front desk. I followed. She asked for our names and the patient's name, and when Kunle told her, she inputted something into the computer and gave us wrist bracelets. She told us the room number and instructed us how to get to the room.

We walked hand in hand, and his warm hands helped calm my nerves. When we got into the elevator and pressed the button for the sixth floor, he brought me in close and our lips met. As I laid my head on his chest, I listened to the rhythm of his heartbeat. I was disappointed when we arrived on our floor.

With my hand still in his, we walked down the hall in search of Room 6425. We read the nameplates on the doors as we walked by. Compared to the first floor, the sixth was empty, with just a few staff members at the front desk and what appeared to be family members in the lobby near the elevator.

"I'm nervous to see her," I said.

"Don't be."

P. Mitchell, the nameplate read. I knocked on the door, and Kunle stepped behind me.

"Just a minute," a woman inside the room said. I recognized the raspy voice.

The door opened to reveal a tall, beautiful middle-aged woman. Her wild, luscious curly hair framed her face, and the gray hairs around her temple were distributed in a way that seemed intentional. She was extremely light, just like Paige. She wore a black t-shirt, jeans, and tennis shoes. She looked too elegant to be wearing such casual clothing.

"Hello. You must be Foma."

"Mrs. Mitchell?"

"Yes, ma'am," she said as she reached for my hand.

"This is my boyfriend, Kunle. Like I told you, he just came to drop me off. He can wait in the lobby."

"Okay, I think that's best for now."

"Nice to meet you, ma'am," Kunle said as he reached from where he stood behind me and took Mrs. Mitchell's hand.

"My pleasure," Mrs. Mitchell said.

Kunle rubbed my back. "I'll be right in the lobby."

"Okay."

He had brought textbooks with him so he could occupy himself.

After Kunle left, Mrs. Mitchell stood to the side to let me in. Until then she had been guarding the door, which was just slightly ajar.

When I entered the room, I stopped and waited for Mrs. Mitchell to walk ahead of me. She walked past a little area which held a sofa and television, and then we entered the part of the room where Paige was lying in bed. Her once vibrant complexion now looked pale, and red circles had formed around her eyes. Her unruly curly hair sat on top of her head in a messy bun. Seeing it made me instinctively reach for mine, smoothing it out. I felt awkward. I didn't know what to do. Paige attempted a half smile.

"Hi, Paige," I said as pleasantly as I could.

"Hi, Foma. It's good to see you."

"How are you feeling?" I asked as I approached her. Mrs. Mitchell went over to the sofa.

"I'm feeling all right." Paige motioned to the chair beside the bed. "I am so sorry about your grandmother," she said once I was seated.

"She's in a better place now," I said without thinking. I pressed my lips together because I realized that this "better place" was what Paige had been seeking when she tried to take her own life.

Paige said nothing, and I sat there uneasily with many questions popping up in my head. I knew better than to ask any of them, especially not with her mother just a few feet away. Although she looked occupied on her laptop, I knew Mrs. Mitchell was paying attention to everything we were saying.

When Paige asked me how my classes were going, I told her that things were rough for me at that moment because I was catching up on the two weeks of class that I missed because of my trip to Cameroon.

"Have you been able to complete any schoolwork remotely?" I asked.

Paige looked over at her mother. "Mom, can you excuse Foma and me?"

Mrs. Mitchell looked displeased, but she got up to leave. "I'll be out doing work in the lobby."

When we heard the door click shut, Paige turned to me and said. "Foma, since you've been away, things have gotten bad for me. Did you hear what happened at our house? I cannot go back to that school. My parents were talking about me going back to school, and I couldn't take it."

"Yes, Paige, I heard about the spray painting and the, umm... noose."

"They're just terrible. There's no way I can show my face on that campus. That incident, me losing most of my friends, the threatening messages I have been getting on social media and to my phone, it is all too much. Now my mother is keeping track of my phone, and I don't go on the internet anymore.

"Everyone has turned on me, including Jamie. I thought he liked me, that we were moving toward something special."

"Did something else happen with him?"

"Jamie was a part of the group that went to our house and wrote that message on our gate and hung that noose."

My mouth gaped open. "How do you know?"

"I recognized him even with the mask. I know his walk. Our outside security camera caught everything."

"Paige, I am so sorry about that."

"I really thought he liked me."

"Maybe they pressured him."

"If he really liked me, he would not have given in to the pressure."

I nodded in agreement.

"It's terrible. When I took those pills, all I could think of was the peace I would feel in the afterlife. This is a cruel world we're living in, Foma. It is so unfair that bad things happen to good people, and that bad people can do pretty much anything they want without consequences."

"Paige, I see where you're coming from. My trip to Cameroon has really shown me how unfair this life is. However, I want you to know that there are people in this world who love you. Your parents love you and I love you. I wouldn't know what to do if you were gone. You have shown me that there is good in this world just by the way you mentored me. It has really meant a lot to me."

"Thank you for saying that, Foma, and I love you too. It's just that when you're in a really dark place, it is hard to have a well-rounded view of everything. Foma, I don't think you understand what it feels like to lose hope. To feel like things in your life will never get better. I hope you never feel the way I felt that night when I drank that entire bottle of pills."

I swallowed hard because I didn't know what to say. She was right. I had never even considered that taking my life was a solution to any of my problems.

"You know, I am still very upset with my mom for finding me so soon. Foma, you could never understand the disappointment I felt when I opened my eyes on that hospital bed and saw that I was still in this world. I love my family and I love you, but when I lay on my bed in my room that night, all I could think of was the peace I would soon feel."

"How are you feeling about the whole thing now?" I asked.

"I'm on suicide watch, am I not? My mother won't let me out of her sight. She doesn't even use the bathroom until I am sleeping. The nurses pop in every thirty minutes to see how we're doing. They're careful when they give me my meds, and they don't leave any sharp objects around me. I couldn't do anything if I tried."

"Paige, these rough times will pass. Please don't make another attempt. Your life is so valuable. When you become a doctor, you can help other women who have gone through what you have. You can be the good that you'd like to see in the world. Please don't let Ray Palmer and all those other people win."

She sank a little deeper into her pillows. "Foma, I don't have the same fight you have."

"Paige, for you to have accomplished everything you have, you must have plenty of fight in you. I look up to you. Please don't make another attempt at your life. All of this will soon be over, and your life will get back on track, I assure you of that."

Paige looked at me skeptically.

"Can you promise me you won't try again?"

She looked at me blankly, and after what felt like a long time, she responded with a simple "Sorry, I can't."

When we left the hospital that night, I had an uneasy feeling that the Paige I knew was gone forever.

CHAPTER TWENTY-TWO

A small group of us met at the Sterling cafeteria the following day to discuss the next steps in advocating on Paige's behalf. After my conversation with her the day before, I wanted us to make our campus safe for her once again.

Larissa was sitting with Chuck, the treasurer of BSA, when we arrived. When we got within view of them, Kunle abruptly let go of my hand. Was it my imagination, or was Larissa scowling at Kunle and me as we approached the booth?

"Hello," I said.

"Hey," Chuck replied.

Larissa nodded her head in acknowledgment but said nothing.

As Kunle and I took our seats, Chris, Jessica's man, showed up. I looked to see if Jessica was trailing behind him, but she wasn't.

When I thought of it, I hadn't seen her since I got back from Cameroon. I noticed she was no longer hanging out with Kara's group of friends.

"We're just waiting for Reggie and then we can get started. He should be here in a few. He said he is around the corner," Larissa said.

"Foma, I was sorry to hear about your grandmother," Chuck said.

Larissa turned to look at me, but she said nothing.

"Thanks, Chuck. Kunle told you about it?"

"Well, not really. I was with him when Ife told him."

"Oh."

"Yeah, how was the motherland?"

"It was nice to be back in Cameroon. I saw family that I haven't seen in years, and I got to do a lot of thinking."

"That's great. I would love to go someday."

"Yeah, you should. You'd love it. There is no place like home."

Reggie announced his presence. "What's up, y'all?" On the few occasions I had been around him, he was a breath of fresh air. He was easygoing and hilarious.

"Okay, since we're all here, let's get started," Larissa began. "I say we write a letter to the university's president calling for him to restrict Ray Palmer's movements around campus until they fully investigate the situation. It is bad enough that the police keep releasing him. The school shouldn't allow him on campus. That includes football practice or playing in games. We can't allow them to place sports above students at this school." Her gaze darkened. "It's not fair that Paige is lying in some hospital bed somewhere while Ray gets to move around anyhow he pleases."

Kunle and I made eye contact when Larissa mentioned the hospital. I was happy he was keeping to the promise he made to me not to tell anyone of my involvement with Paige.

"My problem with the petition is that people might not want their names associated with it because Ray Palmer is our star football player," Chuck said.

"I see where you're coming from, but I think women on campus would be inclined to sign it because a lot of us don't care about sports. The black students would definitely be willing to sign it because of that noose. This case is not just about rape anymore."

"Hmm, okay."

"I'm down with that, and I'm also down for us protesting the school too, even the police station. No justice, no peace," Reggie said.

"That works for me. Get the letter to President Taylor with the signed petitions attached and then have a word-by-mouth protest march so he knows we're serious."

"Sounds like a plan," Chuck said.

"What do you think, Foma?" Larissa asked.

Her question caught me off guard. I didn't have an opinion. I was just absorbing what everyone had to say.

"I think drafting a letter to the president and protesting are great ideas. I for one will help with getting signatures for the petition," I said.

Larissa, without response, turned away from me and began discussing logistics with Chuck. Kunle squeezed my knee, and when I looked up at him, he smiled.

Suddenly, Larissa's attention veered onto us, and a scowl returned to her face. Right then I had the sinking suspicion that Kunle and Larissa had a story. I knew that some people were, by nature, standoffish and that they took time to warm up to others, but I felt like she was being plain old rude to me.

"Ma'am, if that's it, I gotta run. Me and my girl have dinner plans," Chris said. Then he looked at me. "Aren't you and my girl suite mates?"

"Yes, that's right," I responded.

Larissa again frowned at me. I didn't know what her problem was, but I was determined to find out.

"Yeah, I remembered you from that poetry jam."

"Yup, we were there," I said, looking up at Kunle, glad to see I had Larissa's attention. *He's my man,* I thought.

"Cool, cool. Well, see y'all later."

"Bye, Chris," we all said in unison.

"Ready to go?" I asked Kunle.

"We've got some things to discuss for BSA. So, can you stay behind, Kunle," Larissa said suddenly.

I ignored her. "I'll just wait over there while y'all have your discussion." I got up from the booth and walked to a table nearby, where I sat and pulled out my textbook.

Fifteen minutes later, Kunle came over and said he was ready to go. He volunteered to give me a ride to my dorm. As we left the building, I didn't as much as glance Larissa's way.

In silence, Kunle and I walked to the lot where he usually parked his car. Once we got in, and before he could start the car, I asked him outright, "What is going on between you and Larissa?"

"Umm…wh-what? What are you talking about?"

"I think my question is pretty clear. What is going on between you and Larissa?"

"It isn't. What exactly are you referring to?"

"I get funny vibes when I'm around her, and I think it has to do with you."

"Foma, Larissa is not the warmest person when you're first getting to know her. I've told you that."

"Kunle, just answer the question. Do the two of you have a past?"

Kunle looked me in the eye and said, "No, absolutely not. We're just friends."

That was all I needed to hear. I dropped the interrogation. "Well, you should know that she has a major crush on you."

"What're you talking about? We're just friends."

"She looks at you as more than a friend. That's too bad for her," I said lightly. "You're mine."

Kunle raised an eyebrow and chuckled.

The next day, I collected signatures for our petition to restrict Ray Palmer's movements around campus until a full investigation was complete and a determination made on his guilt.

Michelle agreed to collect signatures with me, but Ife refused to help.

"I don't want to be involved because I don't know all the facts."

"You don't have to do anything. Just come with me for moral support," I said.

"I would love to help you, Foma, but I just don't feel comfortable doing that."

"Fine," I barked as I stormed off to Sterling alone to begin collecting signatures.

As I approached Sterling, I saw students standing outside the building, talking. They were black, so I figured they would be an easy sell. I removed my schoolbag from my back and brought it down to my feet to search it for the clipboard that held the petition document. I retrieved a pen from my schoolbag side pocket.

"Hi, how are y'all doing today?" I asked.

There were four of them, two girls and two guys. "Hey," one of the guys said, looking at me expectantly. The other three looked in my direction but continued talking.

I was nervous; they didn't seem interested. "I don't mean to bother y'all, but did you hear about what happened to Paige Mitchell? Ray Palmer, the school's star quarterback, raped her and the school is not doing anything about it. This petition is to force the school to stop Ray from moving freely on campus until this whole situation is figured out."

I now had their full attention.

"Oh, I'm definitely signing that," one of the girls said as she reached for the clipboard. I gave her the clipboard and pen.

"I heard about that girl. But from what I know, she didn't even like black people. That's what she gets for trying to be white. Wasn't she dating that white dude freshman year?" the shorter of the two guys asked his friend.

"Don't say that, stupid," the girl next to him scolded as she tapped his arm. "You black guys date white girls all the time and we don't hold that against y'all. But let a sista do it, and it's a problem."

Something awakened inside me, and I did not know where my next words came from. "She has no problem with black people, she just clicked better with her white friends. And she signed up to mentor a black student this school year. Anyways, even if she didn't like black people, we can't stand by and do nothing when a black woman is raped. What if it were your sister?" I asked him.

"Yeah, that's right," said the same girl who tapped him. I assumed she was his girlfriend.

"I'm just saying. She is fine as hell but showed the brothas no love." The girl tapped him again. "What? It's the truth."

"Man, you're tripping," the taller guy said as he reached for the clipboard. "So, what exactly is this supposed to do?"

"It's supposed to show the school that we, the student body, will not stand for them allowing Ray Palmer to roam around campus like he did nothing wrong."

"But how do we know that he did something wrong? Yeah, she said he raped her, but what if it's not true? We just deprive the man of his education? Don't get me wrong, I support your cause, but just because a girl cries rape doesn't mean she was actually raped."

"Come on, Tim! Why would she make up a story against the star football player, of all people?" the other girl asked as she waited for her turn to sign.

"I'm just saying, stranger things have happened."

"The point of the petition is to keep him from casually moving around campus until this matter is fully investigated. He can still attend classes," I said. "I assure you, she didn't make the story up."

My certainty caught their attention, but I was not going to say anything more.

Inside Sterling, I continued to collect signatures. I had just collected my twenty-sixth when Michelle entered the building. We hadn't seen each other since I got back from Cameroon. We had only texted and briefly chatted on the phone.

"Foma! I've missed you so much," Michelle said when we hugged.

"Aww, I've missed you too."

"How was Cameroon?"

"It was great. I will tell you all about it when we sit down."

We headed to the food court. I was happy that it was just the two of us. Although we made up when Michelle came to see me after Nana Ola's passing, we both agreed that there was much left to discuss.

After getting our food, we found a place to sit at one of the small orange circular tables distributed at the back of Sterling.

"So, tell me all about your time in Cameroon."

"Oh boy, there is so much to tell."

I told her all about Nana Ola's funeral celebration, and she was captivated.

"Wow, y'all have interesting traditions."

"I'm beginning to appreciate it all myself," I told her.

"You should. It's good to know where you come from."

A bout of silence that became too long fell over us. I speared some lettuce and tomatoes and tried to carry along a piece of crouton. Michelle took a bite of her pepperoni pizza. It smelled heavenly, and I regretted my choice of salad.

"So, about that writing contest...I know it didn't go so well last time when we tried to speak about it. So, I thought that maybe we could try again," I began.

"Foma, I want to apologize for not being more open with you about applying for SAWP. It sounded like a good opportunity, but I was almost sure that I wouldn't get accepted, so I saw no harm in not telling you. Also, I thought if we were both accepted, it'd be cool for us to spend the summer together."

"Michelle, I am also sorry. I shouldn't have assumed bad intentions when I found out you applied without telling me."

"Let me finish, Foma. The thing is, you were right—before I started the program, I didn't have a passion for writing. I guess another reason I applied for SAWP was because I wanted to prove to myself that I was just as smart as you. I was always the smart one until I met you. I'm really sorry that I hurt you."

"Thanks for being honest with me, Michelle. I've always

looked up to you, though, because you've always been the popular one. Being smart was the only thing I had going for myself, so it really hurt to think you were taking that away from me. I should've said something months ago, when I found out they accepted you."

"Foma, what are you talking about? You were popular too."

"No, Michelle, I followed in your shadow. You remember middle school. People judged me because of either my African-ness or my dark skin. I had friends because I was around you."

"Aww, Foma, we were just dumb kids."

"I've missed you," I told her.

We hugged it out.

When we sat back down, Michelle said, "So, tell me about you and Kunle."

I told her about everything. How he asked me to be his girl-friend, that crazy night of misunderstandings we had, and then the Larissa situation.

I felt reassured that I made the right decision in staying with Kunle when she agreed that our night of intimacy gone wrong was likely just a misunderstanding. After I told her about Larissa, however, Michelle was resolute that something was going on there.

"I know Larissa is standoffish and all, but I don't see her being rude just for the sake of it," Michelle said.

"That's what I thought. I think she has a crush on him."

"I wouldn't blame her. He's fine."

"He's my man now, so you can't say that," I teased.

Michelle responded with a wave of a hand.

Right after my lunch date with Michelle, I went back to my dorm to take a quick nap. Upon awaking an hour later, I checked my phone and saw a text message from Ife. She wanted to know if I would have dinner with her and Neema. I agreed, though I was still annoyed with her for not coming with me to collect signatures.

"How did your thing go?" she asked as the three of us ate.

I didn't like the condescending way she said "thing," like what I was doing was inconsequential.

"The petition signing went well. I was able to collect forty signatures. When a black woman is hurt, I can't just stand by and watch it happen."

Ife frowned. She heard the accusation in my tone, and I was glad that my message had come across.

"It's not always a black thing," she said. "Yeah, she's black, but I don't like how we always find a way to make everything about race. If Ray Palmer did rape her, you can't just say that he raped her because she's black and he's white. Also, I wasn't there, and I don't know the facts. That is why we have the police to investigate these situations, and they released him, so—"

"I'm not saying that he raped her because she's black. However, the fact remains that she is a black woman, and when a black woman is hurt, all black people should stand up and support her just like white people do when white women are hurt. Do you know that I contacted the feminist group on campus and those white women refused to sign our petitions or help us collect them?"

"Probably because they don't want to get involved without having all the facts. Would you feel the same way if she had accused a black man of raping her?"

"Yes, of course."

Ife gave me an incredulous look. "I don't know if I believe that."

"Believe whatever you want. That noose and threatening message being left by her gate tell me that race is involved. Also, I'm pretty sure that had it been a black student who raped her, the school would've held him accountable instead of allowing him to just walk around campus freely."

"Wouldn't you say that if anything, Ray's hasn't been punished because he's the school's star football player?"

"The fact that he is a white guy from a rich family also helps."

"Whatever you say," Ife began. "What happens if we find out that she made up the whole thing? That's my point. I don't like standing behind things unless I know all the facts. And figuring out the facts is not my job. I'll let the police and the school do their job."

"But that's exactly the point. Ray Palmer has been walking around campus a free man like nothing happened."

"Maybe it's because the police investigated the issue and decided that he didn't rape her."

"Or maybe they let him go because he's a white male and a star football player."

"Foma, don't turn into one of those people," she said.

"What're you talking about? One of which people?"

"It's Kunle. He is contaminating your mind with this black/white thing," she said, clashing her fists together.

"Or maybe he is helping me see things for how they are."

Ife rolled her eyes, which further irritated me. She claimed to be this independent thinker, a free spirit who was pursuing her music career while surreptitiously getting her parents to pay for it as part of her "school expenses." Yet, here she was, criticizing me for being an independent thinker as well.

"You're a hypocrite," I said.

"Okay, ladies, let's just drop this conversation," Neema interjected.

Ife was now riled up. "Okay, Foma, don't go insulting me. But just out of curiosity, how am I a hypocrite?"

"You talk about how you're able to think outside the box and not willing to follow the traditional model of success that our parents laid out for us, but here you are criticizing me when I dare to do the same in Paige's situation."

"It's not the same thing," she said.

"Yeah, I guess not. I think outside the box to help others, while you think outside the box to help yourself."

Ife gasped. I got up and left her sitting there, her jaw on the floor.

I was still upset when I walked into my dorm room. That conversation with Ife had caused me to feel down. I started thinking about Paige. Poor Paige, who had attempted to take her own life because people like Ife refused to believe her.

⌒

I thought about how not so long ago, I was just as ignorant as Ife. I had purposely turned a blind eye to issues involving race because I thought that racism was an African American problem, not mine. After just a few months of college, I was beginning to understand that although I had not faced the same atrocities African Americans faced in the past, I was a black person and at the end of the day, when people looked at me, black was what they saw first, not African.

This train of thought brought back the memory of an incident that happened seven years before. At the time, we had only been in America for a year. Nonetheless, I knew that the downtown Hartford area was a bad area because many African Americans lived there, often in poverty. On the day in question, we were going to the African market to buy food. The market was in the heart of downtown.

"How can people be living like this in America?" Papa asked as we drove by graffiti-laced brick buildings and homes that had plywood nailed to their windows. The homes looked abandoned; yet, we saw black boys congregating on the stoops of some of them. Older black men sat on lawn chairs at the front of a nearby liquor store, playing dominos.

"Why is it that the black people in America live under such conditions? In a country like this with so much opportunity? It is all laziness, I am telling you. Back home we don't have a choice, but here it is pure laziness."

Mama did not say anything. I looked around, uneasy about my surroundings.

Inside the African store, I trailed behind Mama and Papa as

they piled bags of aged hen and other foods native to West Africa into the shopping cart Papa pushed. In our household, we preferred the tough and flavor-absorbing skin of aged hen over the soft skin of the regular chicken sold at the grocery stores.

"Where are you people from?" the Nigerian man at the cash register asked us when he got to us at the checkout line.

"Cameroon," Papa replied. "I'm Gideon, and this is my wife, Rebecca, and my daughter, Foma."

"Oh, my neighbors," the man replied. "My name is Mosby. When did you people come?"

"About a year ago. Is this your store?" Papa asked him.

"Yes. I have had this store for ten years now," Mosby replied. "We will be opening a new store soon. When we first opened, things were not so bad here, but all the white people in the area have left, and every day the value of my property goes down because there are too many African Americans here."

"As we were driving, we noticed that the area is very poor—" Before Papa could finish his statement, we heard chaos outside.

"You not going until you pay my money. I call police," we heard a man yell.

We looked out the window to see him grab a petite black woman by the back of her shirt. Mr. Mosby, who was still checking us out, turned to look out the window.

"That is my friend," he said, as he hurried out of the store.

We followed behind him.

"Get the fuck off me, motherfucker. I found hair in my food. I ain't paying for shit. Now get the fuck off me," the lady yelled, as she tried unsuccessfully to push the short Asian man.

"You eat, you pay," the man responded as he continued holding onto her shirt. He had a good grip, and as much as she tried, she could not get loose.

"You Jackie Chan motherfucker, I said get off me," she continued, still trying to push him.

A younger man came out of the restaurant. I assumed he was the man's son.

"We call police already. You must pay. Ain't no hair in this food. You owe me," the man continued.

"Mr. Huang, what is happening?" Mr. Mosby asked.

"She eat and she no pay, I call police," Mr. Huang replied.

Now the lady began to swing, and suddenly the son threw her down. She was sprawled on her stomach on the pavement, with her hands clasped behind her back, as he held her wrists together. His chubby body enveloped her skinny torso as he squatted over her.

"Why are they holding her down like that?" Mama asked in anger. She tried to intervene, but Papa pulled her back.

"Rebecca. This is not your fight," he said.

"Get off me, you motherfucker. I need to get my babies," the lady was screaming as the young man continued to sit on her.

On the corner I saw a stroller and a black girl about five years old. She watched, eyes wide open, tears falling down her cheeks.

We heard police sirens, and two police vehicles approached with two officers in each vehicle. I breathed a sigh of relief. The younger man released the lady, who now got up quickly and swung on him, missing his face by a fraction of an inch. Within seconds, an officer grabbed her and face palmed her to the ground. Blood gushed from her head. Her daughter wailed as she tried to run to her mother's defense. The other officer pulled her back as she screamed. The officer cuffed the lady and dragged her to the police vehicle. Mama's grip tightened around my hand.

"Y'all have no right!" the lady yelled as the blood continued to flow down the side of her face. I winced as I reached for my own forehead and felt the slight scar from my fall a few years prior. "They come into our neighborhood and sell us their shit and expect me to pay for that? I've been coming here for five years and I make one complaint, and you treat me like I'm some common criminal? You Bruce Lee motherfucker. I need to tend to my kids."

"Ma'am, be quiet. You're resisting arrest," the officer yelled.

"Fuck you! Fuck the police, and fuck you, China man," she continued yelling. The blood now reached her white shirt. "We need to stop eating here. Don't eat at China King no mo', they are racist. They are all racist."

My hands felt sweaty—the sweat was coming from Mama's hands.

The officers closed the backseat door, and from where we stood, we could barely make out what the lady was saying.

Two officers came to speak with Mr. Huang. The officer in the vehicle was seemingly having a conversation with the lady. The fourth officer was still with the woman's children.

Mr. Mosby shook his head and proceeded back into his store. He still had to finish checking us out. We followed.

"Welcome to downtown. That is why I am leaving this place. These people have no respect for themselves," he was saying.

"Ah ah," Mama said. "But why did they have to treat her like that?"

"Mr. Huang is a good man and so is his son. With these people you must be tough, or else they will take advantage of you. Just the other day, one of them tried to fight me because I told him that if he didn't intend on buying anything, he should get out of my store. You should have seen his face. If he had a gun, he would have shot me."

"My brother, make do and get out of here," Papa advised.

"I've been telling Mr. Huang to follow my lead and leave this place, but he said that it is cheap and he makes too great a profit. He asks me all the time why black Americans are not like us Africans," Mr. Mosby said proudly.

That afternoon, as we drove back home, Papa told me, "Foma. You saw how that woman was behaving. Let me not catch you ever acting that way. We cannot be here following the example of African Americans because we know who we are, we know where we come from. These people are just lost. We must respect ourselves."

As I lay in bed, thinking back on this situation, I realized that that was when my prejudice toward African Americans began. Back then, as a girl, I couldn't appreciate the complexities that situation revealed. However, considering what I knew now, my views were totally different. Although the lady could've handled the situation differently, I understood her frustration.

While this situation was not related to the disagreement I had with Ife, lying there, I realized that this memory had surfaced because of the guilt I was feeling. That day I'd been taught that I was different from African Americans. When bad things happened to them, I assumed they did not involve me. That was until someone close to me was hurt...someone whom I looked up to... someone I saw myself in. Ife's ambivalence toward the situation had upset me because of the guilt I felt. Had it not been Paige who had been hurt, I likely would've shared the same sentiment.

CHAPTER TWENTY-THREE

That Friday evening, Larissa hosted a letter-writing party to draft the letter to the university's president, President Taylor. In the email she sent, she had said she spoke to a university staff member who gave her a rundown of the procedures the school must follow when a rape is reported. She had the details we needed to write an effective letter.

We were to meet in a room on the upper level of Sterling. Kunle came to pick me up. He had just gotten a haircut, and he looked as handsome as ever. I had on my best outfit because after the meeting we were headed to a comedy show on campus. I would be lying if I said I didn't also want to show off in front of Larissa.

When Kunle and I arrived, Chris, Reggie, and Chuck were already in the room. Not long after, Larissa came in. She was carrying a big canvas bag, from which she pulled out several legal pads and a box of pens.

"Okay. I guess we can get started. There're legal pads and pens on the table for those who need them. We are grateful for Kunle, who has already completed a rough draft of the letter," she began.

I looked over at Kunle when she said this, but he didn't look back at me.

"I suppose we can read paragraph by paragraph and figure

out how to make the letter better. I took notes from my meeting with Dean Smith of student affairs. I have the printed copies here. Kunle, take one and pass them down," Larissa continued.

We each took a copy of the drafted letter and the notes Larissa took during her meeting with Dean Smith. According to her notes, filing a sexual assault complaint with the school's campus security automatically brought the school on notice because the officers were supposed to write reports and send them to the student affairs office. Upon the filing of a sexual assault complaint, the accused was automatically subject to an interim restriction until a hearing could be held on the matter, and a decision made by the school.

Under an interim restriction, the accused was not allowed to contact or seek out the accuser. Further, the accused would also be restricted to dining at the hall closest to his or her dorm. Entering Sterling for social purposes was strictly forbidden.

Her notes read: *If the accused is found to have violated any of these restrictions, the school may impose further restrictions, which include banning the accused from university housing and only allowing the accused on campus to attend class, and any other restriction the school deems necessary while it investigates the situation.*

While the accused is under the outlined restriction(s), the university appoints one staff member to act as detective, and based on the evidence, make the ultimate determination.

Larissa put question marks around the "one staff member" provision. I understood why she did that. What if that staff member was biased against one party?

After we read Larissa's notes, we were brainstorming out loud on how to improve the letter when Reggie, a senior and the treasurer of BSA, suddenly said, "I know this is a bit out of focus, but I just remembered something that I think is important for us to think about as we draft this letter. Do any of y'all remember that student, I think he was African, Kwame Boateng?"

Nobody seemed to remember. "Man, y'all have bad mem-

ories. Well, he was a student here three years ago, but was suspended for two years after a white girl accused him of sexually
assaulting her."

"Oh, yeah, I remember him, Kwam! He is Ghanaian. I didn't
really know him, but I remember he sent a letter to ASA asking
that we support him because a white girl said he forced himself
on her when he didn't," Kunle said.

"Yeah, he sent a letter to BSA too. He was a smart cat, a chem-
ical engineering major, and he was cold on the sax. He and his
band used to perform right here at Sterling on some weekends.
Anyways, the school suspended him even after they decided that
he didn't sexually assault the white girl," Reggie said.

"Wait, what exactly happened?" Chris asked.

"Here's what I remember," Reggie began. "This Kwame or
Kwam, whatever he goes by, was the only brother in his all-white
frat on campus. One day his frat threw a party. He was there mind-
ing his own business when a white girl approached him and they
started talking. Then she asked him to go to a more private space,
so my guy must have been on cloud nine. He agreed."

I tried to suppress my laughter as Reggie acted out the story.
He was so animated.

"They go upstairs to this room where they start making out
heavy. She's kissing him, she climbs on him, straddles him, and
then she starts reaching for his stuff. She goes down on him, and
then she gets scared because she's afraid her friends will know that
she is messing with a brotha. So, she says she has to go because
she thinks her friends are looking for her. He pulls her arm gently,
saying, 'Please don't go.' But she decides to go and that was that,
as far as he was concerned.

"Then homegirl got to talking with her friends, and they know
she was with Kwam, so they start looking at her funny. That's
when she starts saying that he pressured her. She didn't want her
friends thinking that she willingly hooked up with a black dude.
Then this girl tells her RA and other people that my man sexually

assaulted her, and then the next Monday she goes to the dean to report it, then to the police station. Based on her story, the police say she wasn't sexually assaulted.

"But the school said they had to do their own investigation, so they put him on…interim restrictions. They tell him he can only go to the dining hall near his dorm, and tell him not to go to Sterling, so he can't play his sax there anymore. They also tell him not to reach out to the girl.

"Anyways, a short time later, homegirl goes back to the dean and says he tried to get in contact with her on social media. She gets the feminist group involved, and they urge the school to kick him off campus. Now he can no longer stay in the dorms, and can only be on campus to attend class. He says he never tried to contact the girl and that he has proof, but they don't believe him and don't want to see his proof.

"Frustrated, what does he do? He sends an email to BSA and ASA explaining the situation and asking for help. But my thing is, just like Paige, he wasn't down with the black people before. When they in trouble, they suddenly know how to find us. Anyways, let me continue," Reggie said as he shook his head.

"So, the thing was, he put the girl's name in his email, and the school found out. In the end, the school found him innocent of sexually assaulting the girl, but found him guilty of violating the restrictions by including the girl's name in the email. They suspended his ass for two whole years!"

We were all trying to hold our laughter, not because of the story Reggie had just told but the way he told it. His gesturing and emphasis on certain points was extremely comical.

"How do you remember all of this?" Larissa asked.

"The boy wrote a detailed email, and we all know I have a photographic memory. Also, I was pissed when I read it. Anyways, now when a sista is raped, we all know her name and no one cares, and that punk Ray is walking around campus like he wasn't just accused of raping a girl. All the while, Paige is in someone's hospital, laid up because she attempted to kill herself. This is all messed up!"

After an hour and a half, we felt that we had a good draft. Larissa said she would make final edits before she took it to President Taylor's office. She also asked that we get the signed petitions to her as soon as we could. I pulled my sheet with fifty-two signatures out of a folder and handed it to her as we left the room.

She said thank you, and this time it wasn't accompanied by a scowl or a frown.

We are making progress, I thought, still certain that she had a crush on my man.

Kunle grabbed my hand as we descended the stairs down to the parking lot where his car was parked.

Once we entered the auditorium, I pulled Kunle's hand back when he tried to lead me to the front row. I knew enough about comedy shows to know that sometimes the audience members became the butt of the joke. I was not about to present myself as an open target.

My presentiment was proven correct because right after the headlining comedian got on stage, he targeted a couple sitting at the front of the stage.

"Black women in the audience, do you mind that this man is sitting here with a white woman?" he asked, pointing at an interracial couple. Then he directed his attention to the couple. "Do y'all go together?"

We were seated a few rows behind the couple, and we saw them both nod their heads.

"Does your daddy know you're with a black man?"

The lady eventually nodded.

"Are you sure?" the comedian asked.

This time she nodded confidently.

"Are you a football player?" was his next question to the guy.

The guy nodded his head.

"How did I know that? I must be psychic," the comedian said with a smirk.

We laughed. He was one of those comedians who could draw out laughter with very little effort. It was the effortless yet hilarious way he carried himself, from body movements to facial expressions.

"Would you be with him if he wasn't a football player?" he asked the lady.

She nodded her head.

"Tell me the truth, I won't tell anyone. Would you be with him if he wasn't a football player?"

She nodded her head again.

"Okay, okay, you don't have to be honest. Will you dump him if he doesn't go pro?"

She shook her head.

"Would your daddy let you be with him if he doesn't go pro?"

She nodded.

"The sistas on campus weren't good enough for you?"

Understandably, the guy gave no response.

"Once you go white, black can never be right, is that true?" the comedian asked the guy.

Again, no response.

"Hmm?" the comedian asked, this time smirking at the guy. "Oh, so you're done answering my questions. Black women, you know what that means: after the show, get him!"

More laughter erupted. As I looked around the room, I saw that there was a mixed crowd of both black and white audience members. The white guys sitting beside us were laughing hysterically.

"You see why I didn't want to sit in the front?" I whispered into Kunle's ear.

His eyes widened as he nodded.

I got nerve bubbles in my stomach when Kunle pulled up to my dorm building. I was anticipating our goodbye kiss. After he opened my door and helped me out, he stood in front of me. I looked up at him and admired how handsome he looked with his fresh haircut, and he stared into my eyes before enveloping me in his arms. With my body against his, I took in deep breaths of his intoxicating scent. Then, he lifted my chin and kissed me. This time, it wasn't just a peck, we kissed passionately.

As I climbed the stairs up to my floor, I imagined my life with Kunle; one filled with his sweet kisses. *Mrs. Foma Adeboye has a good ring to it*, I thought. Next, I thought about our wedding and remembered my cousin Mariana's wedding—the only wedding I had attended.

My cousin Mariana's wedding had been a three-day affair.

The first day was the traditional wedding day. For the ceremony, each family—our family and her husband James' family—donned their family cloth. Our family's color was light blue. Mama wore a blouse and skirt made of the fabric. Her long skirt was tight-fitted from the waist to halfway down her knee and then it extended out, like a fishtail. Mama used the remaining fabric as a headband. Nana Ola wore a blouse and a wrapper. On her head she donned a *gele* that was the same color as our outfits, but of a harder, stiffer fabric. Auntie Lulu wore her fabric in a dress with a high slit. In my young age, I hoped to one day have a dress with a slit like that. Mariana wore the purple colors of her husband's family to represent her departure from our family into their own.

Our families negotiated a bride price before Mariana made her appearance. Our family, the bride's family, began negotiations by saying how much we expected James to pay for our daughter, Mariana. They spent hours negotiating until they came to a mutually agreeable amount.

I remember standing there hungry and tired, resisting the temptation to sneak out a piece of meat or puff puff because we could not eat until the bride price was negotiated. The older girls were watching, even as they stood at a distance from the food, talking. When they were called away, I saw my chance and ran to lift the foil from the dish tray, and struggled to pull out two puff puffs surreptitiously. I was not brave enough to go for the meat. I ran to an inconspicuous location and bit into the puff puff, still warm thanks to the hot room.

After negotiations, my favorite part of the wedding began. James would have to identify Mariana and claim her as his wife— the one he had come for. One fully concealed girl at a time made her way through the crowd to enter the circle in which the groom and the most important of his family members sat with the bride's parents and other important elder figures in her life. When the first girl walked past me, as I stood by the door leading to the backyard where the occasion was taking place, I knew that she was not Mariana. She was too short. However, she was so well concealed that I had no clue who she was. The aunties walking beside her held cloth securely around her to conceal her identity.

"Come and take your wife," one auntie said. James was not fooled.

"That is not my wife," he responded.

"This is your wife. Are you calling me a liar?" the auntie argued.

"A beg, I know my wife. That is not my wife. Please, bring me my wife."

The aunties gave him an exasperated look as they returned to the house. When they walked by me, I saw the covered figure was Cynthia, Mariana's best friend.

When the fourth girl walked past me, accompanied by the aunties, I was certain that she was Mariana.

"I have listened to you and I have brought your wife. Come and take your wife."

James hesitated.

"I said, come and take your wife."

James approached, but retreated.

"Ask her to turn around."

"A beg, come and take your wife now, what is this?" the auntie complained.

"Auntie, I beg you. Please, ask her to turn around."

"My dear, turn around," the auntie said to the concealed figure.

The figure turned, and instantly, relief came over James' face. "I knew it!" he shouted. She is the same height as my wife, but I know my wife very well. A beg, take her back, that is not my wife."

"What do you mean?" the other auntie argued. "I am telling you, this is your wife."

"Auntie, I know my wife. That is not my wife. Please, go and bring my wife."

When the fifth girl came down, once again accompanied by the aunties, I did not know what to believe, so I did not bother deciding whether it was Mariana.

After some debating, James asked the fifth concealed figure to turn. When she did, he shouted, "I have found my wife!" The cloth came down and Mariana's identity was revealed. People shouted, and James' brothers hugged him. He had found his wife.

"Take this palm wine to the man who you say is your husband," an uncle said after the hoopla calmed.

Mariana sauntered away from where our family was seated, her purple flowy dress moving to the sway of her hips, the wooden horn that held the palm wine in hand. She approached James and his family's table. She stood next to him, and he looked at her longingly. He tapped the seat beside him for her to sit. When she sat down, she extended the wooden horn to his lips, and he drank. The backyard erupted in cheers. Mariana found her husband. It was time for us to eat!

The next day was the white wedding, when the bride wore her white dress and the wedding was officiated in church. I was one of the flower girls. Since Mama told me about my position months before, I longed for my moment to walk down the aisle throwing flowers. After I told my friends all about it, they agreed to help me practice—only we used leaves from the papaya tree in our backyard instead of real flowers. Even so, I felt prepared. As I strolled down the aisle, all eyes on me, I carefully distributed the flowers in a discriminate manner, to make sure I had enough left to take me down the aisle.

After the church wedding was the reception. That night, my cousins and I danced our best dances. I danced myself to exhaustion and fell asleep in Mama's arms right at the reception hall.

On the third day was a sendoff party at Uncle Paul's lavish house to wish journey's mercies to those who came from far, and send Mariana and James off to begin their new life together.

I admired Uncle Paul's house with a high metal gate with broken glass bottles encircling each of the iron bars that extended at the top. When we first arrived in Buea, I asked Uncle Paul why he had those glass bottles on his gate.

"To protect my house from thieves, Foma," he had explained. "If they try to climb my fence to steal my things, those bottles will take care of their hands." I had shrieked when he said this, imagining the sharp glass piercing through my skin.

Protecting his house from thieves was a top priority for Uncle Paul, because he also had a gateman, Cyril, who slept outside to look out for strange activity. "These thieves have gotten smart. They tie their hands now before they steal. If they make it past the bottles and Cyril, I have Sheba here to eat them alive," Uncle Paul told me.

That night I tossed and turned as I slept. I had a nightmare about the humongous Sheba. His mouth was open, I could see his teeth, he was salivating at the mouth, eyeing me ferociously, longing for a taste of my African flesh.

Tonight however, thoughts of my future with Kunle filled my mind when I laid my head on my pillow. Then, I became sad, thinking that he was several months away from graduating. *We can make it work*, I thought as I drifted off to sleep.

CHAPTER TWENTY-FOUR

I spent the rest of my weekend getting my school affairs in order. I hadn't done as well on my quizzes as I wanted, so I was a bit panicked. I had goals for that semester, and I was not about to let myself down.

Michelle agreed to join me at the library on Sunday after we had brunch together.

"Where's Ife?" Michelle asked as we sat down in a booth.

"I don't know," I said. "I'm upset with her right now."

"Oh, what happened?"

"Just a little drama. She refused to go with me to collect signatures for the petition because she said she didn't know all the facts."

"Oh."

"Isn't that messed up?"

"I mean, Foma, if she doesn't want to help you collect the signatures, she doesn't have to."

"I know, it was just that she accused me of trying to make everything about race."

"Not everyone is going to be on the same page as you, even your friends. You can't force people to see what they can't see."

Deep down, I knew that Michelle was right. I understood that my still being upset with Ife was partly due to my wanting her to see things my way, but I still thought she was a hypocrite and I did not like the condescending way she had spoken.

"Is Larissa still making googly eyes at Kunle?"

"I'm over it. He's my man and she can suck it if she doesn't like it."

Michelle chuckled. "Okay, I hear you."

"I trust him, so I'm not even worried about her."

On Monday, the prosecutor's office released a statement saying that they were not pressing any charges against Ray. Larissa called for a meeting to discuss the news.

We were seated at a booth in Sterling discussing the matter, as I read the newspaper article. I'd had two quizzes that morning, so I hadn't even thought about reading the paper after class as I usually did. Also, I had rushed to Sterling for the meeting, so I felt I wasn't caught up on everything. Thankfully, Kunle had forwarded me Larissa's text calling the meeting. She hadn't bothered to include me in the thread, despite the fact that I had attended all the meetings so far.

"It's because she is a black woman," Larissa said once we were seated at our usual spot at the Sterling food court. "We get no respect."

"Did you send the letter to the president's office?" Kunle asked.

"Yes, I personally delivered it to his assistant this morning, but I feel like we need to do more. This is unacceptable."

"If they say there isn't enough evidence to prosecute the case, why was he arrested in the first place?" Chuck asked to no one in particular.

"That's what I'm saying. Like, they know he had sexual contact with her, and she is saying he raped her. I think there's good cause to prosecute this matter in court," Kunle said.

I sat there thinking about Paige, wondering how she must be feeling.

"I better not see him in Sterling. I also better not see him at that football game," Chuck said.

"Oh, he better not play at that homecoming game," Larissa said.

I was the only one who hadn't said a word, and they noticed.

"Yeah, this is all so messed up," I said.

When I got to my dorm that evening, it was clear that my floor was filled with Ray supporters.

"RP!" Mark said as he walked down the hall.

"He's free!" Thomas finished.

An hour later, Kara entered the room. Neither one of us greeted each other. I was totally fine with things being like that. We had made a truce after Nana Ola's passing, but now things were back to normal. My towel still lay on that bathroom floor, so until it was washed, I decided to pay her dust.

"Did you hear?" Shannon asked Kara after she popped her head into our room.

"Hear what...Oh, yeah, RP, he's free. Mark and Thomas have been saying that all afternoon."

"I hope he gets to play at the homecoming game. I knew she lied about the whole thing. Like, his girlfriend is Dawn."

It took a lot for me not to say anything. I knew they only thought he was innocent because they couldn't believe that he would want to rape a black girl.

The next morning, we found out that Paige's parents had pulled some strings and Mrs. Mitchell was going to be on the prime-time show on a national news network. I agreed to attend a viewing party at Kunle's town house. He and Chuck also invited Reggie and Larissa.

Kunle picked me up from the library, and we went straight to his place. I was going to make queso for the tortilla chips he bought so we could snack while we watched.

By 7:55, we were all gathered in the living room, waiting for the program to start.

The news reporter opened the show by introducing Dr. Rhonda Mitchell, an esteemed African studies professor at one of the nation's top universities. Then the camera shifted to Dr. Mitchell's face. She did not look happy, and I did not blame her.

"Thank you for joining us today, Dr. Mitchell, however unfortunate the circumstances that brought us together may be."

"Thank you for having me."

"So, your daughter has accused a student at her university of rape."

"Yes, Ray Palmer, a student and star football player, raped my daughter," Dr. Mitchell said bluntly.

"What you're saying is, your daughter, Paige Mitchell, reported Ray Palmer of rape?"

"Yes, he raped my daughter."

"Okay, it has been alleged that he raped your daughter. You say that the school and your local prosecutor's office have not been handling the accusations as delicately as the situation requires?"

"Yes, they all have let my daughter down. The school has allowed her rapist to walk around campus with impunity, violating its very own procedures for such cases. Also, despite the evidence showing that my daughter's injuries are consistent with rape, and Mr. Palmer admitting that he had sexual intercourse with my daughter that day, the prosecutor's office refused to prosecute Mr. Palmer.

"Even before we get to that point, when my daughter reported the rape, the school should have warned him against uttering her name, and they should have outlined consequences in the case he did not abide with the rule. However, from what we are learning, they did not do that. As a result, Mr. Palmer was able to drag my daughter's name through the mud.

"She hasn't been back at school since she reported this rape because her friends won't speak to her and she feels unprotected.

While the young man has lost nothing, my daughter has lost everything. She is now a nervous wreck. There is a great chance she will be accepted into one of the most prestigious medical schools in the country, yet she can barely get out of bed."

"Speaking of that. I know this is a very sensitive matter, but we heard reports that your daughter allegedly tried to commit suicide. I think it would be helpful for you to clear this up if there is no truth to the allegation."

"I'm not going to entertain that. I am not here for that. I am here to bring awareness to the fact that Ray Palmer raped my daughter and no one wants to do anything about it."

"Have you spoken to the prosecutor's office to find out why they have decided not to prosecute?"

"Yes. They've insisted that they don't have enough evidence to go to trial, which is preposterous. They're blackballing my daughter."

"Why do you think that is, Dr. Mitchell?"

"I think it is all a cover-up because they don't want that young man to miss any football games."

"You think that the prosecutor's office won't charge Mr. Palmer with the rape because of football?"

"Absolutely. We all know that the American culture is infatuated with celebrity. This young man has been the best they have seen in a long time, and understandably, the community wants to see him make it big. Because of him, we have scouts from the best pro football teams at our home games. However, I assure you of this one thing. Whatever future success Mr. Palmer may have as a football player will not be at the expense of my daughter. We will fight till the bitter end."

"Okay…apart from his value to the football team, why else do you think the university and the prosecutor's office would want to protect Mr. Palmer's image at the expense of trying your daughter's case?"

"Money," Dr. Mitchell said unflinchingly.

"Money?"

"Yes, we all know that college football is big business. The school earns revenue from the games in which he plays, and they also earn money from sporting apparel with his name and number: jerseys, shirts, mugs, bobble heads, helmets, you name it. The fact is, as a star, Ray Palmer is a cash cow."

"I see. Is there any other reason you would say the school and prosecutor's office are not handling the situation as delicately as you feel it should be handled?"

"Because a black woman was raped and she is accusing a white man. Well, not just any white man, a white athlete."

"So, you're saying this is about race?"

"I certainly am. Imagine if this were a white woman raped by a black athlete? They would stop at nothing to prosecute him. In fact, we have heard the cases of black boys and men going to prison for rapes they did not commit simply because a white woman batted her tear-filled eyes and accused them. But what else do you expect in a society that has historically elevated white women and oppressed black women?"

"What would lead you to this conclusion?" the reporter asked.

"As you know, I am an African studies professor. As such, I am a curator of black history. I've studied the great African civilizations before the European colonization: the Kingdoms of Kush, Aksum, and Zimbabwe, the land of Punt, ancient Carthage, and the Mali, Songhai, and Ghanaian empires. I've also studied all the ills of the Middle Passage and beyond, where black women had no control over their bodies. The same European conquerors who lauded their white women snuck into slave quarters to rape enslaved black women. In America, our bodies have never truly belonged to us. We were used as experimentation tools. Ever heard of Henrietta Lacks, whose cells were exploited, or James Marion Sims, who made advances in the study of gynecology by operating on enslaved black women without anesthesia?"

"What I am hearing you say is that you believe your daughter is being exploited?"

"That's not what I am saying. What I am saying is that in our society, black women are often viewed as disposable, not worthy of the same protections that white women receive. That is why Ray Palmer remains able to move around the school campus unrestricted and no charges have been filed against him for raping my daughter, who is currently experiencing an emotional crisis."

"To synthesize what you've said, you believe the state and university are not doing their due diligence in investigating and prosecuting this matter because your daughter is a black woman?"

"Yes, that's correct."

The news reporter nodded his head. He was a middle-aged white man who was known for his liberal views on race and equality. In the few times I watched his program, he interviewed in an objective manner.

"As I mentioned, had it been a white girl accusing a black male athlete of raping her, the laws would have been swiftly executed against him. Remember Emmett Till? He was savagely beaten and lynched to the point that his face was unrecognizable just because they thought the fourteen-year-old whistled at and was sexually crude toward a white woman. Might I add, she recently admitted that he had not been sexually crude toward her. Nonetheless, she lied to her white husband and said he had, leading to the beating, lynching, and shooting of Emmett. Despite all the evidence against them, they were found not guilty! That's what this is about."

"Yes, I'm aware of that case. My question to you is, you've mentioned all the ills that black people have historically experienced. However, would you say that things have gotten better for black people over the years as we, as a society, have come to grips with our problematic past?"

"The sins of the past always find a way to haunt the present. Unfortunately, when they see us, they think we can only be aggressors, not victims. This goes to both black men and women alike.

Ray Palmer must be prosecuted for what he did to my daughter. I will not let the color of his skin, his superstardom, or his parents' influence shield him from paying for his crime."

Then music started to play, indicating that the segment was coming to an end.

"Wow, that was very powerful, Dr. Mitchell. I hope justice prevails in your daughter's case. We hope to see you again."

"Thank you all for having me."

For several seconds none of us uttered a word. We were in awe of how Dr. Mitchell handled that interview. Her points were clear and succinct. Deep down, I knew that this interview had lit a fuse to something much bigger.

CHAPTER TWENTY-FIVE

The morning after the interview, I woke up to a group text from Kunle, forwarding Larissa's message calling for a meeting that morning to make plans for our march.

When I left my biology class early to attend the meeting, Ife looked up at me, lifting her eyebrows as if to ask me where I was going. I gave her a slight wave as I left the hall.

At Sterling, Kunle, Chuck, Reggie, and I listened to Larissa speak. She wanted us to have a peaceful march from the administrative building that housed President Taylor's office to his home, which was located on the outer limits of campus.

This route was intentional: we wanted him to use his office to bring about justice for Paige, and the walk to his home was intended to bring what happened to Paige to his doorstep so that, hopefully, until he resolved the situation, every time he arrived or left home, he would remember our protest and think of Paige.

"What if they say that we are trespassing by going to his home?" Kunle asked.

"As I see it, our tuition dollars fund his stay at that house. He lives there because of his position as president of our university," Larissa said.

"What if they say we are threatening him by walking to his home?" Kunle asked again.

"It's a peaceful protest. There will be no threats involved," Larissa responded.

"Okay. I'm down, but I just want to make sure that everything is well thought out."

After the meeting, I made it to my next class on time. An hour and fifteen minutes later, as we were leaving class, Ife asked me where I was headed. I told her to a store on Main Street to buy construction paper. She volunteered to come with me.

"What's this for anyways?" she asked.

"I'm making a poster."

"What for?"

"Calling for justice for Paige."

"Oh. That was an interesting interview last night, wasn't it?"

"Yeah, it sure was."

"It's really messed up what the school and police are doing."

"Yeah, it really is. If that happened to me, I would want people to stand up for me. That's why we're holding a peaceful march tomorrow."

"Oh, who's we?"

"Me and some BSA members. I was planning on sharing the information at our ASA meeting this evening."

"Okay. Yeah, I think we should get involved."

"Yeah, we should," I said, happy that Ife had said that. I supposed she had gotten the facts she needed to join us.

When we got to the store, we searched for a poster board that wasn't too big but also not too small. Once I picked out the one I thought was best, Ife picked up a duplicate poster board.

"I wanna participate in the march, even though you didn't ask me."

"No need to be asked. If it moves you to join, join."

As we walked to the residence hall together, I felt silly for having been so upset with Ife. I was happy she was now coming around.

After an early dinner, we went to the lobby on my floor so that we could make our poster signs for the protest. The ASA meeting started at seven, so we only had an hour and a half to finish. I had a container filled with markers, glitter, stars, and about everything else you could imagine, thanks to the arts and crafts camp that Michelle and I attended our eighth-grade summer.

On my poster board, I wrote in large letters: JUSTICE FOR PAIGE. The words took up almost the entire board.

Good, nice and visible, I thought.

In a little spot at the bottom right corner, I drew a stick figure behind bars, then wrote #LOCKHIMUP right below the animation.

As we were working on our posters, I noticed some of my floor mates walking by, peering through the glass that encased the lobby, trying to see what we were doing.

"They're so nosy," Ife said.

"Tell me about it. Since this thing happened, they've been trash-talking Paige. Screw them. I want them to see."

After we finished making our posters, Ife went to her room to store her poster. We agreed that we would meet in the courtyard. I placed my poster on my desk, face up. I also placed my arts and crafts container on top of the poster, then grabbed my backpack and headed out to meet Ife.

At the ASA meeting, Ife and I sat next to Neema in the middle of the classroom. She had other commitments before the meeting, so we had agreed to meet her there.

Ife and I were relieved when Gillian showed up to the meeting with boxes of pizza in hand. Right behind her was Chad with liters of soft drinks. We had been in such a hurry to get back to the dorms to make our posters that we had not had much to eat at dinner. I excused my healthy diet for just this night.

The meeting started as usual. We went over the minutes from the previous meeting and started strategizing for our Taste of Africa event, the major ASA event of the school year.

The premise of Taste of Africa was to celebrate African culture.

The plan was to open the event with a choreographed African dance performance. We also planned on presenting the different sides of Africa with the aid of photographs that showed the modern continent—a view seldomly shown in western media. Someone also had the idea of creating video reels of "the things African parents say" and "growing up in an African household."

When Gillian opened the floor to special announcements, I raised my hand and went to the front of the classroom. My palms were sweating. I didn't like speaking in front of a large group of people. Yet, I remembered the words in Nana Ola's final letter about being courageous. As I began to speak, a long-suppressed side of me came out.

"ASA family. As I'm sure that many of you know, recently, one of our fellow students reported a rape that was committed against her. It has come to our knowledge that the school hasn't followed the appropriate procedure in investigating the matter. They have allowed her accuser to casually roam our campus in violation of their rape procedures.

"Several years ago, a black student—African, in fact—was accused of sexually assaulting a white female student, and the school applied those procedures in his case, even though from the girl's statement the police immediately determined that he had not sexually assaulted her, and the school later found the same.

"We as black students cannot stand by and allow the school to get away with this travesty. Accordingly, tomorrow we will be participating in a peaceful protest to call for the school to apply its own rules to Ray Palmer's case, and call that he not be allowed to participate in the upcoming homecoming game."

"Yes, I saw the interview with her mother yesterday. I'm interested in participating," Chad said.

"Wait, do we actually know whether the school has punished him already for being around campus?" Gillian asked.

"The fact that students continue to see him at Sterling implies that they have not."

"My problem is that I don't want us to participate in a protest if we don't know all the facts."

I rolled my eyes. I was getting tired of this "facts" thing. "But did you try to get all the facts after you heard about the rape accusation?"

"Well, no," Gillian replied.

"I think that's one of the problems. We as Africans need to stop turning a blind eye to these types of situations," I said.

"What situations exactly are you talking about?" Gillian asked.

"Situations that involve race," I said.

"Who said anything about race? You're asking for us to participate in a march to call for the school to act. I don't see what race has to do with anything."

"It involves race because, as I said, a similar incident happened with an African man and the school wasted no time in applying their procedures in that case. In that case, the African student, Kwame, was restricted from moving around campus, and when he made his accuser's name public, the school kicked him out for just that reason, even though they determined that he hadn't sexually assaulted her. In Paige's case, though, everyone knows she's the accuser, and the school doesn't seem to care, while Ray Palmer has free rein on campus."

"Yes, I see you're passionate about this, but in these situations we have to be objective," Gillian said.

"I'm tired of Africans being objective in these types of situations. Just so you know, if this can happen to Paige, it can also happen to you."

"Foma, I'm not trying to dismiss what you're saying. I just wanted to make sure I know what I'm getting myself into. That is the problem with some black people, they lack independent thought. They'd rather follow the crowd than think for themselves. I'm not one of those people."

"All I'm saying is that I know Paige personally, and I believe her one hundred percent. If we don't speak up for her, I guarantee you, no one else will. The all-white feminist group on campus refused to join our cause."

"Okay, I hear you."

"Because we're in America, we also need to fight for racial justice. We're able to live the lives we do in this country because of the African Americans, who in the face of great oppression, stood up for black people."

"Okay, I understand. You've made some great points. Everybody, please see Foma if you want details about this peaceful protest. For now, meeting adjourned," Gillian said.

Several students approached me after the meeting to express their interest in participating in the march. I gave my contact information to those who didn't have it already, and I told them I would keep them updated on the details.

"Wow, that was powerful," Neema said as we began our walk back to our side of campus.

"Thank you, Neema." I took that as a major compliment, because Neema hardly spoke.

"Yeah, that was very powerful. I'm looking forward to this march tomorrow."

"You're going?" Neema asked Ife.

"Yes, I am," Ife responded.

I was proud of myself. It felt great to speak up and say what was on my mind, and I was happy that what I said seemed to change how people viewed the situation.

When I got back to my dorm that evening, though, I noticed that my poster had been disturbed. My art container was set to the side—no longer on top of my poster. I was tempted to ask Kara who touched my poster, but I decided against it. We hadn't been speaking and she would claim she didn't know.

Thursday seemed to speed by. We received a group text from Larissa saying that the plan was to meet at Sterling that afternoon before heading over to the administrative building to start our walk to the president's house. She included me in the text this time.

When Kunle and I got there, we found a group of other black students standing, waiting for the march to begin. Larissa thanked the crowd for showing up. She stated the objective of the peaceful march, and away we went, walking the two and a half miles to the president's house.

"What do we want?"

"Justice!"

"For who?"

"Paige!"

As I was marching with Kunle by my side, Ife came from behind and tapped me on the shoulder.

"Glad you could make it!"

"I rushed after practice," she said. Ife was now a member of On Pitch, a campus choral group.

"What do we need?"

"Restrictions!"

"On who?"

"Ray Palmer!"

As we walked, our group continued to grow. We started with only around twenty-five of us, but by the time we were halfway to the president's mansion, it had doubled. I was pleasantly surprised when Gillian found us.

"We've got to stick together," she said. I smiled at her.

I saw a girl who looked like Michelle, but when she turned around, I realized that it wasn't her. Michelle had a doctor's appointment she could not miss.

The farther we went, the group kept getting larger. Then we noticed a helicopter trailing us. About three-quarters of the way to the president's mansion, we saw police cars blocking the path to the front. I counted five police cars and ten officers standing by the vehicles. Right behind them were a few news reporters and their cameramen.

I got nervous. My mind began to race, thinking of all the things that could go wrong. I was put at ease by the fact that Kunle was by my side. Kunle, seemingly sensing my angst, rubbed my back and I was instantly comforted. I smiled up at him.

"You cannot come any closer. Turn back!" an officer said as he used his hands to signal for us to move back.

Larissa was front and center, and she didn't look like she was going to back down.

This girl fears nothing, I thought.

"We have every right to be here, officer. We're not trying to cause trouble. We just want to make sure our voices are heard. This is a peaceful protest."

"Ma'am, you all are entering private property. It is illegal to trespass."

"Sir, we're tuition-paying students. Our tuition dollars keep the lights on in that house. We have every right to be here. We're not trying to jump the fence, I assure you. We are going to keep our protest in front of this gate."

"Ma'am, I will repeat: this is private property. Do not come any closer, and that is an order."

The male students rallied around Larissa to make sure that she was protected, including Kunle. I started taking deep breaths to calm myself down. I was seeing things escalate and I did not want anyone to get hurt.

Then President Taylor approached. He was a tall man with salt and pepper hair, wearing a nice suit. His rectangular glasses added to his distinguished look. He went over to the officer who was addressing Larissa and tapped him on the shoulder. It seemed like he was telling him to back off. Then he walked over to our group with the officers by his side.

"Good afternoon. I hear you all are looking for me?" he asked with a smirk. He was trying to defuse the tension with humor.

"Yes, sir, we've been looking for you," Larissa said.

"Okay, now you have me, how can I help you?"

"We're here because one of our fellow students, Paige Mitchell, accused Ray Palmer of raping her. Yet we don't see the school enforcing its own policies to restrict Ray's movements on campus."

"Okay. I assure you that we're taking care of the matter. Henceforth, and until we complete an investigation and hearing, Mr. Palmer will only be allowed on campus to attend class."

"Why wasn't the policy instituted immediately?" Larissa asked.

"Things fall through the cracks. However, now I assure you that the matter is being taken care of. Mr. Palmer has been notified."

"What about the homecoming game? Will Ray Palmer be allowed to play?" Larissa asked.

The president hesitated. "As of now, we have not made a formal decision, but I assure you that we're looking into that. There are a lot of moving parts involved here."

"Aww," we all said in disbelief.

"Sir, that is just not enough," Larissa said.

"I'm doing the best I can," he said, raising his hands to indicate his helplessness. "I love to see your activism—in fact, I support that. Our society moves forward when young people like yourselves fight for a cause you believe in. It was great speaking to you all this afternoon," he said, and with a wave of his hand, the officers surrounded him and he walked back to his house.

"President Taylor, we have more to ask you," Larissa yelled.

However, the cops were standing in front of her, making sure that she did not get a step closer. Chuck touched her arm, indicating that any other step would escalate tensions. The best thing was for us to leave.

CHAPTER TWENTY-SIX

"Hold on," I said to Ife when we were leaving class. I stooped down and reached for a newspaper in the rack right at the front of our building. Because this was how developments in Paige's case were communicated, I picked up the habit of reading the newspaper every day after class.

When I looked at this local newspaper, the first thing that caught my eye were the words *President Calms Down Angry Mob and Institutes Policy in the Paige Mitchell Rape Case*. Right below the caption was an image of us at the protest. I could see my face clearly. My mouth fell open. My entire face was hot, and the heat creeped over to my ears.

"What in the world?" I began as I read the paper frantically.

"Foma, what's going on?" Ife asked.

"Pick up the paper and read for yourself."

Students began to pass by, so I stood to the side. It was drizzling outside, so I didn't exit the building. Ife followed me over to the corner, newspaper in hand as well.

"Yo, this is messed up," Ife said.

Amy West wrote: *A group of angry students marched to President Taylor's residence, livid about the school's handling of the Paige Mitchell rape case. Nonetheless, President Taylor, in a show of great restraint, calmed the mob of angry students and listened to their concerns. Early this morning, we got word that President Taylor restricted Mr. Palmer's movement around campus. News as to whether Mr. Palmer will play in next week's homecoming football game is yet to be disclosed. Nonetheless, President Taylor assured the group that he will do all he can to ensure that the best decisions are made.*

"It was a peaceful protest! It's already bad enough that we felt played yesterday. Oh man, people are about to be really upset."

By "people" I was referring to Larissa. She had cussed up a storm on our walk to Sterling after the protest.

"What do you mean by you felt played?"

"Larissa was just saying that President Taylor must have gotten wind of us marching to his house and called the cops and the news reporters so that he had protection and the news reporters on his side."

"Oh, if that is what he was trying to do, it worked, because this article makes him look like the hero."

"Now my image is on this newspaper that's portraying me to be a part of an 'angry mob' that went to the president's house to harass him. This is just bull crap!"

The following Monday, Paige and her mother came to pick me up. Paige had texted me earlier that day asking if I wanted to have dinner at her house. I had a lot to do, but I agreed. Paige was finally released from the hospital and I wanted to show my support. Also, I could not pass up the opportunity of being in her mother's presence again. If there was one thing Nana Ola taught me, it was the importance of surrounding myself with greatness. I still got goosebumps when I thought about Dr. Mitchell's interview.

When I slid onto the tan leather seats of Dr. Mitchell's luxurious car, I felt elevated. Paige was sitting in the front passenger seat. I did not know much about cars, but I was certain that it was the best vehicle I had ever ridden in.

"Foma, I appreciate you accepting our invitation."

"Yeah, Foma, thanks for coming," Paige said as she turned around and gave me a closed-mouth smile.

"It's my pleasure. Thanks for the invitation."

"We saw you in the paper," Dr. Mitchell said.

"Oh," I muttered.

"Paige should be honored to have such a great friend like you."

"Yeah, Foma, I couldn't believe that was you in the paper. I'm very thankful. People say that the best way to know who is in your corner is to go through hard times. You're one of the few people out of all my groups of friends who've really stuck by my side, and I appreciate that."

"Paige, you have no idea how just knowing you has made me a better person and student. We can't allow the school to disrespect you like that. Heck, we can't allow them to disrespect any black woman like that. You were the black face of the school and look how they have treated you."

"It's not right, Foma, but I can't say I am all that surprised."

"Also, by the way, despite what the paper said, we were not angry. Yes, we were chanting as we marched, and yes, Larissa was passionate when she was talking to President Taylor, but it was a peaceful march and that's how we conducted ourselves. They twisted everything."

"Foma, that is nothing new, honey. We're not permitted the privilege of just being passionate."

The Mitchell family lived in a mansion, one of those homes you assumed came with a butler. When the gates opened and we pulled in, I felt important. Our five-bedroom, three-and-a-half bath house paled in comparison. The home was made entirely of white brick, and they had a massive driveway. To the right of the driveway was a garage that was separate from the home, but connected by a breezeway to a corner entrance to the house. The lawn was perfectly manicured. I had never seen grass so green.

Dr. Mitchell parked in the three-car garage next to Paige's car. I assumed Mr. Mitchell parked his car in the empty bay. As we walked into the home, I saw the cascading central staircase. High up on the walls, I could see old-fashioned paintings of Paige and her parents. She was an only child just like me. Their flooring was a cool light gray color. Their home reeked of abundance.

Dr. Mitchell reached her hand out to me, indicating that she wanted my coat. She looked as elegant as ever. Her graying hair was now tied to the back, and she wore the most beautiful diamond earrings, which glistened under the light of the elaborate crystal chandelier.

"Foma, come up with me while Mom gets dinner started," Paige said as she led me up the stairs.

"Ladies, dinner should be here in thirty minutes, and so should your dad."

"All right, Mother," Paige said, and in that moment I felt like we were back in high school.

The stairs were that same cool light gray color as the floorboards. As we ascended, with me at her heels, we passed framed photos. I tried to look at each one. The photos displayed a happy family. One that went skiing, traveled to beautiful islands, and attended holiday parties.

In all the photos in which she appeared, Paige had a megawatt smile and bright, engaged eyes. She looked as though she did not have a care in the world. That was the same glow I had seen at the hospital that summer. The glow that I hoped Ray Palmer's crime would not permanently erase.

"Oh, my gosh! I am so happy to be with someone beside my mom. I love her, but I can't have her hovering over me like this much longer," Paige said as she shut her door.

"How is it being out of the hospital?"

Ever since I found out she was released, I had been nervous because of her refusal to promise me that she would not attempt to take her life again. Now that she was out, she would have less supervision. That frightened me.

She shrugged. "It's all right. My bed is much more comfort-able. Even with the private bedroom we got, that bed was crap."

"How've you been feeling?" I asked.

"I'm taking my meds, and I'm seeing a therapist now. So, like I've told my mother a thousand times, you don't have to worry about me, I'm all good now."

"Okay, I'm happy for you. So, what've you been doing all this time?"

"Reading books. That's the only thing I can stand to do."

I decided against asking when she would be returning to school.

"What's been going on with you?" she asked.

That was the opportune time to tell her about Kunle, but I wasn't sure how she would feel hearing about men after all she had been through, so I tested the waters.

"I'm currently involved with someone."

"Oh, do tell, who?" she exclaimed.

Okay, she's ready.

"Do you know Kunle Adeboye?"

"Of course I do! You're with him?"

"Yes, he's my boyfriend."

"How long has that been going on?"

"A couple months."

"He's a great guy. You know, we lived on the same floor of our freshman year residence hall."

"Oh, did you?"

"Yeah. I spoke to him a few times, but you know, our circles were different."

"Do you know Larissa from BSA?"

"Yes, why?"

"Just curious," I said. While Larissa was now cordial, I still noticed her stealing glances at Kunle every now and again when she thought no one was watching.

"All I know about her is that she used to be around Kunle a

lot freshman year. She was always on our floor, but I think they were just friends."

Instantly, the wheels spun in my head. Maybe Larissa had always had a crush on Kunle, but things never developed. Or maybe they had a thing in the past, which he was not willing to cop to.

"What's going on, Foma?"

"I think Larissa likes Kunle."

"Why do you say that."

"It's the way she looks at him. I felt like they had something going on, even though he assured me that they never did."

"Has he given you a reason to feel that way?" she asked.

"No, it's just something in my gut."

"Then, go with your gut, I guess. If you're not feeling right, there's a reason."

"Yeah, but I trust him. I can sometimes think too deeply into things. I'll just let it go and see what comes of it."

"If that works for you," Paige said as she went into her closet.

When she came out, she had a sandwich bag in hand. It was filled with white pills. She placed the bag on her white desk and gulped a few pills down with the water from the water bottle beside her gold desk lamp. It was awkward. I thought it weird that she would be taking pills from a sandwich bag, but it was not my place to ask. Besides, Mama sometimes put her vitamins in sandwich bags, to take them at work.

"So, I'm seeing someone too," Paige blurted.

I tried not to show my confusion. Not to say that a girl who was just raped should not be dating, but it felt off that she would be dating after both the rape and the suicide attempt. She just got out of the hospital a few days ago. Nonetheless, I sat there and listened while she told me about this guy, Jeff.

"Does he go to our school?" I asked.

"He did, but he got kicked out."

"For what?"

"I think for fighting."

"Umm…okay…how did you connect with him?"

"He had something I needed."

Before I could ask any further questions, Dr. Mitchell called up, saying dinner was ready.

I trailed behind Paige as we went downstairs. We passed French double doors with glass windows as we headed down to the dining room. One side of a long opulent oak table held food from a local Greek restaurant. There were four place settings. I supposed Mr. Mitchell would be joining us for dinner. I sat to the left of Paige, and Dr. Mitchell sat across from us.

"Did Dad say he was going to make it home in time for dinner?" Paige asked.

"Yes, he did," Dr. Mitchell responded, and shortly thereafter, we heard the garage gate ascending.

Moments later, we heard Mr. Mitchell open the door from the garage. For some reason, I had expected to hear the jingling of Papa's keys, but I realized I was not home.

When Mr. Mitchell appeared in the dining room, I saw that Paige was a carbon copy of her father. They had the same oval face and thin nose. Mr. Mitchell was a handsome man with a mustache. He had a full head of graying hair, and he was just slightly darker in complexion than Paige. He was a thin and tall man, and his posture was impeccable. He wore the typical attire of a lawyer: a dark suit and blue-collared shirt with a striped tie.

"Oh, we have a visitor," he said. His voice was deep.

"Yes, this is Paige's friend, Foma."

"We've heard a lot about you, Foma," Mr. Mitchell said as he hugged and kissed his wife. Then he made his way to Paige, whom he kissed on the head, and then he held his hand out for me to shake. His grip was firm.

As we ate, I could not allow another moment to go by without me acknowledging Dr. Mitchell's interview from the week before.

"Many of us black students on campus really appreciated your interview."

"Oh, I hadn't realized that you saw the interview," Dr. Mitchell said.

"Yes, a group of us got together and watched. It was much needed. In fact, it inspired us."

"I have to say, it was great to see that you all stood up for Paige last week," Mr. Mitchell said. "My cellphone has been ringing off the hook since that interview and now that protest. I'm not sure if you understand, Foma, but many people who contacted me have been really impressed by you all taking action and calling for the school to act."

"Thank you, sir. We just want to make sure that justice is served. However, the article painted us in a bad light. We were having a peaceful protest and everything stayed peaceful despite what it may have portrayed."

"People are seeing through that," Mr. Mitchell said. "I wouldn't worry about any negative blowback."

Coming from a lawyer, I was assured.

"Foma, one thing Mr. Mitchell and I wanted to tell you during this dinner is that even though Ray Palmer has been released, we have a strong handle on what's going on. We are calling in our networks to make sure that he doesn't get away scot free with what he did," Dr. Mitchell said.

"Absolutely. We don't want you all to feel as though things aren't being done in the background. I would never discourage young people from protesting, but I just want you to know that Paige's mom and I've got this."

As I spoke to her parents, I could not help but notice that Paige appeared withdrawn. She had gone from being present to sitting there, seemingly out of it.

When dinner was over, Paige said she was tired, and Dr. Mitchell alone took me back to campus. On our way back to my dorm, we spoke about my recent trip to Cameroon, and she told me about the research project she was conducting on Botswana women in politics. I told her about my idea of creating Our Women Create Our Future, to help build women's health practices in Cameroon.

"That's a great idea, Foma. Please, when you start the non-profit, reach out to me. I would love to help."

I could tell Dr. Mitchell was genuine, and I couldn't wait to tell Papa that we had a supporter. Thanksgiving break couldn't come soon enough. I was ready to get the non-profit up and running. I didn't yet have professional backing, but it pleased me to know that I had my father's.

"Thank you for having dinner with us, Foma. I hope we'll be seeing you again soon. I think your visit really lifted Paige's spirit," she said.

As I walked to my building, I wondered if she had noticed how withdrawn Paige had become during dinner, or her plate full of barely touched food.

I took the elevator up to my floor. I felt too lazy to climb the stairs as I usually did. As I walked from the elevator to my room, I fumbled with my purse to retrieve my keys. I was not paying much attention to what was in front of me. At my door, I looked up to see a piece of white computer paper taped to the door. I unfolded it and read, *BLACK BITCH, YOU'RE NEXT*. To the side of the paper was a stick figure whose face was colored in black—behind jail bars. Right below the image was the hashtag *#LOCKHERUP*.

My face was hot, my hands were shaking. I did not know what to do. Then I heard my suite mates' door open. Out of the corner of my eye, I saw someone peer out at me and then immediately bolt inside, closing the door. Then I heard laughter coming from the room.

Those fools did this, I thought.

I opened my room door slowly and walked inside quietly. Kara was not there. Also quietly, I opened the bathroom door as lightly as I could, and I tiptoed to my suite mates' room door. I put my ear to the door and I heard them talking in low but audible voices.

"I don't think she saw me," I heard Casey say.

"That's what she gets. She's been such a bitch to Kara," Shannon said.

"I'm not in this." That was Kara talking.

I was so upset! As I stood there, I felt tears rushing to my eyes. I backed away, went back into my room, and called Kunle. I packed my toiletries and searched for a change of clothes.

CHAPTER TWENTY-SEVEN

Kunle was at my dorm within fifteen minutes of me calling him. I met him outside. As I approached his vehicle, he exited and came walking toward me.

"You said you don't know who wrote the note?" he asked. I had never seen him so upset.

"No, I don't. I just heard those girls laughing."

"Let me see the note."

I handed it to him.

He read the note carefully. "A dude wrote this note. I have the mind to go up there and find out which one."

"Oh, no, you're not. Let's go," I said as I pushed him toward his car. It was cold outside and the tears that had fallen down my face stung in the cool evening breeze.

"Only cowards would do a thing like this anyway," he said.

In his car, I pulled out the poster that I had made for the protest the week prior from the floorboard of the backseat of Kunle's car. I showed him the jail bars *#LOCKHERUP* sign that had been written on the note, and we compared it to the *#LOCKHIMUP* one I had written on the poster for the protest, with a stick figure of Ray behind the jail cell.

"You see, I think this is why they left me that note. I knew that someone had tampered with the poster when I got back to my room. Someone had moved the art box container I had placed on top of the poster. Also, some of the guys saw Ife and me in the lobby working on the posters."

It was already past eight when we got to Kunle's town house. Chuck was nowhere in sight.

"I can sleep out here if you'd like," Kunle said as we stood self-consciously in his living room.

"No, you don't have to sleep on the couch," I said.

We headed into his bedroom. Once in his bedroom, I placed my bag down. I sat in the chair by his desk. It had wheels. He sat at the edge of his bed and pulled the chair toward him with me in it. Once we were face to face, he opened his hands, asking me to go to him. I sat on his lap. He hugged me, and his head fit perfectly in the curves of my neck.

I trembled as I felt his soft kisses on my neck. I was feeling things I had never felt before. In my mind, I debated whether I should tell him to stop, but I knew the words would not escape my mouth. Before I knew it, I was straddling him, and we were kissing. I shuddered when he placed his hand in my shirt to grab my waist. When he tried to retreat, I pulled his hands back to where they were.

I could tell he was taking his time with me, with slow caresses and soft kisses. Before I knew it, we were lying on his bed. Something deep down told me to tell him to stop. But I said nothing because my body did not want him to stop. My body froze when I thought of Nana Ola. I remembered that day in Cameroon when she told me to be careful about who I allowed to take my flower.

As Kunle lay on top of me, still kissing my neck, that thought too faded away. I did not stop him when he reached into his nightstand to get protection. When our bodies connected as one, I was relieved to find that my experience was not clouded by the pain that Michelle had described to me junior year when she lost her virginity.

Our bodies swayed to the sound of their own drums. The feeling that had started off strange now felt natural. Shortly after I gave him permission, Kunle collapsed to the right of me, pulling me in close, so my head rested on his chest. In that moment I became aware of our nakedness and I was embarrassed, but seeing how calm and unaffected he was calmed me.

"How was it?" he asked.

"It was good," I said as I told myself that I had not been too hasty in taking this step with him.

As my eyes closed that night, my body entangled into Kunle's, I hoped that I would not come to regret my decision.

When I woke up the following morning, I felt different. Kunle let me get ready first, and as I sat on his desk chair, waiting for him to get ready, I studied myself in the mirror that hung behind his door. I wanted to see if I looked as different as I felt.

We walked to his car, hand in hand. I felt like an adult when he placed his hand on my thigh as we drove into campus. We had entered a mature phase of our relationship, and I hoped the spontaneous decision I made the night before did not blow up in my face.

When Kunle dropped me off in front of my class building, we kissed. After I exited the vehicle, I watched him drive off to the parking lot where he would keep his car for the duration of his day on campus.

After class, I told Ife about the note. We were standing in one of the vacant halls of the building. "Oh, my gosh! This is awful. Who wrote this?" she demanded.

"I have no idea who wrote it, but I think I know who was involved."

"Who?"

"My suite mate Shannon. I heard them talking after I found the note. Something tells me she had something to do with this."

Ife agreed to go with me to report the note. I had placed it neatly into a folder in my schoolbag, and I had decided to take it straight to the campus officials as opposed to our hall director because of the threatening message within the note. I was anxious about what they meant by I was next.

The housing affairs building was just a five-minute walk away. When we got to the right floor, we were told to sit and wait to be attended. As we sat, I told Ife all about my visit to Paige's house. I did not mention my night with Kunle.

"Hello, I'm Mrs. Rogers. You are Forman...Foter..." The lady began to say my name. I had filled out the sign-in sheet with my full name, instead of writing Foma F., as I usually did. It always made me cringe when people tried to pronounce my names.

"Fomanju Fotabeng," I corrected her.

I got up and walked over to her. Ife followed me. We went through the open door and let the middle-aged blonde lady guide us to her office. Mrs. Rogers motioned for us to sit down.

"How can I help you ladies?"

"I would like to speak with you about this note I received yesterday," I said as I slid the note over to her.

"Oh, my! How did you receive the note?"

"Someone taped it to my door."

"You're sure it was directed to you?"

"I'm the only black person in my room."

"Okay, I see. So, you don't know who wrote this note?"

"No, I do not. However, some girls were in my suite mate's room and one of them popped her head out to see me reading the note, and then bolted back inside, and I could hear them laughing inside the room. When I went to listen, I heard them saying that I deserved it for being mean to my roommate or something to that effect."

"Hmm...have you spoken to your RA and hall director about this?"

"No, I don't trust that they'd be able to help, because I've been having problems with my roommate, and every time I report the different incidents of disrespect, things don't seem to change.

My RA has been just useless. At least our hall director has tried to help. However, for now I'd like to lodge a formal complaint about this note."

"Who's your hall director? Sarah?"

"Yes, that's correct."

"What are these other incidents you are referring to?"

"Well, I had an incident where my roommate used only my towel to clean up someone else's bathwater without telling me. When I asked her to wash my towel, she refused. Then she moved the room around, removed my rug from where I placed it by my bed, and put the trashcan near where I lay my head. When I put my rug back under my bed, she came to the dorm one night and pulled the rug right from under me as I slept. I've been dealing with a lot of disrespectful things with my roommate. So, I am not one bit surprised by this situation with the note."

"That's all unacceptable. What's your roommate's name?"

I gave her Kara's first and last name, which she wrote down.

"I'm going to take care of this matter. I will email you. No worries. I'll handle it."

"Thank you, ma'am."

"Do you feel safe in your dorm? Is this a matter where we need to get campus security involved?"

I thought about it, but then decided not to. I wasn't afraid of them. Whoever wrote that note was a coward because they could not say those things to my face.

Anyway, the tone of her voice was assuring, and I was relieved. Ife and I walked to our resident dining hall to have a late lunch.

When I got back to my dorm after lunch, everything looked normal. I took a nap. I was woken when Kara and her posse walked into our room. It was six o'clock, and I saw that Ife had texted me asking if I wanted to get dinner.

"Who put that note on our door?" I asked Kara squarely.

"What're you talking about?" she asked, feigning ignorance.

"You know what I'm talking about, and so do you," I said, pointing at Casey, who gave me a nasty look. "And, I deserved that note, right?" I asked Shannon pointedly.

Shannon responded with a smug look. At least she was true to herself. Her other friends were pretending like they didn't know what I was talking about.

"You're being paranoid," Shannon said, still with the smug look on her face.

The nerve of her, I thought. I just wanted those girls out of my room.

"And you're a liar," I responded.

"I don't have time for this," Shannon said. "Kara, did you find your wallet? I want to get out of here."

"Yes, get out of here," I barked.

They left without saying another word.

After dinner with Ife and Neema, I returned to my dorm. Kara, Jennifer, Casey, Jared, Thomas, and Mark were in our room. I was ready for them.

"Do any of you know who put that note on my door, or are y'all going to play dumb like the rest of your friends?"

As I said this, my gaze was directed at Jennifer, Jared, Thomas, and Mark. Jennifer looked away. I took that as a sign of guilt or shame. Jared would not meet my gaze.

Sell out, I thought.

Black men like him who did not stand up for black women disgusted me. I knew his mother was black, and if he had a sister, his sister was also black. However, with his white friends, my presence seemed to be a burden to him. I knew why, because no matter how hard he tried to fit in, my presence reminded him that he was black, just like I was.

Nobody said a word, they just looked away.

"What about you, my brotha?" I asked, looking pointedly at Jared.

He always referred to himself as a "brotha" when he was

around his white friends, so I made sure that when I said "brotha" I put the same amount of emphasis on the word that he usually put. The pained look he gave me provided me comfort because it showed he knew I was mocking him. He looked down at his feet and turned to leave the room.

"Coward," I said under my breath, but just loud enough to where I knew he heard me. He turned around and threw a nasty look my way before turning again to leave.

"You need to calm down," Mark said in an authoritative tone that I did not care for.

"And what if I don't? Who do you think you are?"

I maintained a gentle, measured tone as I spoke to make sure my words sank in. I did not want to give them cause to dismiss me as the angry black girl.

"Don't bring that ghetto stuff here," he said.

"Don't bring that superior stuff here. You don't intimidate me," I said, looking him directly in the eye to show him that I would not back down.

"I'm sick and tired of people like you always complaining about how bad you have it. Always trying to play the victim with the race card. It's always white people's fault, huh? If you all get off your fucking asses and actually be respectable people, you'll find that people will respect you for once."

Jennifer touched his arm, indicating to him that he had gone too far. Even his other friends looked uncomfortable. At that moment I knew in my gut that it was Mark who wrote that note. He was one of the guys who walked by the lobby as Ife and I were working on the poster.

"No, let him talk. Let him reveal who he is. FYI, I respect myself. It's you who needs to respect yourself to realize that it's off the backs of people like me that you are able to stand here with your entitled attitude. Respect yourself!"

"In the good ole days, you wouldn't be able to speak to me like that!"

"Mark!" Jennifer bellowed.

"Too bad for you it is not, and here I am, speaking to you any way I like."

He stormed out of the room. I was happy that I was able to bring out his true character. *How was Jared rooming with this guy?*

"Oh my gosh, I am so sorry about that," Jennifer said.

"I'm not. Looks like I found out who wrote the note, after all."

Thomas hung his head but said nothing. I took that as confirmation.

I grabbed my schoolbag and left the room. I went downstairs to the courtyard. Tears were streaming down my face; I had been holding back the tears since I left the room. There was no way in the world I was going to let them see me cry. I did not want them thinking they caused me pain.

I spent the night at Ife's dorm. I couldn't stomach being on my floor that night. I decided against saying anything to Kunle because I knew he'd be upset, and I didn't think I'd be able to stop him if he decided to confront Mark.

CHAPTER TWENTY-EIGHT

Ife, Neema, and I had brunch that Saturday morning. After brunch, I went back to my room. Kara was not there. I figured she and her friends had gone tailgating for the big homecoming game that afternoon. I had told Michelle what had been happening, and she said what I needed was a fun day out. She suggested that I meet her at her dorm so that we could go to the cookout that the Black Student Center was hosting. Ife couldn't make it because she had to prepare for an On Pitch performance that evening.

As I began the long walk to Michelle's dorm, I saw students piling onto the school's shuttle buses. The bus was filled to capacity, and many were left standing because there were not enough seats for everyone. Their apparel gave away that they were going to the game. Many wore football jerseys. Some girls had on short shorts, long socks that went up their knees, and tennis shoes. Most didn't have on coats, while I was bundled up in my jacket and still felt chilled.

By the time I made it to Michelle's dorm, I had warmed up. The sun had just begun to shine on a beautiful Saturday afternoon.

"I'm sorry about those jerks on your floor," Michelle said once we got up to her room. "Now that you're here, tell me what exactly happened."

I told her everything.

"Black guys like Jared make me sick. He really is a coward. He should've stood up for you."

"I wrote an email to Mrs. Rogers, the lady over at housing, right after the situation happened. She emailed me yesterday to let me know that Mark will no longer be on my floor. She didn't say much else. I wasn't going to let it go."

"You shouldn't let it go, shoot."

We entered her room and Michelle began getting dressed.

"How are things going with Kunle?" she asked.

"Things are going all right," I said as I played with my bun.

"Okay, what's really happening? You know I can tell when you're holding back, right?"

"How can you tell?"

"I'm not giving up my secret."

"Okay. Well, Kunle and I did it," I said as I hid my face with my hands.

"Did what?" she teased.

I gave her an annoyed look. "Did it, stop playing."

"Ahhhhh! When did that happen?"

"Well, when I found the note on my door, I called him because I didn't want to stay at my dorm. He came and picked me up. We went over to his place, and one thing just led to another."

"Oh, my gosh, Foma, I can't believe this. I never thought I'd see the day. Little miss innocent Foma got down and dirty," Michelle said as she did a belly roll.

"Oh, hush, I'm not all that innocent."

"Well, not anymore. Kunle made sure of that."

We laughed. This was what I missed.

"It just happened."

"How was it?"

"It was good. After hearing your story about your first time, I was freaked out, but things went better than expected," I said, trying to hide the smile on my face.

"Foma, you just made my day with this revelation."

"I aim to please."

At the cookout, I kept an eye out for Kunle but I didn't see him. I had texted him to let him know that I was there, but I knew he was helping with the event, so I figured I'd see him sooner or later. In the air was the hip sound of old school rap. I swayed from side to side as Michelle and I stood together.

Michelle's friends Tracy and Leticia were supposed to meet us there. As we stood observing the crowd, we heard a whistle and members of one of the black fraternities began strolling. I was captivated by the uniformity they maintained as they strolled.

I scanned the yard for Kunle once again, and in the process, I spotted Tracy and Leticia. I waved them over. I looked for a place to sit while they went to the food table. Michelle was going to get my food.

As I sat, I spotted Reggie. He was talking to someone, and he seemed fully engaged in the conversation. When I saw Chuck, I knew that Larissa had to be there too, but I couldn't spot her.

Soon, Michelle and the two ladies returned with plates of food. I checked out the plate Michelle placed in front of me: the mac and cheese and grilled chicken wings looked delectable. We swayed to the music as we ate. I was in good company, listening to great music, and eating good food. I felt like life could not get much better than that.

After we were done eating, Michelle said she needed to use the bathroom, and I told her I would go with her. Tracy and Leticia said they would stay back to secure our table. The bathroom was located inside the Black Student Center, which was basically a house converted into a center.

I had been to this center on several occasions with Kunle so I knew my way around. When we stepped in, only a few people were inside. They were seated on the sofa right across from the front door.

"You can take that bathroom," I told Michelle, pointing at the bathroom on the first level.

"Okay."

"I'll go to the one upstairs to see if it's free."

As I headed upstairs, I kept my step light because those floor-boards always creaked. The creaking sound bothered me. As I approached the last step, I heard people talking. I froze because I recognized the voices.

"Listen, I've already told you, I'm in a situation right now, so we gotta stop this thing."

"Oh, so where was your situation several weeks ago? You were the one who made the first move, remember that?"

"Yes, I know I was wrong. We shouldn't have gone there again, but now that we have, I'm saying we need to cool this off."

"So, it didn't mean anything to you?"

"You know I care about you, but we both know that this isn't going to work. People's feelings are involved here."

"What about my feelings?"

"Larissa, Chuck is my roommate. If you haven't noticed, he has liked you since freshman year."

"Don't you think I know that?"

"Then you understand."

"No, I don't. We both care about each other, so why don't we see where things go?"

"I told you, I have a girlfriend."

"You came running to me when you were with her. You weren't thinking about her then."

"Come on, Larissa."

"I already told you, I want you. I don't know what you see in her."

"Larissa."

"But, Kunle, I want you."

My heart was beating out of my chest when I heard tussling coming from that room. I already knew what was going on, but I had to see for myself. I climbed that last step quietly, walked to the door where they were, and pried it open.

When I peeked inside, I saw Larissa and Kunle rolling on the couch, kissing, Larissa on top of Kunle, and Kunle stroking her back as they kissed.

I pushed the door open to get their attention. Kunle looked up and saw me, bewilderment in his eyes. I had caught him. He had lied straight to my face that there was nothing going on and I had caught him red handed. Larissa was smirking. She was happy to be caught. I was frozen. I could not move.

"Foma," Kunle said as he got Larissa off him, but I turned to leave.

He chased me down the stairs and caught me right when I got to the front door. He grabbed my arm. I flung it back, my elbow hitting his chest. He winced. Michelle was just coming out of the bathroom.

"What's going on?" she asked, looking between us.

The people seated on the sofa were now looking at us, trying to figure out what was happening.

"Get off me," I told Kunle as I jerked my arm away one last time.

"It's not what it looks like," he was saying, but I didn't care.

"Let's go, Michelle," I said, and we left the house.

"Foma! What happened?" Michelle asked.

"I don't want to talk about it. I need to go back to my dorm."

"I'll come with you."

"No, you can stay. I just need to get out of here."

"I'm going with you. I'll text Tracy and Leticia that we had to leave."

I felt like my heart was going to beat out of my chest as we walked to my dorm. I could not believe what had just happened.

"What happened?" Michelle asked.

I told her everything I heard and saw.

"That's so messed up! You had that gut feeling too. Argh, I am so mad for you. You should've slapped him. Heck, maybe even slapped her."

"I'm done with the two of them. They can rot for all I care."

"Some girls are like that, just ruthless."

"She's a fraud. Here we are fighting for Paige while she's there purposely trying to hurt another black woman."

"I am so mad for you!"

CHAPTER TWENTY-NINE

I woke up from my nap to my phone ringing. It was Mama calling. Michelle had stayed with me for a few hours when we got back to my dorm, but she left after I told her that taking a nap was the only thing that would help me feel better.

As the phone continued ringing, I thought about not answering it. Yet I needed to feel loved at that moment. When I answered the phone, I regretted my decision.

"Foma, what are you doing at that school? We saw you in the newspaper. You were involved in a protest?"

I took a deep breath. The protest was the last thing I wanted to think about. Besides, it happened over a week ago; how was she just finding out that I was involved? "Mama, good afternoon to you too. Yes, I participated in a protest."

"And this protest was against the president of your university?"

"No, Mama, it wasn't against anybody. It was just to call the school's attention. It was for Paige. Against its own policy, the school had been allowing her rapist to walk around campus without any restrictions, so we wanted to bring awareness to that."

"What is your purpose of being in that school? To be a student or a revolutionary?"

"Mama, I am here to be a student. But what's wrong with me being a revolutionary if I choose to advocate for justice?"

"Foma, we want you to focus on school, not get involved in insurrection. Who knows how things like this could end?"

"Mama, didn't you and Papa tell me stories about how when you two were students at your university in Cameroon, you participated in a protest when the government brought French teachers to teach at your English school?"

"Yes, but that was different."

"How was it different? They are both protests in school."

"We couldn't have teachers coming to our English schools and teaching us in French."

"Well, I can't go to a school that allows the rapist of a black woman to just walk around freely. What if it had been me?"

"Don't say that. It couldn't have been you."

"Mama, if it could happen to Paige, it could happen to me. We can't allow people to think it's okay to hurt a black woman and get away with it. We need justice!"

"Dear, all I am saying is that I hope you are making time for your books."

"Mama, I have to go."

After I hung up the phone, I slammed it on my pillow and pulled my comforter over my head. I felt like I was in a nightmare that I wanted to wake up from.

Ife texted me to see if I was still at the cookout. She was done with her rehearsal for that night's concert, and she was headed back to the dorms. I told her I was in my room, and she said she would come over.

Ten minutes later, Ife texted me to tell me that she was across the hall. I went and let her in, and we headed to my room.

"What's wrong with you?" she asked.

"Oh, Ife, it's such a long story."

"I've got time."

I told her everything.

"Oh, my gosh!" she said. "I can't believe Kunle would do something like that. Have you spoken to him since?"

"No, I've just been here."

"That's crazy. I'm sorry this happened to you."

I began crying heavily. My chest was heavy with pain. Kunle's betrayal was especially heartbreaking because I had given him my virginity just days ago. Now, here I was, feeling like a fool.

"Ife, there's something I haven't told you."

"What is it?"

"I slept with Kunle."

Her jaw dropped. "What?"

"Yeah, it was unexpected, so now I feel really stupid. I should've known better," I said as tears streamed down my face.

"Foma, don't cry. You didn't know. You can't beat yourself up."

"Ife, deep down I knew, but I just ignored it."

"That Kunle. If I had known he was capable of doing something like this, I would've told you."

"He had us all fooled."

"I can understand if you won't be able to make it to my concert."

"That's right, Kunle got the tickets. I'm definitely not going with him."

"If you're up to it, I'll get you a ticket. Don't worry about that."

"Okay, I'll come. I will be too depressed just sitting here alone all night."

"I'm about to get ready. You can get ready with me and we can go together? Neema is coming too."

"Okay. Would you happen to have an extra ticket? I want to see if Michelle can come too."

"I can figure out how to get more tickets if she's coming."

I started to pack the clothes I was planning on wearing that night.

"You're gonna wear that?" Ife asked me with a scowl on her face.

I held my tongue. She was nice enough to invite me. "Okay, how about you decide what I should wear?"

"Yes, it will be my pleasure," she said as she went into my wardrobe and started searching through clothes.

"How about you just wear these jeans and you can wear one of my tops? I have a pink top that would go good with the jeans. Also, you should wear those blush flats. It's not too cold outside."

"Yes, ma'am," I said as I packed the clothing and shoes she had selected. "Can you help me fix my bun?"

"Yeah, sure."

The call I had been dreading didn't come until I was in Ife's room, sitting on her bed while she took a shower. My phone started vibrating. It was Kunle. I stared at the phone, not sure of what to do. I was livid, but I did want answers.

"Foma, I am so sorry. Words cannot express how sorry I am."

I was silent.

"Hello?"

"Yes, I'm here."

"I understand you're upset, but at least give me a chance to explain."

"What is there to explain? I heard what I heard and saw what I saw."

"Foma, please. If you're in your dorm, I can be there in five minutes."

I thought for a second. Did I really want to see him? I did want answers, so I replied that he could come.

When Ife came out of the bathroom, I told her that I was going downstairs to talk to Kunle.

"Do you need me to come with you?"

"No, I can handle this."

"I'm planning on leaving in an hour."

"Okay, this won't take long."

Ife squeezed my arm. "Let me know if you need me."

My chest tightened when I saw Kunle's car. *I should kick it,* I thought. *If I had a can of paint, I would throw it on his car.* I told myself to remain calm. I didn't want to give him the satisfaction of seeing how much his actions hurt me.

Kunle stepped out of his car when he saw me. I opened the passenger side door before he could. I didn't need him being a gentleman. I didn't want him doing good guy things. I had already come to see him as a selfish, self-indulging jerk, and that is how I wanted to keep it.

He stopped halfway when he saw me open the door. As I got into the vehicle, he turned around and went to the driver's side.

When we were both seated in the vehicle, I stared at my hands, waiting to hear what he had to say.

"Foma, I am very sorry about what happened. I do really care about you and I do want to be with you. The situation with Larissa was a mistake."

"When she said you went running to her, was it before or after I left for Cameroon?"

Kunle was silent.

I turned to look at him, to look into those same eyes that just days ago had assured me that nothing was going on between the two of them. He was a good liar. After all, didn't he want to become a lawyer? Wasn't that what they did?

"Uh…uh. It was about a month ago, right when you were leaving for Cameroon," he said, putting his head down.

"So, when you told me there was nothing going on with you and Larissa, you were lying, right?"

"We had a talk about the situation before you came back, and I told her that I wanted to be with you. I only went over there in the first place because you'd gotten super upset with me after that misunderstanding that night. She was the only girl I could talk to about something like that."

"Okay, so what exactly happened when you went to talk to her?"

He was silent.

"Umm, are you not going to answer?"

"We fooled around," he said.

"You had sex with her?"

He said nothing. Then he pleaded, "You can't tell Chuck about any of this."

This felt like a blow to me. Here we were having a conversation about how he had betrayed me, and the only thing he could think to say was to tell me not to reveal his dirty little secret to his best friend?

Even though I had no intention of speaking to Chuck about the situation, I decided to play with him, just as he had been playing with me this whole time.

"And why shouldn't I tell him?"

"Because he has had a big crush on Larissa since freshman year."

"And you knew this when you went over to see her, right?"

"Everyone knows."

"Have you been with her in the past other than just that one time? Based on the conversation I heard, it seems that you all have had a thing for a while."

"She's been my friend since freshman year. Yes, we fooled around sophomore year but that was it."

"So, you've been betraying Chuck for years."

"Foma, please, don't say anything to Chuck. He's my best friend."

"What a best friend you are."

"It's complicated."

"Kunle, if you wanted to be with her, you should've been a man about it and put your cards out on the table with Chuck. That was the respectable thing to do. Now you have both me and Chuck wrapped up in your mess."

"Easier said than done. Besides, I already told you that I want to be with you."

"Too late. You should've been honest."

"Had I been honest, you would not have wanted to continue our relationship."

"Had you been honest, I would not have given my body to you."

Kunle put his head down. "Foma, what we shared that night was special."

"What we shared that night was founded on a bed of lies. Goodbye, Kunle, enjoy your life."

CHAPTER THIRTY

Michelle, Neema, and I sat at the front row of the hall where On Pitch was performing. Ife had gotten us tickets and Michelle got Kareem, the guy she was seeing, to drop us off at the building.

On Pitch was popular on campus because they did their own renditions of famous songs that we all knew and loved, and the singers sang exceptionally well, which is why it was quite an accomplishment for Ife to have been selected to become one of its twelve members.

As I sat there, listening to them perform, I tried to forget about everything that happened earlier that day. However, as much as I tried, I kept thinking about Kunle and Larissa. I felt used. He had lied to my face, and naïvely, I had allowed him to take what Nana Ola had said was so precious to me.

After the concert, my friends convinced me to attend a party with them. Michelle arranged for Kareem to give us a ride. The four of us piled into his car when he arrived.

"It's crazy out there," Kareem said as he drove.

"Crazy? What's going on?" Michelle asked from the front seat.

"They're out there going crazy because we lost the game. They think we lost because Ray didn't play. We only lost by like two points."

"Going crazy? What are they doing?" Ife asked.

"A big group of them are walking on Main Street yelling, 'Free RP.'"

"You've got to be kidding me," I said.

Earlier in the day, I'd heard word that Ray was not playing in that afternoon's game. That had been the one good thing to happen to me.

"That's privilege at its finest. They want to be victims so bad that they'd riot over some stupid shit like that," Michelle said.

"Are they doing anything else? Other than walking around yelling?" I asked.

"Not that I saw, but these things have a way of escalating. It wouldn't surprise me if it turns into a full-on riot."

"I kinda want to see it," Michelle said.

"Oh, no way, I want no part of that. They can get away with that stuff 'cause they're white. Who knows what'd happen if we get roped in?"

As we drove on, Kareem's phone started ringing. He picked it up and spoke to the person on the other end.

"Oh, that's wild," we heard him say.

Shortly thereafter, he got off the phone and told us that the cops had shut down the party and that they were out in full force that night. He made a U-turn to take Ife, Neema, and me back to our side of campus.

When I got off the elevator, my floor was abuzz, with people gathered in the hallway talking. I approached the group, but stood to the side to listen to what they were saying.

"Oh my gosh, they burned down a car by the overpass. You know, the one near Smith Hall?"

"They're also on Main Street, smashing storefront windows. This is so crazy. They should've just let Ray Palmer play that game. Now everyone is going crazy because we lost."

I was still behind the crowd, listening to everything they were saying. Then, someone turned around and they all turned. There I stood, alone, while they all looked at me. They knew who I was, because I was the only black girl on our floor. The look in their eyes told me that they saw me as a troublemaker who got Mark kicked out of the dorm. I was certain he dragged my name through the mud before he left to go to God knows where.

They stepped to the side and I walked past. I ignored the whispers that erupted behind me. When I slipped into our room, I was relieved to find that Kara was not there. However, I saw that my towel was now folded and placed on my desk. I opened it, inspected it, and then sniffed it; it smelled of laundry detergent.

Kara's parents were in town that weekend because it was also parents' weekend. I was certain that her mother had washed my towel.

I had just come out of the bathroom from taking a shower when I heard my phone vibrating. I checked my phone and saw text messages from Michelle. I opened the images. In the first one, I saw the image of a burning car and the faces of white students. The flames in the background distorted their faces. The next image was of storefronts with broken windows. Then an image of students looting the stores.

As I viewed the images, I wondered how the news media would refer to the riot. I could already see the headlines: *Passionate Students Express Themselves After a Big Football Loss.*

I slept in until late the following morning. When I woke up, I got ready to go over to Paige's town house. The evening before, she told me she had moved back to her place near campus. The plan was for her to start school that Monday. She asked if I wanted to come over for brunch. I agreed. Although I wanted to lie in bed and forget the weekend had happened, I was happy to see Paige, and I was proud of her for being brave and deciding to come back to school.

Just as my luck would have it, as I walked to the elevator, I turned around to find Jessica and her parents right behind me. They were also getting on the elevator. It was too late for me to turn around. I wished I had taken the stairs.

I forced a smile in their direction and Jessica did the same. Since our exchange after the poetry jam, we had barely acknowledged each other.

Seeing her parents confirmed everything I knew: Jessica was black. Her father was very fair and had silky hair, but he had black features. Her mother, on the other hand, was darker, of a caramel complexion, with fine-textured curly hair.

As the elevator descended, her mom was frowning at her arm. "See how dark you've gotten."

"Mom, stop."

"You need to stop tanning with those girls. When we brought you here, you weren't this dark. You can't tan like them, *mi hija*; they're white girls, they can do that, but you can't afford to do that. You will be dark like this for months!"

Jessica looked frustrated and I pitied her in that moment. I stayed in my corner, engrossed in my phone, while her mother fussed at her. As soon as the elevator reached the first floor, I rushed out without saying a word.

Once outside, I sat on the black metal bench at the front of the building, waiting for Paige. Jessica and her parents walked by me, and her mother was still fussing at her.

"Who's gonna want you but *negritos* with a tan like that?"

"Sabrina," Jessica's father said sternly.

"What? Don't you want the best for your daughter?"

I sat there amazed at what I was hearing. *We are all products of our environment,* I thought as I came to realize where Jessica's complex about being black came from. Little did her mother know that Jessica was already seeing a *"negrito."* From what I saw, she and Chris were still going strong. I was certain her parents didn't know about him.

A few minutes later, Paige's silver car approached. When I opened the passenger door and got into the vehicle, I was happy to see that she was looking more like herself. Her hair was tied up in a neat bun, and she even had on makeup.

"You look great, Paige!"

"Thanks, so do you."

"Don't lie, we both know that's not true."

"Are you okay?" she asked.

I blurted out all that was happening between Kunle and me.

After I was done pouring my heart out, she said quite frankly, "Larissa and Kunle deserve each other. I know you are hurting and that it will take you some time to get over what just happened, especially since you lost your virginity to him, but just be happy you found out about that whole situation sooner than later."

"I'm just mad at myself for being so naïve."

"Foma, it's all a part of life. Things happen, we make wrong choices. Don't fret, just learn from those choices. Besides, think about it this way: they're both seniors and you won't have to see them next school year."

"Good point," I said. My mentor was back, and I was relieved.

The elegance of Paige's town house still amazed me. I sat down at the breakfast bar while she made breakfast. I tried to help, but she told me that she had everything handled.

"Want a mimosa?" she asked.

"Umm, I am under twenty-one," I said.

Paige gave me a knowing look. "We both know you've been indulging."

I laughed, and told her that yes, I did want a mimosa.

I sipped my drink as I watched Paige make the batter for German pancakes. My stomach growled as I watched her pour the rich, light brown batter from the glass bowl into the metal baking pan. *Liquid gold*, I thought.

"'Morning," I heard a voice say from behind me. I turned to

see one of her roommates descend the stairs. I'd never met this one.

"Hey, 'morning, Sophie," Paige responded.

Sophie went to the fridge and got out a bottle of water. She and Paige did a dance as they tried to get out of each other's way. Sophie headed back upstairs. When I was sure she was out of earshot, I asked Paige, "How are things going with you and your roommates?"

Paige shrugged. "Things are all right. Sophie and I have never been close to begin with. I do my thing and she does hers."

"How about with Monica?"

"Things are good between us. She feels torn because she's also friends with Dawn, but we've been getting along just fine."

"Okay, that's good. Are you ready to be back on campus?"

"I have no idea. I suppose we'll see when I get there."

After Paige and I ate our breakfast of German pancakes, scrambled eggs, and turkey bacon, we went to her living room space in the basement to talk. I didn't mention the riot that took place the night before, but Paige opened the door to it.

"Foma, I have to be honest with you. Ever since I found out about the riot last night, I've been more nervous about going back to school. Also, I'm so behind."

"Have you spoken to your professors about that?"

"I've been emailing them, and they said they will let me take make-up tests."

"That's good that your professors are willing to work with you. And I wouldn't worry about that rioting."

"He has so many supporters on campus, and Dawn has turned people against me."

"Paige, this is your last school year. Before you know it, you'll be off to medical school."

"Yeah, I guess you're right. I start finding out about schools soon. I'm pretty sure I'll be attending medical school in Massachusetts."

"I'm happy that's all working out!"

"Yeah, I'm so glad I applied for schools early before this whole mess began. I created a timeline for myself for when to take the MCAT and when to apply for schools. I can share them with you if you'd like."

"Okay, that'd be great, thank you."

We were still talking when we heard the doorbell ring.

"That must be Jeff," Paige said.

"Jeff?" I asked.

"Yeah, my friend. The one I was telling you about when you came over."

"Oh, okay," I said uneasily.

Paige went upstairs, and within minutes she and Jeff came down the stairs.

"Jeff, meet Foma, and Foma, meet Jeff."

I nodded and smiled at Jeff. He was tall and light-skinned; his hair and features gave away that he was black. On his head, he sported a mohawk. Jeff sat at the other end of the sofa, and Paige sat between us. Jeff reeked of weed. I wondered why she had invited him over if she knew I was going to be there.

After a few minutes of us trying to make small talk, Paige and Jeff excused themselves and went into her bedroom. I sat in the living space, watching television and wondering why I was still there. Then I realized that I had no choice because I had no car and it was not practical for me to walk back to my dorm.

When I got tired of hearing the bed squeak, despite the loud music that came from Paige's bedroom, I went upstairs to wait for her there. I felt disrespected. As I sat upstairs, I tried not to think about all the productive things I could be doing.

Almost an hour later, Jeff came upstairs. Paige wasn't with him. He headed toward the front door.

"Is Paige okay?" I asked.

"Yes, she's more than okay," he said with a grin on his face that I did not care for.

After he left, I went downstairs to see what was going on with Paige.

"Paige?" I called as I knocked on her bedroom door.

I heard no answer, so I pried the door open.

"Paige?" I called again. I saw her lying on the bed, her white sheets covering her body.

"Foma, I'm so tired," Paige said, without lifting her head. Her bun, scattered, flopped toward the front of her head.

"Are you all right, though?" I asked.

"Foma, I'm fine, just tired. I'm going back to sleep now."

It was already after three and Paige was in no position to give me a ride back to my dorm. As I turned to leave her room, annoyed by the whole situation, I spotted a sandwich bag of pills on the floor, near her leggings and underwear.

I shook my head and left the room. I wished I had brought my school things with me because I had a quiz the following morning which I still had to study for. In my desperation, I even contemplated asking Kunle to pick me up and give me a ride back to my dorm, but I came to my senses.

I was upstairs sitting in the living room when Monica descended the stairs.

"Hi," she said.

"Hey."

"Where's Paige?"

"She's downstairs, sleeping."

"Is she okay?"

"I suppose so."

"Was Jeff here?" she asked with a knowing look on her face.

"Yes."

"Do you need a ride somewhere?"

"Back to my dorm, please, if you wouldn't mind."

"Sure, let me grab my keys."

When Monica came back downstairs, we bundled up in our coats. Fall whipped around us with a vengeance. I wrapped my scarf around my neck. I trailed behind Monica to her car.

"I'm worried about Paige," Monica said as she drove.

"I am too, especially after all that has happened this weekend."

"What do you mean?"

"The riot that happened yesterday." I didn't want to mention Ray's name.

"Oh, yeah. But I'm worried about Paige because I think she needs to go to rehab."

"What are you talking about?"

"Have you not noticed that Paige has a problem?"

"What kind of problem?"

"A drug problem. When Jeff came, he brought pills, right?"

I remembered the sandwich bag on the floor of Paige's room. However, I felt I would be betraying Paige if I answered in the affirmative.

"I don't know what Jeff brought."

"Trust me, he brought her something. That's what they do. He brings her a stash and she gives him sex."

I sat there not knowing what to say.

"She needs to go to rehab," Monica said again.

CHAPTER THIRTY-ONE

"**I** knew they were going to do this," I said, reading the newspaper to Ife as we stood near the entrance to the building where our biology class was held.

As predicted, the paper referred to the rioters as *passionate, frustrated, students with a lot of school spirit*. These words were written right below the photograph that displayed a burning car and broken storefront windows.

The students' damaging and looting stores had cost an estimated million dollars' worth of property damages. I was relieved that I could not pick out a black face in the sea of white faces displayed in the photograph. At least no one could blame us for this one.

"This is just not right," Ife said as she read the newspaper over my shoulder.

At noon, President Taylor sent a university-wide email stating that the occurrences that weekend were unacceptable and that steps were being taken to hold the students involved responsible for their actions. He also asked that anyone who recognized the students involved in the rioting contact the dean of student affairs to reveal their identities.

I studied the photograph below President Taylor's message, but I couldn't make out the students.

After English class, I went to the library, and Ife went to an On Pitch practice.

As I sat at a little wooden desk overlooking a window, I could not concentrate on my schoolwork. I had a chemistry quiz the following day, but my spirit was unsettled by everything that was going on. Kunle had proven to be a jerk, white students on campus had rioted because they lost a stupid football game, and Monica had just revealed that Paige had a drug problem.

Although my computer sat in front of me, I took out my note-book and a pen and began venting my frustrations, as I used to do in high school. This time, instead of writing a poem, I freestyled, writing whatever came to mind. I didn't care about rhyme or flow. Before I knew, I was finishing off the third page and moving on to the fourth.

As I wrote, a thought came to mind. *Maybe I should get an op-ed published in the newspaper.*

I typed the local newspaper's name into my search engine and saw they accepted personal submissions. Excitement filled my chest. I sat there and began typing what I had written. Afterward, I edited my work.

My heart beat fast when I hit send. Initially, I was going to submit the op-ed anonymously but saw that they did not accept anonymous submissions. When I began thinking about backing down, I thought about Nana Ola's letter about being courageous.

I was still in the library studying when Chuck texted me asking if we could meet. I told him I was busy that evening, but we could talk the following day. I was certain he wanted to talk about Kunle and Larissa, and I figured the conversation would give me the closure I needed.

Chuck and I met the following day at the dining hall closest to the library. I walked there after my late morning class. I was seated by the window, so I saw him walking into the hall. He saw me too and waved. I waved back. He did not look as high-spirited as he usually did.

With a tray of food in hand, Chuck sat across from me. "How are you doing?" I asked him.

"I'm all right. How are you?"

"I'm doing well. Thank you for reaching out."

"Thanks for agreeing to meet with me. Considering everything, I wasn't sure if you would."

"So, we're here," I said, hinting for him to get to the topic at hand. The anticipation was killing me.

"I heard you and Kunle broke up," he blurted out.

"Yes, it's done between us. Do you know why?"

"Kunle broke it down for me a few days ago."

"What did he say?"

"You know, he told me about him and Larissa."

"Good, I'm glad he stopped being a coward. How do you feel about that?"

"It is what it is. I'm glad he finally came clean after all these years. He knew how I felt about her, but he didn't bother to let me know that they had a thing going, and he had the nerve to call himself my best friend."

"I'm sorry about that, Chuck. It must be hard."

"Like I said, it is what it is."

I studied Chuck. He had nice features that came together to create a handsome man. However, I was certain that girls often overlooked him because of his height and the fact that he was very skinny. It was hard to notice him when he stood next to Kunle, who stood at over six feet, was buff and had that smile that revealed his impeccably aligned pearly whites.

When Chuck and I parted ways after lunch, we hugged.

"Take care of yourself, Foma," he said before he walked away.

Our separation felt final. I didn't like that. I had come to like Chuck.

A week after I submitted the op-ed, I had yet to hear any-thing from the newspaper. However, when I checked my email on Wednesday morning, I was notified that my story would be printed in Monday's paper.

Nerve bubbles formed in my stomach because after a week of not hearing from them, I assumed my story hadn't been selected for publication. Now I would have to face the consequences, what-ever they were.

A few days later, the state attorney general announced that he was pressing charges against Ray Palmer. Relief filled my chest when I got the news update. I had subscribed to receive emails from our local news station, and I received the notification just minutes after the attorney general made the announcement.

I texted Paige. Although I had reached out and we had texted on a few occasions, I hadn't seen Paige since I left her town house that Sunday evening. We texted briefly on the Monday following my disastrous visit to her town house, but she had responded saying that she didn't go to class because she wasn't feeling well.

I suspected that whatever she took that Sunday had some-thing to do with her not attending school. I wanted to ask, but it was not my place. Also, I was too busy with my own schoolwork to worry about anyone else's.

That evening when I got to my dorm, people on my floor were talking about the charges being pressed against Ray. Although he was taken into custody earlier in the day, he was released on bond that evening. Displayed on the news was the image of his father shielding his face from the cameras with his sports coat.

"That's not right," Shannon said when she, Kara, Cassie, and Jennifer walked into the room talking about Ray's arrest. I had overheard that Shannon and Jessica were no longer seeing eye to eye, so Jessica stopped hanging around with the group. I didn't care enough to find out what had happened between them.

While usually I would ignore Shannon and her comments, I decided to humor her this time.

"What's not right about it?"

They looked at me, shocked. However, I knew Shannon well enough to know that she would take my bait.

"It's not right that they've arrested an innocent man and are holding him out to be racist."

"How do you know he is innocent?"

"I just do. I don't need to explain anything to you."

"So, you're saying that Paige made the whole thing up?"

"I'm not saying she made everything up. I just don't think he raped her."

"How can you be so sure? And don't bring up how pretty Dawn is again."

"A guy like Ray doesn't need to rape anyone, let alone the likes of someone like Paige," Shannon said.

"Let's go," Jennifer began, but I was ready for blood.

"A black girl like Paige, right?"

"Don't put words in my mouth, I never said that."

"You didn't have to. I know what you mean."

"Let's go," Jennifer said again, this time pulling Shannon's arm.

"The truth comes out," I said.

"Whatever, Foma. You can stay on this racism kick if you want, but so you know, you're hurting no one but yourself. You're not going to bait me like you did Mark."

"Whatever, Shannon. You were perfectly willing to believe Ray raped someone until you found out the victim was a black girl. Don't try to act like it's not true. I notice everything."

"Good day to you, Foma," Shannon said as she walked away. The three girls followed behind her. Jennifer turned and gave me pleading eyes, but I ignored her. In my book, her complacency made her just as bad as Shannon.

I waited in my room for a few more minutes before I left for dinner, which I'd already planned with Ife and Neema. I didn't want them to think I was following them. As I was walking down the hallway, I saw the coward Jared himself. Since the incident with Mark, he had stopped coming to our room, and I had only seen him once, but he had been far ahead of me so we hadn't interacted. However, that evening when he stepped out of his room as I was walking to the elevator, he stepped back in quickly to avoid interacting with me.

"Coward," I said, loud enough for him to hear me as he shut his door. I didn't care.

On Monday, the day my op-ed was to be published in the local paper, I woke up earlier than usual. When I checked my phone, I saw I had a missed call from a number that I did not recognize. I listened to the voicemail. Dr. Mitchell, Paige's mother, was the caller.

She was calling to see if I had spoken to Paige because she hadn't heard from her in a few days and she wasn't answering her calls. I waited until seven to call her back to let her know that I had not heard from Paige all week.

Concern set in as I thought about Jeff, the pills, and what Monica had said about Paige needing rehab. Then I started thinking about the worst-case scenario. What if Paige had overdosed on the pills? At that moment I wished I had taken Monica's number.

An hour later, after I took a shower, I called Dr. Mitchell. She answered on the first ring.

"I haven't heard from Paige in about a week. I texted her last Friday, but I still haven't heard from her," I explained after we greeted each other.

"Foma, I am so worried. Her roommates say they haven't seen her since Wednesday and that the last time they saw her she was with some guy named Sean?"

"Not Jeff?" I asked.

"No, I'm pretty sure Monica said Sean."

"Dr. Mitchell, I've never heard of this Sean guy, but I can ask around," I said.

"Please, Foma, if you could do that, I'd really appreciate it. I'm worried sick about her. She missed her appointments with her therapist, and from what Monica told me, she has been self-medicating. Did you know about that?"

I did not know what to say. I had seen the pills and I had seen her take them when I was at her parents' house. However, at that time I wasn't certain that they weren't prescribed, even though they had been in sandwich bags.

"Ma'am, I've never witnessed Paige abuse drugs," I said. That was the most honest answer I could muster.

"Okay. Anyways. Her father and I are worried sick. Please, do ask around."

After I got off the phone with Dr. Mitchell, I knew I had to contact Kunle. Of all the people I knew, he was the one most familiar with Paige. I began crafting the message I would send him, one that showed I meant business and was by no means trying to get back into his life.

Good morning, Kunle, this is Foma. I hope all is well. I am contacting you because Paige has gone missing and her parents are worried sick about her. They've asked me to help find her. The last time I saw her, she was with a boy named Jeff, who used to go to our school but was kicked out for fighting, I think. He is light-skinned, tall, and has a mohawk. Also, her roommates said she was with a guy named Sean recently. If you know anything about these two guys, I would really appreciate your help in getting in touch with the guys for me.

When I thought the message was detached enough, I hit send, and rushed out the door so I wouldn't be late for class.

I had forgotten all about my op-ed. My mind was on Paige. I was worried about what could have happened to her. While I was in class, my phone began buzzing. I put it on silent and checked to see who was texting me. Several members from ASA had texted. Then texts from Reggie, Chuck, and Kunle. My heart skipped when I saw Kunle had texted me, which caused me to become angry at myself. He did not deserve any heart skips.

Discreetly, I opened the text messages, saving Kunle's for last. The senders congratulated me on my op-ed in the paper. The end of class couldn't come any sooner. I wanted to see my op-ed.

When I got to Kunle's text, I saw he had asked me if we could talk about the Paige situation over the phone. He hadn't seen my op-ed yet, I supposed.

After class ended, I turned to Ife. "Let's go check out the newspaper stand. I heard my op-ed was published in the local paper."

"What?"

I hadn't told Ife or anyone about writing the op-ed.

"I submitted an op-ed with the local newspaper, and they published it today."

"Oh my gosh, Foma, that's amazing," she said as we speed-walked to the front of the building.

I pulled a paper off the stand and I was surprised to see that my op-ed had made the front page. It wasn't the headline, but nonetheless, there my name was underneath the words, *I Am a Black Woman at UC and I Feel Unprotected*. As I stood there reading my words, I felt a cocktail of contradicting emotions, vulnerable yet powerful, and afraid yet courageous.

Ife and I stood by the side of the front door, out of everyone's way, reading.

I Am a Black Woman Attending UC and I Feel Unprotected

Fomanju "Foma" Fotabeng, UC Student

This past August when I arrived on our university campus, I was excited to explore all the opportunities that awaited me both academically and socially. Brochures I had received prior to finalizing my enrollment displayed a diverse body of happy students, learning and participating in the vast number of activities UC offered. Those images solidified my decision to accept UC's proposal for admission. I looked forward to being one of those students.

However, two months later, I am disappointed to say that I have become disillusioned, after coming to grips with my second-class status on our university campus.

The process of disillusionment first began when my white roommate, to whom I had shown nothing but respect, knowingly used my towel to wipe up someone else's dirty bath water without my permission. Mind you, other towels were within an arm's length of mine, yet she only used mine. Second, she moved our room around and placed our trashcan right by the head of my bed where I laid my head. Most recently, while I slept, she pulled my rug, which was held down by the legs of my bed, right from under me because she decided that that was not where she wanted it. At each turn in my dealings with her, I have had to be the bigger person out of fear that should an altercation result between the two of us, I would be viewed as the aggressor because of the color of my skin.

Next, my mentor, a black woman, reported that she was raped a few months ago. Yet the school did not follow its own policy in restricting the accused rapist's movements on campus. Also, racial obscenities were spray-painted on her family's gate along with a hanging noose shortly after she reported the rape. While my mentor was dealing with the resulting emotional terror, the accused, a white male, openly walked around campus, visited our student center, and in front of a large body of students, ate and joked around, as a group of adoring fans surrounded him.

When a group of us black students decided to stand up for my mentor by holding a peaceful protest, local media characterized our peaceful march as rebellious, and insinuated that we were being violent. Later, a racist, threatening note was hung up on my door. When I tried to get to the bottom of the note, one of my white floor mates told me, quote, "In the good ole days, you wouldn't be able to speak to me like that." Subsequently, white males, just like himself, participated in a riot resulting in over a million dollars' worth of damages because our school lost a football game in which the accused was not permitted to participate. Local media characterized these white rioting students as "passionate" with "a lot of school spirit."

All these circumstances have led me to now feel unsafe on my own university's campus, as I come to realize that the promises of a great experience at UC do not extend to me because of the color of my skin. I am a black woman attending UC, and I feel unprotected.

"That was beautiful, Foma," Ife said when we both finished reading.

"Thank you. I can't believe I wrote this."

"I'm glad you did."

I checked my phone and saw more streams of messages. I replied to Kunle, telling him when I was available to talk.

Michelle called me screaming as Ife and I headed to our second class of the day.

"Foma, someone told me about your article in the paper. I couldn't believe it until I read it. Thank you for speaking up for us. Words cannot express how much I appreciate your article, especially with everything going on around our campus right now."

Hearing all the great feedback made me feel so happy. However, I told myself not to get too puffed up. I was proud of what I had written and that was all that mattered. *They can knock you down as easily as they can build you up*, I thought.

When Professor Ross pulled me aside after English class, I was nervous. I knew she wanted to talk about the op-ed. I noticed her glancing at me all through class.

"I'll wait for you outside," Ife said.

I nodded.

"Foma, I wanted to talk to you about your op-ed in the paper today," she began.

"Okay."

"It was such a refreshing read."

"Thank you, Professor Ross."

"I'm so sorry about all that you experienced this semester, from the issues with your roommate and the people on your floor to your friend's rape. With all that, including the passing of your grandmother, you've been able to do so well in my class. I just want to tell you to keep up the good work. I'm not sure what you plan on doing with your future, but I want to encourage you to continue writing, because you're so good at it."

"Thank you, Professor Ross."

"No, thank you, Foma."

I felt like I was walking on cloud nine when I left the classroom.

"What did she want to talk about? The article?" Ife asked.

"Yes, the op-ed."

"She had good things to say, I hope?"

I nodded.

I received Kunle's call later in the afternoon. I was upset with myself when once again my heart skipped a beat upon seeing his name appear on my telephone screen.

"Foma, I read your op-ed. It was very well written," Kunle said matter-of-factly.

"Thank you."

"What inspired you to write it?"

I was annoyed that he was talking to me as if we had not just had a messy breakup just a few weeks prior.

"Circumstances. So, you have information on Jeff or Sean?" I asked bluntly.

I heard him take a breath on the other end of the phone. I

knew I was being curt, but I didn't care. I had no time for small talk with him.

"Uh…yes, I think I know who Jeff stays with, and I have an idea of who this Sean guy is."

Kunle went on to describe Jeff, and his description matched the Jeff I had met. I didn't know what Sean looked like, but I assumed if this Sean that Kunle knew ran in the same circles as Jeff, he must be the same one whom Monica saw Paige with.

"I was hoping this wasn't the Jeff you were talking about. He is into some very dark stuff. Last time I checked he was on some heavy drugs, and he sells them too."

My heart dropped.

"Paige's parents want to know how to find her. Any information you can give me would be very helpful."

"Wait a minute. I'll get their contact information and text those to you," Kunle said.

"Okay, thank you."

"It was nice speaking to you, Foma, and I really appreciated reading your op-ed."

"Thanks," I said. "Looking forward to your text."

Kara was in our room when I got back to the dorm that evening. I was surprised that her posse wasn't with her.

"Hey," she said.

From the way she looked at me, I knew instantly that she read my op-ed.

"Hey," I responded.

I went about my business, taking off my coat, scarf, schoolbag, and shoes. It was freezing cold outside.

Kara was sitting on her bed, a book on her lap. She was looking up at me and I could tell she wanted to talk. I gave her the opportunity.

"What's up?" I asked.

"I read your article," she said.

"Okay, good."

"I didn't use your towel to clean up that bath water because you're black. Also, I didn't move the room around because you're black. I'm not racist. I really don't appreciate you calling me out like that."

"I never used your name."

"You didn't have to. Everyone knows that you were referring to me."

"I spoke my truth."

"But your truth is one-sided."

"Yeah, that's the point. I wrote what I felt. We are all entitled to our own opinions. I wrote a fair op-ed based on the things I experienced."

"Well, you did not experience any racism from me."

"Why did you use my towel to clean up someone else's bath water, Kara?"

"I was in a desperate situation and I used what I saw first."

"If that's the case, how come you didn't use the towel that was hanging up on the towel bar in the bathroom?"

"I didn't know whose towel it was."

"So, you didn't feel okay using that towel in the bathroom because you didn't know who it belonged to, but yet you chose to use mine even though your own towels were just a few feet away?"

"If I knew it was going to be such a big deal, I would've just used mine."

"But you didn't and that's the problem. You didn't even ask who caused the flood. You just used my towel. Why, though? Why would you do that? I find that to be very disrespectful. I have been nothing but respectful to you since I met you. However, you've greeted my kindness with nothing but disrespect. That's why I've had nothing to say to you."

"I wasn't trying to be disrespectful or racist," she said.

"No one called you racist. You're ascribing that title to yourself."

"Your article implied that I was racist."

"I'm not going to argue with you about that. We're having a conversation now and I'm calling your behavior disrespectful. You do see how you've been disrespectful toward me, right? You moved our room around without telling me and put the trashcan by my bed, on the side where I lay my head at night."

"I think you're thinking too much into things," she said.

"I think you're not doing enough thinking. Imagine if I did all those things to you?"

She was silent for a moment. "I guess I wouldn't like that," she said finally.

"Then why did you think it was okay to do that to me?"

"Foma, I don't have an answer for you."

"And that's the problem. All I ask is that you show me the same respect that I've been showing you. We have another semester to dorm together, unless you are planning to move out. So, hopefully we can respect each other from now on."

"I never meant to be disrespectful to you."

"But somehow you were. Hopefully, you can find it in yourself to figure out why you thought it was okay for you to treat me and my property the way you did."

"Foma, I already said I wasn't trying to be disrespectful or racist."

"Well, whether it was subconscious or intentional, I just hope you think about it just as long as I have."

CHAPTER THIRTY-TWO

On Thursday morning, I was rushing out of my dorm to make it to the student affairs building on time for a meeting with Dean Williams, one of the deans of student affairs, and the others invited to attend. I was dreading seeing Kunle and Larissa.

A few days prior, I had received an email from the dean regarding my op-ed. When I first saw the notification, I panicked, expecting him to chastise me for exposing the school the way I did. However, I breathed a sigh of relief when he praised my op-ed as well written and heartfelt.

He said he wanted to speak with me and a group of other black students on campus about how UC could improve our on-campus experiences. He asked for me to recommend a group of students who would be interested in participating.

Still feeling relief from his kind words, I had been tempted to give an excited and flattering response, but then I remembered how President Taylor had tactfully silenced us during our peaceful protest. I almost didn't reply to the email at all, but on second thought, I realized that as a black student at UC, I could not pass up this opportunity to get our voices heard.

I replied saying that we could only participate if he guaranteed he was genuine in his request to meet with us, and would listen to what we had to say.

After I sent the email, I thought about the students I would recommend. To my chagrin, Larissa and Kunle made the list at each turn. I could not leave them out of such an important meeting. They were the ones who inspired my social activism in the first place.

Because I knew I would be seeing them, I got up extra early to get dressed. I had to look fabulous. My hair strands, now a few weeks free of the braids in which they had been confined for months, sprang as I released them from bantu knots I had tied the night before, revealing soft curls. I wore the yellow shirt that teased just a little cleavage and brought out the luscious brown of my skin, and then donned those jeans that hugged my curves in just the right places, all topped with knee high tan boots.

My hair bounced around my face as I rushed down the stairs, desperate to catch the shuttle, all the while wrapping my scarf around my neck and tying the belt of my dark purple peacoat. It was too cold outside for me to walk, but luck was on my side. When I stepped outside, I saw the shuttle approaching.

Speed-walking from where the shuttle stopped, I made it to the dean's building with several minutes to spare. As I approached the appointed door, six white middle-aged faces greeted me, along with one older black lady. A few were seated at a long oak table in the conference room, while behind them a group was standing around the refreshment table, with styrofoam cups in their hands. When I stepped farther into the room, I saw Larissa, Kunle, and Reggie seated at the far end of the table.

Kunle looked down when our eyes met, and Larissa greeted me with a scowl. I ignored both as I smiled at Reggie.

"You must be Ms. Fotabeng," one of the white males began. He was holding out his hand for me to shake. I was impressed that he said my name correctly.

"Yes, I am, a pleasure to meet you, Dean Williams," I said, reading the name plate on his coat.

"It's my pleasure to meet you, Foma," he said as he grinned at me.

I took my seat at the end of the table, away from the other three students. As I was taking off my peacoat, Chuck entered the room and took a seat next to me. We smiled at each other. We were now bonded by mutual betrayal.

While I was still upset with Kunle, I was grateful for his help in getting not only phone numbers for Jeff and Sean, but also Jeff's address. Even though Dr. Mitchell texted me saying they were not able to find Paige with the information, I was nonetheless grateful for his willingness to help.

Chuck and I made small talk and waited for the meeting to officially begin. As I stood up to get a cup of tea, Chris entered the room. I gave him a smile as he walked by.

"Great article, Foma," he said.

I thanked him and popped a teabag into a cup. I was not a coffee drinker; it made me nauseous. Shortly after I took my seat between Chuck and Chris, Dean Williams commanded the attention of the room.

"Thanks to you all for coming. As I assured Foma the other day, we are sincere in calling this meeting to address the African American experience on our university campus. We know we don't always get everything right when it comes to diversity and inclusivity, but we'll continue trying."

We introduced ourselves, and I was impressed to find that most of the staff before us were deans on campus, except for Ms. Diane, the director of equity and inclusion. After introductions were made, Dean Williams asked each of us to give ideas of how they could improve the culture of the university for black students.

Of course, Larissa was the first to raise her hand and she had very compelling ideas. While I disliked her, I could not deny that she was very intelligent and well-spoken. I tried not to be bothered by the smirk she gave me after she made her points. I was certain it pained her that this meeting was spurred by my actions, not hers.

Her suggestions were that the school employ recruitment strategies geared toward enrolling more black students. She recommended having better financial aid packages and making resources available. She also requested that the faculty and staff receive diversity training before the beginning of each academic year, and hold programs where black students interacted with faculty and staff in hopes of promoting respect and opportunity between the two groups.

"Okay, your recommendations are more robust recruitment efforts for minority students, better financial packaging and access to resources, diversity training, as well as programs focused on socializing faculty and staff members with minority students," Dean Williams summarized.

"No, I meant specifically for black students. The term 'minority students' is a broad characterization that includes white women, Hispanics, Asians, and the like. Black students are the ones who have been marginalized here. I thought this meeting was supposed to be about black students," Larissa said.

"I'm sorry for mischaracterizing your words, Ms. Turner," he said.

I caught Reggie's eye and we gave each other a knowing look. We understood that whatever resulted from this meeting would be marketed to not solely benefit black students but rather all students who identified themselves to be something other than the generic Caucasian male. That semester, I had come to realize that benefits geared toward black people alone made others uncomfortable, so other groups were included to make them more palatable to society at large.

In that instant, I knew that nothing much would come of the meeting. The point was not to give black students an advantage over other students by providing us with more resources, but rather to acknowledge that our experiences on campus were not comparable to that of non-black students, and facilitate programs to get us closer to equity.

After the disappointing meeting, I hurried out of the room and into the bathroom, where I played with my hair in the mirror, waiting for Kunle and Larissa to leave the building before I departed myself. I was desperate for our paths not to cross. Imagine my surprise when I looked to my right to see Larissa opening the door to the bathroom. I turned my head abruptly back to the mirror, keeping my gaze at my reflection.

Larissa went into a bathroom stall, and I began gathering my things, which I had placed on the marble counter to the left of me. Before I could finish gathering my belongings, from my peripheral vision I saw her standing next to me.

"You've won. Are you happy?" she said as she glared at me.

I stood there dumbfounded. "Larissa, I don't know what you're talking about," I said finally.

"Sure, you don't. I'm about sick and tired of you. Everything was good in my life until you came with your holier than thou attitude and screwed everything up. Now my best friend isn't talking to me. By the way, Kunle only likes you because you're weak. This whole meeting was supposed to be your big idea, but you could barely get a word out. I may be leaving this campus soon, but you can never take my spot."

She spoke softly and calmly, but the hatred in her voice left me with goosebumps. My instincts told me to run, but I gained control of myself.

"I don't know what you're talking about, but I want no part of it. I'm competing with no one but myself. Focus on you and do you, and I'll do me," I said, trying to keep my tone calm, I did not want her to know that she had rattled me with her venom.

My things in hand, I left the bathroom and stormed out of the building, ignoring Kunle, who was standing by the exit.

"Uh, Foma—" Kunle began, but I marched right past him without giving him as much as a glance.

I was in my last class of the day when I got a text message from Kunle. I was inclined to ignore his text, as I assumed it was about that morning. However, something told me to read it. *I know where Paige is. I am going to find her. I think it's best that you come with me.*

My heart beat fast. *When are you going?*

Now. I can pick you up by the overpass.

I rushed out of class.

When Kunle's car approached, I could think of nothing other than finding Paige. I decided against letting Dr. Mitchell know that we had located her daughter, out of fear that I would get her hopes up for nothing.

In the car, I questioned Kunle about how he found out about Paige's possible location. He said he told everyone he knew to alert him if they saw Paige, and a friend said he saw her in a house not too far off campus.

At our destination, I looked around. All I saw were the town houses that were typical for that area, sort of like the town homes where Kunle and Paige lived.

"Stay in the car, just in case," Kunle said.

"No, it'll look funny for you to go in there alone to get her."

He thought about it for a second, and then told me to stand behind him. He had changed from his crisp button-down shirt and peacoat. He was now wearing a hoodie and puffy jacket. His hood was pulled up on his head. I stood behind him as he knocked on the door.

"Yo, what's up, Jeff," I heard Kunle say when the door opened. I peeked around Kunle and made eye contact with the same guy who had been in Paige's town house.

When Jeff saw me, the pleasant look on his face turned into a glare. Kunle gave me a chastising look.

"Whatchu doing here? Man?"

"Paige's parents want her home," Kunle said softly.

"Well, she doesn't want to go home," Jeff said.

"Jeff, I don't want any trouble, man, but I can't leave without her."

"And I told you, she's not going anywhere." As he said this, I noticed he was about to shut the door.

I didn't give him a chance. I bulldozed my way past him, yelling, "Paige!"

"Whatchu doing!" Jeff screamed behind me, quick at my heels. I felt someone grab me—Jeff. Before he could do anything further, Kunle charged at him. I ran around the disarrayed town house calling out Paige's name.

"Foma?" I heard a weak voice say from one of the rooms. I ran in. Clothes, fast-food bags, and drug paraphernalia were strewn about the room. The stench was alarming. Nonetheless, when I saw Paige lying on a dirty, ripped-up sofa, I went to her. She was lying on her back in wrinkled clothes. Her hair was all over the place, and red circles were around her eyes. A plastic band was tied around her arm, and I noticed a red bump on the skin below the band.

"Paige, I'm getting you help. Your parents are worried sick about you."

Paige began to scream. "No, no, I want to stay here! I'm not going back to school. They don't want me back there! Look what they've done to me!"

"Paige, honey, who?"

"You know who! They don't care about me."

"I'm not taking you to school, Paige. I want to show you something, come with me," I said as I tried to get her up. The smell that exuded from her body was overpowering.

She took my hand, and I wrapped her arm around my neck as I tried to lead her outside. I took small steps with her.

"Kunle!" I called out as we walked.

"You've got her?" I heard Kunle ask from the other room.

"Yes."

"I've got him, you can come."

"Where are we going?" Paige asked, still in a stupor.

"I want to spend some time with my mentor," I told her.

"I love you, Foma," Paige said.

"I love you too."

Once we got close to the door, I saw Kunle and Jeff. Kunle had him restrained in a headlock; Jeff's hands were swinging in the air.

"I've got him, go," Kunle said as Jeff struggled to no avail.

"Jeff," Paige called as she tried to walk toward him.

"Don't let 'em take you, Paige. They're taking you back to school, back to Ray," Jeff wailed.

Paige freaked out and started fighting me off. We struggled until I could not keep ahold of her. She ran out the door. I chased after her.

"I don't wanna go back there," she screamed as she ran, without a coat.

I chased after her, but she was too fast. Before I knew it, Kunle was at my heels.

"Foma, get in the car, let's go."

Jeff now stood by the door, panting. I watched Paige run farther and farther away.

"She's a hoe anyway," I heard Jeff say as he panted.

Once in the car, we drove around, trying to find her, but we did not have much luck. I was relieved that I had not told Dr. Mitchell that we had located her. I was coming to realize there was nothing I could do for Paige. She was in a dark place that only she could get herself out of.

As we drove around the area looking for her, I was certain that no matter what came of Ray Palmer's case, the Paige I knew was long gone.

That night when I got back to my dorm, my emotions were running wild. Visions of Paige lying on that dirty sofa, high out of her mind, flashed in my brain. Her once soft, luscious hair had felt like dried grass, and the thought of that strap she had around her arm made me quiver. I could still smell the stench of the mucky room. A stark contrast to the rooms in which I had grown accustomed to seeing her.

My heart ached to think of what Paige had been reduced to. The pounding in my heart was crippling. I slid into the chair by my desk. I needed to release the deep emotions lodged like a stone in my chest.

I opened a desk drawer, pulled out a sheet of paper. Pen in hand and shoulders huddled over the sheet of paper, I released those emotions the best way I knew how. As I sat there writing, I watched as tear drops hit the sheet below me.

By the time I finished writing, I knew that, just like Paige, I too was forever transformed. The innocence that had glazed my vision just months prior was now long gone.

Who Will Mourn for the Woman?

I still get visions of the woman you used to be
Luscious brown skin, sweet, hopeful, dazzling eyes, you had the
world at your feet
However, that same world which you held in high regard,
Has left you forever scarred.

Now, for your protection, scar tissue has formed over your once soft skin.
Those who see your tough exterior judge you without knowing
what you hold within.
Will you remind them that it is from you that humankind began?
How could you, when to utter those words, you barely can.

You are viewed as strong, loud and boisterous.
However, deep down you know you have been silenced.
Afraid to reveal the real you, you allow others to remain oblivious.
Now for you, being vulnerable means an invitation to violence.

Around, the world spins.
Counter clockwise,
They admire your plump lips and thick thighs,
All the while, deep down a part of you dies.

Imitated but never duplicated,
Where would the world be without you?
When no one can clean dirty laundry quite like you do?

Who will care for the woman,
Who gives with nothing left but an empty shelf?

Who will mourn for the woman,
Who is too torn to mourn for herself?

ACKNOWLEDGMENTS

Special thanks to my family and friends who have been supportive of me during this process—especially those who provided me feedback as I decided on the cover art and design for this novel. Also, I am grateful to my editor, John, for guiding me as I wrote this novel, and in the process, helping me to become a better storyteller.

Last but certainly not least, I am thankful for the black authors whose work inspired me to dare dream that I too could one day become a novel writer. Representation is powerful.

A NOTE FROM THE AUTHOR

Dear Reader,

Thank you for your support of my debut novel, *Respect Yourself*. Writing this novel has been one of the best experiences of my life. In writing this novel, I wanted to create something that provoked thought, and kept its readers on their toes, wanting more. The countless hours of brainstorming, writing, and editing have all been worth it, as I feel that *Respect Yourself* will both entertain and stimulate much needed conversations about sensitive social issues that continue to plague our human race.

Historically, we have separated ourselves from each other based on superficial assumptions or unfounded stereotypes about our relative races and/or ethnicities. Occasionally, when this practice backfires, we resort to symbolic gestures without fully addressing the issues that divide us. Over the years, we have seen that shallow measures solve nothing, as there continues to be frustration, discord, and fatal incidents that have taken the lives of countless people. It is my strongest belief that the best way for us to grow as a people—regardless of our respective races, ethnicities, or creeds—is to acknowledge the things that divide us, and have open, honest, and respectful conversations about them. It is also important that we listen to one another for understanding, not rebuttal. I hope *Respect Yourself* catalyzes such conversations.

Also, through *Respect Yourself*, I wanted to expose the masses to the rich African culture. The African continent is an opulent one not just because of its natural resources that fuel our world, but also because of the people who inhabit the land. In *Respect Yourself*, readers experience a piece of the West African culture, one filled with delectable cuisines and unique customs and traditions.

Again, I am thankful for your readership, and I hope you enjoyed Foma's story as much as I enjoyed writing it.

Joyce Asong

DISCUSSION QUESTIONS

1. How does the first chapter forecast the remainder of the novel?

2. Can you understand Foma's frustration with her parents and Michelle? Do you agree with how Foma handled the situation with Michelle?

3. In regards to the teasing Kunle and Foma experienced when they first came to America, do you think xenophobia towards Africans exists? Why or why not?

4. How does the issue of colorism surface throughout the novel? Would you have handled the situation with Jessica differently had you been in Foma's position? Does the scene with Jessica's parents cause you to sympathize with Jessica? Why or why not?

5. What are your thoughts on the Bridging the Gap event? Can you relate to any of the issues discussed?

6. Do you think the African students were unreasonable in their request to hear the facts before engaging in the different protest activities the BSA was sponsoring? Do you agree with Foma's observation that Ife was being a hypocrite?

7. How do you think Foma's relationships with Paige and Kunle affect her transformation in this novel?

8. Could the students have advocated for Paige in a better way? Are marches still effective in calling for justice?

9. What are your thoughts on Dr. Mitchell's television interview? Do you agree with any of her assessments?

10. Do you think Paige's downward spiral would have happened had the school been more vigilant in handling the matter? How does her situation tie into the greater theme of the experiences of black women in America? What did you think of Foma's poem at the end of the novel?

11. What emotions did Foma and Mark's exchange of words after the note incident stir in you? Do you think Jared knew about the note? And what are your general thoughts on Jared?

12. Do you feel that race played a part in the different disrespectful incidents between Kara and Foma? Do you agree with how Foma handled the situation with Kara? Why or why not?

13. What are your general thoughts about Nana Ola and her and Foma's relationship? Had Foma not had Nana Ola's influence, do you think she would have made the decisions that she made in the novel? Why or why not?

14. Would the novel have had the same impact had Foma not returned to Cameroon? How did going to Cameroon change Foma?

15. What do you make of Kunle's resigned attitude as it relates to the situation in Africa? Did you expect him to respond differently?

16. What are your perceptions of Larissa in this novel? Can you relate to her? Can you understand her frustration with Kunle and Foma's relationship? Between Larissa and Kunle, who was more in the wrong?

17. Does Kunle deserve Foma's forgiveness? Do you believe Kunle cared about Foma? Overall, what did you think about their relationship?

18. Is there anything you learned from reading this novel that you would like to share?

www.ingramcontent.com/pod-product-compliance
Lightning Source LLC
Chambersburg PA
CBHW030808210726
48290CB00002B/478